Damascus & The Wildfire

Lone Star Mavericks MC Series
Book 2

Rachel Esterline

Venturesome Publishing

First Edition

Ebook ISBN: 978-1-968862-01-5

Paper cover ISBN: 978-1-968862-04-6

Hard cover ISBN: 978-1-968862-05-3

Cover design by Mel Purdy of PawsitivelyPurdy (etsy.com/shop/PawsitivelyPurdy)

Content editing by Pinpoint Editing (pinpointediting.com)

Venturesome Publishing

PO Box 144

Haslett, Michigan 48840

VenturesomePublishing.com

VenturesomePublishing@gmail.com

To My Husband, Jeremy

"You are, as I've always known,
the perfect fucking wife."

*I'll always choose you over my book boyfriends because you say
romantic shit like that to me.
Maybe someday I'll let you read my books.*

Trigger Warnings & Content Reassurance

Scan to view trigger warnings or visit
rachelesterlineauthor.com

The dog featured in this story is <u>never</u> in danger and lives happily ever after.

Key Terms

Church: Official club meeting attended by officers of the motorcycle club where business, rules, and votes happen.

Cut: The sleeveless leather vest worn by members with their club patch.

Old Lady: A wife or steady girlfriend of a club member.

Out Bad: When a member is kicked out of a club due to a serious violation of the club's code.

Patch Over: When one club merges into or is absorbed by another. May be voluntary or forced.

Prospect: A potential member undergoing a probationary period before becoming a fully patched member. Often required to do grunt work for fully patched members to prove their loyalty to the club.

Rockers: The curved patches above (top rocker) and below (bottom rocker) the club emblem.

Sweetbutt: A woman who is sexually available to club members but doesn't hold the status of an Old Lady.

Playlist

Listen on Spotify:

Lifetime • Three Days Grace
Fuck It • New Medicine
Empty • Letdown.
I'm a Mess • Racyne Parker
Life Is Beautiful • Sixx:A.M.
Leave a Light On • Papa Roach
Built From Broken • Georgia Phantom
Just Pretend • Bad Omens
Warrior • Beth Crowley
Baggage • Kelsea Ballerini
Beauty in the Struggle • Bryan Martin
For A Boy • RaeLynn

Chapter One

In the six days since I'd moved to Texas, I'd knocked back more tequila shots than an entire frat house during welcome weekend.

The morning sun stabbed daggers into my skull as I rolled up the long driveway leading to the clubhouse owned by the Lone Star Mavericks Motorcycle Club. I stepped out of my Range Rover, holding onto the door as I swayed slightly. I'd hoped the drive would settle my stomach, but the world still felt off-kilter, like I'd just stepped off a tilt-a-whirl. I closed my eyes for a moment and sucked in a breath, counting on the warm Texas spring air to clear the fog from my mind.

My best friend, Eva, waited for me, leaning against the hood of her chili pepper–red Jeep with ice-cold drinks from Maisie's Bakery clutched in each hand. Her blue-gray eyes looked annoyingly bright for someone who'd matched me, shot for shot, less than twelve hours ago.

Eva's gaze raked over my face, and she grinned. "You look like shit."

I caught my reflection in the window. Dark circles cradled my green eyes, and a light sheen of sweat shimmered across my forehead. Tendrils of red hair stuck to my damp skin despite the light breeze.

I snagged the iced coffee she offered and took a few gulps, my empty stomach rolling in protest as the cold, bitter liquid swirled with the lingering tequila. "Next time Rhetta offers me a margarita, remind me to say no."

Eva chuckled, patting me on the shoulder. "Last night reminded me of college. This morning reminded me that we're not in our twenties anymore."

I started to shake my head but stopped as dizziness threatened to knock me off balance. "Never again."

"You say that every time."

I scoffed. "This time, I mean it. How do you still look annoyingly beautiful after a night of drinking? It should be illegal."

Eva shrugged, flipping her long, dark hair over her shoulder. "Guess I just handle my liquor better than you."

We walked into the clubhouse like she owned the place. Maybe it felt that way because Eva was head over heels for the club's vice president, Reaper. The guys treated her like royalty—a biker princess in a vest they called a cut.

The clubhouse hit my senses all at once. The place smelled of leather, pine cleaner, and a hint of motor oil. Underneath it all, there was the unmistakable musk of stale beer, a reminder of wild nights that had come before.

I pitied the prospects—the new guys, still earning their patches— who were stuck mopping up spilled liquor and God only knew what else from the polished concrete floors. For all the debauchery I'd heard about when it came to the rough-and-tumble biker crowd, the Mavericks seemed surprisingly particular about cleanliness.

Maybe it was just Thane, their president.

"Want a drink from the bar before our meeting?" Eva teased.

I groaned. "Fuck. No. If I even get a whiff of tequila right now, I'll yack on Thane's desk."

Eva laughed. "I don't recommend it. He would be thoroughly unamused if you violated his office like that. He's got a thing about puke. Says that's why he never became a parent."

Rhetta strolled toward us with a wide grin, her blonde curls framing her bright-blue eyes. I cringed as she stopped at the bar to add a splash of Bailey's to her steaming coffee cup.

"Sugar, we need to get your tolerance up if you're going to hang with the club," she drawled as she sipped her spiked drink.

As the president's wife, Rhetta wore her cut with queenly pride— the bottom rocker declaring her "Property of Thane." Still patriarchal as fuck, if you asked me. But, as Eva reminded me last time I ragged on her about the "Property of Reaper" claim on the back of hers, no one had.

Rhetta swept us down the hall toward Thane's office. The air grew thicker with the scent of smoke and whiskey. I breathed slowly in through my nose and out through my mouth, willing my stomach to settle.

"The guys have Church in an hour, so let's get this meeting out of the way, and then we can grab brunch," Eva said.

"Church." I scoffed, trying not to roll my eyes. I dropped my voice into my best National Geographic narrator impersonation. "Here, we witness the rare and secretive biker species in their natural habitat where they participate in a sacred, men-only ritual for mysterious 'club business.'"

Eva pinched my side and shot me a glare. I offered a sheepish smile.

Rhetta glanced back at us and chuckled. "You're not wrong. But if you want to keep your sense of humor—and your fingers—I'd suggest not doing that in front of Thane."

Her tone was light, but a warning shone in her eyes that sent a shiver down my spine. As we trailed Rhetta toward Thane's office, I considered the possibility that she might not be joking.

The Mavericks weren't just a bunch of guys who liked to ride bikes. They were outlaws. And you didn't become president of a motorcycle club by handing out hugs and rainbows. My gut told me Thane had earned his place at the head of the table with grit, loyalty, and a reputation for making hard choices.

A lamp glowed in the corner of the ample office space, emanating warmth from the knotty pine walls. Thane stared at a pile of papers, his weathered face schooled in a frown. Rhetta knocked on the door, and his lips shifted beneath his graying goatee into a genuine smile.

"Hey, darlin'." Thane stood, wrapping his arms around Eva in a warm hug. He glanced at me. "Kenna, glad you could join us."

He reached a calloused hand out to shake mine before gesturing to the cowhide chairs before his oak desk, lighting a Marlboro, and taking a long drag. "This year's our fiftieth anniversary."

I tried my best to control my grimace as the smoke curled around him, but Thane shot me a knowing smirk. He knew I hated the smell, but he didn't give a shit.

"I'd like to throw a shindig next month," he said, tapping ash into a mangled clay ashtray. "Live music, good food. Celebrate our history and honor the men we've lost over the years."

Eva pulled a notepad out of her back pocket. "Can you get me a list of names? And more photos?"

Always so damn prepared. If she weren't my best friend, I'd hate her for it.

Thane nodded. "Ask Linc. He can get that for you. I'll dig out a box of shit I have in storage, too. Rhetta wants this to be a family affair that's open to the public, so no strippers." His eyes sparkled with mischief as he glanced at his wife. "My old lady likes to take away all the fun."

Eva laughed as my eyebrows rose in question.

"You don't need strippers at every party," Rhetta chastised. "Wasn't it enough that I got them for your birthday?"

Thane grinned, unrepentant. "Never enough, darlin'. I have half a mind to hire them to hang out full-time in the clubhouse. Think it would bring us more prospects."

I ground my molars and bit back a sigh. I had no problem with any woman who wanted to dance for a living. Hell, I respected their strength and talent. But I was surprised Rhetta was so nonchalant about it.

"Since it's a family event, how about some games for the kids?" I suggested.

Thane nodded. "Whatever you think. I'm giving this entirely to you two."

"Consider it handled," Eva chirped.

Thane grinned at her, his coffee-colored eyes crinkling in the corners. "I always do when you're at the wheel, darlin'," he said, his voice thick with affection.

The way he looked at Eva—like she was his long-lost daughter—sent a pang through my chest. There was something gentle beneath his gruff exterior, a fatherly instinct that reminded me of my dad.

Thane shifted his gaze to me. "How's Texas treatin' you?"

"It's great. Sun's hot, beer's cold, and there are cowboys everywhere. But I didn't realize your drivers were worse than they were in D.C. I've been cut off by three trucks in two days."

Thane's gravely laugh echoed through the room, but a knock interrupted us before he could respond.

The door opened, and my heart jolted at the scarred face that peeked in.

Merrick glanced at Eva and me before shifting his steely, dark eyes to Thane. "Prez, we've got a situation."

Thane grumbled and nodded. "Sorry, darlin'. I'm going to have to push you out the door. You've got a blank check and the prospects at your disposal to make this happen."

Rhetta kissed Thane's cheek, leaving behind a smudge of maroon lipstick, before ushering us toward the parking lot. The heavy, humid air hit me in the face, blanketing my skin in a damp sweat.

"We're having a bonfire tomorrow for Fuse," Rhetta said as she hugged Eva. "You should both come."

I tensed, already apprehensive about the emotions the week

would bring and ready to make up any excuse to avoid a crowd on the day of the year I most dreaded—but Eva got there before I could open my mouth.

"We wouldn't miss it," Eva said brightly. "I can't wait to hear the stories he'll tell me about Roman."

Rhetta shook her head with a grin. "Fuse is going to give Reaper so much shit for finally settling down and letting a woman call him by the name his mama gave him."

Eva laughed, her cheeks pink and eyes shining. I'd never seen her fall so hard, so fast. The reckless joy and happiness radiating from my best friend only reminded me of the hollow space where my heart used to sit.

"It'll be a pretty tame night," Rhetta said, pulling my focus back to the present. "We don't want to overwhelm Fuse. It'll take a while for him to adjust after Coffield."

Rhetta headed back inside. I sidled up to Eva and lowered my voice. "Coffield? The prison?"

Eva rolled her eyes. "Don't make a big deal out of it."

"Prison is a pretty big deal. Did they check him for shanks before letting him out?"

Eva sighed dramatically. "He's not bad. I promise. It's not my story to tell, but trust me. He's a good guy who got caught up in a shitty situation."

I bit my lip. "Are you sure we're safe here? Some of the guys seem cool, but honestly, some look at me like they want to eat me for breakfast—and not in a fun way. Like, legitimately murder me before crunching on my bones."

"They're wary of outsiders, but they're loyal to the club. To their brothers and the people who matter to them. Every man here would protect you with their life because you matter to me. They would literally take a bullet for you."

I looked at Eva skeptically. "I'd never ask that of someone."

Her lips tipped up in a half smile. "When you're a part of this family, you don't have to."

I shook my head. What kind of world did these bikers live in, where loyalty was paid in blood?

* * *

"You have to come to the bonfire tonight," Eva pleaded over the phone, her voice too chipper.

I rubbed a hand just below my neck where the pressure suffocated me. "I just want to stay home. Maybe drink some wine. Watch some bad movies."

Silence hummed between us for a beat. I wanted to wallow in peace, but Eva seemed to have forgotten why. I hadn't. I couldn't. Despite the years that had passed, the ache of this day and the memories that haunted me lurked just beneath the surface.

"Please," Eva said, her tone softening. "I want you to get to know them. They're my family."

"Eva, I just—"

"I'm not taking no for an answer," she interrupted. "I'll drag your ass there if I need to. You need to make friends. Besides, I already told Hatchet you'd be making an appearance."

She dangled the pretty, blonde-haired, blue-eyed biker who'd helped us unpack my moving truck the week before like catnip. His charming grin and the short beard shadowing his jaw made him look reckless. Guilt pulsed beneath my ribcage as I considered how much I'd enjoyed the way he made me laugh.

I rubbed my temples. "You're not going to let this go, are you?"

"I promise you'll have fun. Besides, when have you ever said no to a party?"

I released a deep sigh, relenting. "Fine. I'll come. But I'm leaving at nine."

"We'll see about that," she sing-songed.

I choked in a shaky breath. "I need to go for a run. I'll talk to you in a bit."

My fingers trembled as I slipped my cell phone into a pocket.

The walls in my small home leaned in, and my mind spun as I attempted to press away the memories I'd shoved to the back of my mind. But they were always there, waiting for a moment of weakness. I needed to relieve the pressure building in my chest before I exploded.

Within minutes, I laced my running shoes and bolted out the door with plans to hit the shaded trail around the corner. Despite the early evening, the thick and oppressive Texas heat clung to the air, making each breath feel like a struggle. But I welcomed the burn in my lungs, the ache in my legs—anything to distract me from the storm brewing inside.

I focused on the rhythm of my feet hitting the pavement, trying to outrun the ghost who haunted me. But the pressure in my chest only grew heavier. My breath caught in short, shallow gasps as the panic threatened to engulf me.

I grumbled and forced myself to slow my pace, opting to try the grounding technique my therapist constantly and annoyingly suggested. She promised it'd help me focus on the present when the past bit at my heels.

Name five things you can see.

Trees. The trail. A weather-worn bench. A crushed Coors Light can. Alec's broken body slumped against the steering wheel.

Fuck. No, not that. Trees, the trail, a bench, a crushed can, and a patch of petunias.

Name four things you can feel.

The paved path beneath my running shoes. The sticky Texas heat on my skin. My necklace bouncing with each stride. Alec's blood dripping down my fingers.

Name three things you can hear.

Birds chirping. Children shouting. The crunch of metal.

Name two things you can smell.

Leaking gasoline. Burnt rubber on pavement.

Name one thing you can taste.

Regret.

I slowed to a stop, placing my hands on my knees as I tried to catch my breath. My lungs burned nearly as much as my grief as I shoved the memories back.

Three years later and the guilt still crashed through me in unforgiving waves. I sucked in sharp, ragged breaths, but it seemed like the oxygen was sucked out of the air. I squatted on the side of the trail, and the world spun for a moment.

"You OK, ma'am?" a man asked as he and his wife walked past, their faces creased with concern.

I nodded and flashed a thumbs-up as I averted my gaze from them. "I'm fine," I lied.

I pulled the small backpack from my shoulders, digging for the medication at the bottom with shaky hands. I swallowed the pill dry and chased it with a splash of warm water.

You can't run from grief, I reminded myself. But that didn't mean I had to face it.

Tonight, I'd do the next best thing.

Drink.

* * *

Eva insisted on picking me up, clearly intending to foil my plan to leave the party early. But at this point, I was ready to surrender and end the night completely hammered with no memory of why this day made my chest ache.

She chattered about a recent meeting with a local editor while I snuggled Hawk, her Malinois puppy, in the front seat. When we pulled up to the clubhouse, I took in the scene before me. A row of Harleys lined the driveway, each with gleaming chrome and shimmering paint jobs. An irresponsibly large bonfire crackled in the yard, its smoke curling around the surrounding Adirondack chairs.

"I'm glad you came," Eva said. "I need my best friend."

I offered a small smile. "For you, I'd join a cult. Which, technically, isn't that what this club is?"

Eva rolled her eyes. "Smart-ass. It's not a cult. It's a club."

"If I get kidnapped by bikers tonight, you're explaining it to my mom."

"Oh, fuck that. I'd rather be tied up beside you than have to call your mom."

As soon as we parked, I beelined for the makeshift bar and poured myself a whiskey on the rocks in a plastic red cup.

"Thought you were never drinking again," Eva teased as she tipped a bottle of water into a bowl for Hawk.

"Desperate times," I deadpanned, forcing a smirk. I wondered how she could forget. I considered reminding her, but then I'd have to see her blue-gray eyes mist and answer endless questions about how I felt. And talking about my feelings wasn't exactly high on my list for the evening.

Eva looped an arm through mine as she insisted on another round of introductions amidst the low thrum of laughter, chatter, and country music.

"You introduced me to almost everyone last week," I whined as I tried to pull away. "Reaper, back me up here."

Reaper held up his palms, his tall frame backing away. "Nope. I find it's best just to do as she says."

I scowled at him. "You're not nearly as tough as you look."

Reaper laughed, waving me off as he walked away with the pup biting at his heels. The man might have been a hardened biker and veteran, but he was a marshmallow when it came to Eva.

The parade of names and faces began again. A few I'd met already. Don and Maisie, a sweet couple that would fit in at a retirement home if they weren't clad in leather cuts. Linc, a wiry, dark-eyed man who looked exactly like his brother, Reaper, but seemed younger and lighter.

Eva dragged me across the yard to another group.

"Jack, meet my best friend, Kenna."

Jack stretched out a grease-stained palm. "A pleasure," he said in a Southern drawl.

Before I could respond, a woman with a hot-pink pixie cut pressed up beside him.

"This is Leah, my old lady." Jack kissed the top of her head as she suspiciously eyed me like I might try to steal her man.

I forced a polite smile as I bit back a comment about the old lady label. *Their world, their rules*, I reminded myself.

"Nice to meet you both," I said. I threw back the rest of my whiskey, savoring the burn as it slid down my throat.

A roar split the air as a Harley rumbled up the long gravel driveway.

The man who swung off the bike was massive, all muscle and tattoos. His presence commanded the attention of everyone in the yard.

"That's Fuse," Eva said, excitement clear in her chipper voice. She glanced at my now-empty cup. "Let's grab another drink and go say hi."

"Sure, let's go meet the prison biker who could snap me in half," I grumbled, though curiosity coursed through me. I'd never met anyone who'd done hard time.

"Trust me. He's a good guy," Eva chided as she poured more whiskey into my glass before filling her own. "Don't judge him before you get to know him." She pressed the drink into my hand with a warning glare before spinning on her heels.

I sipped my whiskey and watched in rapt fascination as a group surrounded Fuse. They gave each other the manliest hugs I've ever seen, concluded by bruising back slaps.

It was a far cry from the old money country club world I'd grown up in—all handshakes and air-kissed cheeks, polite applause, and passive aggression. Instead of polo shirts and linen pants, these men wore leather and patches steeped in testosterone and tobacco.

Reaper waved us over. "This is my old lady, Eva, and her best friend, Kenna."

Fuse's intense gaze swept over us both, lingering just long enough to make me shift and tense.

"Reaper has good taste," he said in a gruff voice as he wrapped his bear-sized hands around Eva. He lifted her off the ground and twirled her around in a circle. She giggled as her drink arced through the air and splashed onto the grass. Hawk let out a high-pitched yip, leaping to follow his human.

"You are absolutely stunning," Fuse said as he set Eva down.

"Hands off my woman before I cut them off," Reaper growled possessively.

Fuse glanced at me and smirked as I subtly stepped back.

"Relax," he murmured. "It's just been a long time since I've seen so many beautiful women. You can't blame me for being a little enthusiastic."

I kept a careful distance and studied Fuse as he turned to greet Thane. Every inch of him up to his neck was covered in tattoos. Scarred knuckles marred his fists. The unyielding confidence and flicker of challenge in his eyes made him magnetic.

From across the yard, Hatchet caught my eye. He was laughing with Linc, but when he saw me, he winked. My face flushed as I offered a small wave. He sauntered to the bar before heading my way with two drinks in hand.

"What's this?" I asked, sniffing the one he offered me.

"I hear you and tequila are taking a break, so I took a guess with a vodka tonic." He embraced me with a side hug. "I'm glad you could make it."

Hatchet stood close enough that I could breathe in his cologne mixed with leather, motor oil, and maybe even bad decisions.

"Thank you. Eva forced me. She thinks I need to make *friends*."

A crooked grin tugged at his lips. "I'll be your friend," he said smoothly, his ocean-blue eyes sparkling.

I sipped the drink, the ice and citrus biting my tongue. "Being my friend means Bloody Mary brunches, shopping, and dancing. Are you prepared to agree to those terms?"

Hatchet snorted. "Brunch? Absolutely. I like a woman who starts drinking in the morning. Dancing? I've got moves you've never seen, doll. But shopping? Sorry. That's where I draw the line." He grinned at me as he took a long drink of his beer.

I hid my smile behind my glass as I pretended to consider. "What if it's for lingerie?"

Hatchet choked. I laughed as he sputtered, delighted to have caught him off guard.

He wiped his mouth. "Fuck. You trying to kill me?"

I feigned innocence. "I wanted to see if you truly drew the line at shopping. Friendship requires flexibility."

He leaned in closer. "If that's what friendship with you looks like, I'm willing to negotiate."

I arched a brow. "What exactly are your terms?"

"Hmm," Hatchet hummed, stroking his beard as he pretended to ponder the question. "First, I get to take you to my favorite taco truck for brunch. Second, I always get to pick the music in my truck. Third, I have a strict no-pants-after-midnight policy."

I nearly spat out my drink. "It seems we may be at an impasse, biker boy. I always pick the music."

Hatchet grinned as he closed the last bit of distance between us. He reached up and tucked a strand of hair behind my ear. "I'll agree to that, as long as you don't play any Taylor Swift," he said in a low voice as his fingers lingered on the side of my neck. "I have to draw the line somewhere, sweetheart."

For a heartbeat, I let myself enjoy the warmth of his touch and our easy flirtation. Then the world tilted, and I froze as the unwanted memories flooded my mind once again.

Taylor Swift blaring in my Lexus. Tires screeching. The cry of metal on metal. Steel piercing through Alec's chest. My hands, cut from shattered glass, covering the wound. The smell of copper filling the car as blood flowed under my palms. Alec's shaky fingers tucking a strand of hair behind my ear as he called me "sweetheart" one last time and apologized over the approaching sirens. His expression went slack, his eyes blank, before I had a chance to insist that I was the one who should apologize.

A crushing weight pressed on my chest as I stepped backward. "I'm sorry. I need a minute."

Hatchet's brows furrowed as I stumbled toward the edge of the clubhouse, my lungs clawing for air as the laughter and music faded behind me.

Chapter Two

The scent of woodsmoke drifted on the warm Texas breeze, wrapping around me from where I sat in the shadows near the edge of the bonfire.

After a long week dealing with a clusterfuck of a misunderstanding with the Red Rock Riot, a New Mexican MC led by two men who made Thane look like a teddy bear, and planning a sitdown with the Fort Worth mafia, I needed a drink.

Kenna's laughter floated above the bonfire's crackling and the twang of Hank Williams. She was all fire and warmth, offering too much light for a dark soul like mine. But that didn't stop the envy from pooling in my chest as she flirted with Hatchet.

He lit up the space. Sometimes I wanted to hate the prick. He made it look effortless, drawing people to him in a way I couldn't imagine. He might be my best friend, but it still grated on my nerves.

I forced my attention back to Fuse, a longtime friend. But even as we talked bikes and business, my gaze kept drifting back to Kenna. The chatter between her and Hatchet quieted, and I couldn't quite place the mix of emotions that flickered across her face. One moment, she was soft and happy, her eyes alight with laughter. The next, something brittle and broken flashed through her expression. She flinched, and the light in her eyes snuffed out like a birthday candle on a windy day.

I knew pain when I saw it. I'd lived with it long enough in my forty years to recognize it in others.

She muttered something to Hatchet, then slipped into the darkness.

It certainly wasn't the response Hatchet expected. He shoved his hands in his pockets, his easy smile faltering before he strolled over to where we sat, his usual swagger muted by confusion.

I narrowed my eyes and glanced back to the darkness where Kenna had disappeared, the shadows swallowing her whole.

"Where's Kenna?" Eva's question cut through the music and chatter as her eyes searched the area.

"She kind of stormed off." Hatchet sounded uncertain—a tone I rarely heard from him.

Reaper leveled a look at him while Eva shot him a murderous glare.

"What did you do?" she demanded.

Hatchet held up his palms and took a step back. He'd seen what Eva was capable of, and he sure as shit didn't want to be on the receiving end of her retribution. I'd laugh at the sight of our enforcer backing down from a five-foot-something woman if I wasn't worried about why Kenna pulled away.

"Nothing. I swear. We were talking about music. She just ... fell apart."

Eva's anger flickered to guilt as understanding dawned on her face. "Shit. I forgot," she said, barely above a whisper.

"Forgot what?" I asked.

Eva shook her head, glancing over to her friend. Pain colored her expression as she spoke in a voice thick with sadness.

"It's today. The anniversary," she explained. "Her fiancé died in a car accident the day before their wedding. It's been three years."

Silence fell over the group.

"I should check on her. I can't believe I made her come tonight."

I let out a breath I hadn't realized I'd held in my chest. I cleared my throat. "I got it," I said as I stood.

My voice came out hoarse, and all eyes shifted to me. I rarely volunteered for anything that wasn't club business or generally fucking things up.

Eva started to object until Reaper grabbed her hand and gave her a look—one that said he'd explain later why I was the best person to talk to Kenna tonight.

It wasn't a secret. Any man who'd been a part of the club six years ago knew about the moment my life crumbled.

I grabbed both a fifth of Jack Daniel's and a bottle of water and stalked quietly toward the darkness. I found Kenna perched on top of a picnic table behind the clubhouse, her shoulders hunched and her hands clenched in her lap. She stared into the inky-black night. For a moment, I just watched her.

"Hey," I said, my voice raw.

Kenna flinched, startled, but she didn't look at me.

"Thought you might want a drink."

She kept her eyes trained forward, her face bathed in shadows.

I held both bottles in front of her, and she grabbed the whiskey, unscrewing the top and swallowing a long pull. She wiped her mouth with the back of her hand and glanced at me. The corners of her glassy eyes pulled in anguish.

I slid the bottle of water closer and sat beside her, keeping space between us. The silence stretched, broken by the occasional laugh at the bonfire and the distant melody of country music.

I grabbed the whiskey bottle from her hands, taking a long drink before starting to speak. "Anniversaries are hell."

Kenna stared at the trees. Her expression stayed unreadable. "Eva figured it out?"

I gave her a slow nod as I swept my gaze over her tense body.

"I hate this day." She let out a shaky breath. "This isn't the anniversary he deserved. That we deserved." She grabbed the whiskey and took another sip before handing it back.

I swallowed a shot of my own. "Six years ago, I was on a run. My old lady was on the back of my bike. We'd fought all day. I was fuming. Distracted." I took another swig of the whiskey and handed it to Kenna. "We were passing through a school zone. A teenager changed lanes. Didn't even see us. I reacted too slowly."

Kenna swallowed another mouthful of liquor and glanced at me.

My voice cracked as I continued. "Rose flew off the bike. I hit the pavement. She was gone before I could stand up."

Kenna stayed silent for a beat before speaking in a flat, acerbic tone. "Is this the part where you tell me everything happens for a reason? Or that Alec is in a better place? Or that he wouldn't want me to be sad?"

I gave Kenna a grim smile and swiped the bottle from her. "No. This is where I tell you that you're not alone and offer you more liquor to take the edge off."

She managed a hollow laugh. "Does it ever work?"

"No. But it's never stopped me from trying."

She let out a deep, shaky sigh. "Once I let myself think about Alec, once I open that door, I can't stop it. It's like a dam breaking. The guilt, the memories. They drown me."

Grief bubbled up in my chest, and I pressed the feelings down. I stared at my scarred knuckles. "For me, it's like sharp rocks on a sandy beach. Some days I can walk across it just fine. Avoid the rocky areas. But other days, the pain cuts me. Makes me bleed. Sometimes it brings me to my fucking knees."

We sat in heavy silence for a long time. I'd heard people say talking about loss helped. Those people were full of shit.

After a while, Kenna exhaled. "I think I want to go home."

"I'll take you."

She scoffed. "I am not getting on a bike right now."

I laughed, but there was little humor in it. The pain was too salient for that. "I'll borrow Eva's Jeep. You want to say goodbye, or should I let them know you need space?"

"Space. Please." Her small voice was barely audible over the singing cicadas and katydids.

"Drink this," I ordered as I handed her the water and helped her stand. "I'll meet you at the Jeep."

I strode to the group, the remnants of sadness swirling in my chest. The warmth from the fire did nothing for the chill in my soul. Eva looked at me with concern and sympathy, and I grimaced, knowing Reaper had shared pieces of my painful story.

"Kenna wants to go home. Can I borrow your Jeep?"

Eva stood, concern etched into her face. She ran a hand through her hair. "I should talk to her."

I shook my head and handed her the liquor bottle. "She asked for space. I'll get her home safe. She'll be fine."

Reaper tossed me the keys, and I made my way to the gravel parking lot.

I found Kenna already in the passenger seat, her clenched hands twisted in her lap. The drive was quiet, the rumble of the engine the only sound that filled the air.

Kenna stared out the window until her breath fogged the glass. I kept my eyes on the road, giving her as much privacy as I could in the small space.

It wasn't until we pulled into her driveway that Kenna broke the silence. Her raw voice echoed across to me, pulling my own pain to the surface.

"Does it ever get easier?"

My hands gripped the steering wheel until my knuckles were white, and I put the Jeep into park. "No." Any other response would be a lie. "You learn to live with it. Like a slice in your skin surrounded by scar tissue."

I killed the engine and stepped out of the Jeep. Kenna fumbled with the passenger door handle before I opened it for her. The liquor was hitting her hard, and she swayed as her feet hit the ground. Her perfume wafted over me—jasmine, geranium, and rose—reminding me of the smell of my mother's garden in the mornings.

I steadied Kenna with one arm as I guided her to the front door. She entered the key code three times before crying out in frustration.

"Damn it. I can't fucking number the numbers."

"Let me." I gently pushed her aside and keyed in the code Reaper had given me when Eva lived here. The lock whirred, and I opened the door.

She stepped inside and turned to face me. "Merrick?" Her voice was soft and uncertain. She stared at me with glassy eyes and flushed cheeks.

"Yeah?"

"Thank you," she whispered.

Her gaze moved up to mine, and my breath caught as she ran a hand down my chest.

"Kenna," I said in warning, catching her wrist.

Her lips parted as she blinked up at me. "What?" Her voice was innocently high, a desperate edge beneath it.

"I can't stop the pain."

"You could try." She stepped closer to press her body against mine.

Fuck, I wanted to. I could help her silence the memories. She could help me drown it out, too. But only for a couple of minutes. The ache that lived in my heart for years wouldn't go away. I'd fucking tried. I spent the first year after losing Rose numbing myself with bodies and booze, only to feel emptier each morning after.

I shook my head and forced myself to step back, releasing her wrist as I gave her space. "It won't work. Trust me."

She bit her lip, looking up at me. Emotions flitted across her expression—sadness, annoyance, frustration.

Disappointment.

"Get some sleep. Drink some water. You'll feel better in the morning. I promise."

"Fine," she grumbled, stepping away before slamming the door in my face.

* * *

The bitter heat of my morning coffee bit my tongue as I waited near the clubhouse bar. The others would be dragging ass after the party, but I'd crashed early after taking Kenna home.

Thane's text before dawn calling an urgent meeting at eight had been a gut punch. No details. That never meant anything good.

Hatchet strolled in first, his legs unsteady and his veins probably filled with more liquor than blood. "Mornin'."

I nodded at him and then leaned in a bit closer as I peered at the red mark streaking his neck. Typical Hatchet. "You might want to scrub that lipstick off before you start the day."

Hatchet smirked, saying nothing as he circled the bar for a napkin and some water. I'd seen him flirt his way out of trouble, into trouble, and through trouble so many times. But that was Hatchet: all charm and no strings. He could be texting his next date while still tangled in the sheets with the first with not a single word from his conscience—if he even had one. The man lived for the chase. He never thought beyond the moment, unless he was planning his next conquest. He wasn't the type to get attached, and anyone who thought otherwise was setting themselves up for heartbreak.

Maybe that's why watching him turn his easy charm on Kenna the night before had made my jaw clench. She deserved better than him.

She deserved better than any of the Mavericks.

Reaper's boots scuffed the floor as he walked in. "How was Kenna when you got her home?"

I stared into my coffee. "Drunk and sad."

"Eva's worried. Kenna didn't answer any of her calls or texts last night."

I sighed. "She needed space. She probably passed out as soon as she hit her bed. She could barely stand."

"Thanks for making sure she got home. And for talking to her. I know it's not something you like to rehash."

I shrugged stiffly. I never spoke of Rose. I'd buried part of me with her.

But Kenna's pain mirrored my own. Despite her warm smile and laughter, she had scars and sharp edges like me, and hollow spaces that nothing could fill.

Some wounds just didn't heal.

Linc approached, his tablet in hand, with Thane trailing closely. Reaper and I exchanged glances, gut instinct telling us shit was about to hit the fan.

Thane moved behind the bar, adding whiskey to his coffee mug before he sat. He sipped the spiked brew as his gaze moved around the table. "There's no good way to say this. We have a rat."

I stiffened. "The fuck you mean?"

Linc spun his tablet to face us. "A while ago, I breached a few law enforcement systems. I need to be careful snooping around in there, so I've built scripts that flag keywords related to the club. It runs through their databases and emails, plus some third-party vendors."

"Local or federal?" Reaper asked.

"Both now," Linc said with pride. "Federal took me a lot longer. I only just got the scripts set up this week. Details were scarce, but it looks like the feds are working on an investigation to nail a Texas club on firearms trafficking."

"There are a lot of clubs in Texas. What's the chance it's us?" I asked.

Linc tapped the screen. "One report mentioned meeting a confidential informant in Conroe. Could be a coincidence." He shrugged.

I shook my head. "I don't believe in coincidences. One of our brothers is talking to the feds. Un-fucking-real. A rat." I spat out the last word with disgust.

Thane's eyes narrowed. "I want this information to stay between the four of you. I don't want to believe one of our other officers could be a CI, but it's happened before. Merrick, I want you to investigate. Quietly. Loose lips sink ships."

Reaper contemplated for a moment before speaking up. "I'm pausing the deal with the Riot. If the feds are watching, we can't risk going near the warehouse. And we sure as fuck can't transport a load of weapons to New Mexico."

Thane nodded. "Everything we do needs to be squeaky fucking clean for the foreseeable future. Above board, legit business only. Shut down the rest."

I rubbed my temples. "What about Dixon? He accepted a contract earlier this week. The kill is in New York. With the distance, the risk should be minimal."

Reaper shrugged. "We already got the wire. Have Dixon finish the job. Just remind him to not fuck it up."

Thane rolled his eyes. "Fucking mercenary. Pain in my ass. But that payout should be enough to float us for a while."

Linc typed away on his tablet and then glanced up. "It wouldn't hurt to let him know we're facing some heat right now. He needs to be more careful than usual."

"He needs to be careful, period," I growled. "Fucker acts like he's invincible. Like the goddamn patch is an invisibility cloak."

Reaper took a long sip from his coffee thermos. "Tell him to drive and wear a disguise. We don't need a flight manifest tying him to New York. It's a high-profile contract. It'll make national headlines."

I nodded. "I'll talk to him. He was planning to head out on Monday."

Thane stood and strolled back to the bar, this time pouring Jack Daniel's into his now-empty coffee cup. "Find the rat and fucking end him."

I nodded once his way as the rest of the men stood to leave. "Hold up," I said to Hatchet. "Let's make a plan."

Hatchet grumbled. "Too early for this shit. Let's just shake everyone down and see who sweats."

I pressed my fingers to my temples to ground myself. Sometimes I wondered why I put up with him—except I knew precisely why. I trusted Hatchet with my life, even if he drove me up the goddamn wall with his antics and lack of self-control. "No. We keep this quiet. We don't need the rat getting spooked. Linc will pull the security footage. Phone logs, too. If they're smart, they're using a burner. But only a fucking idiot would be a rat in our club. We need to look over the evidence before we bring anyone in."

Hatchet rolled his eyes. "While you're busy playing detective, someone is leaking our business to the feds. Your way is too slow."

"And your way is too risky. If we spook the rat, he could go underground. Right now, he thinks he's safe. We keep it that way. We can't show our hand before we're ready."

Hatchet's eyes hardened. "You always want to play it safe. Risk this, risk that. It's always about risk with you."

"Minimizing risk. It's not just about the rat. The last thing we need is for our brothers to lose faith in each other. Mistrust is a cancer. We do this my way. Quiet and methodical. That's a fucking order."

Hatchet scoffed and stood. "Fine. But when your way fails, I'm not holding back."

He stalked out, and I sat in silence, the weight of the club and the night before heavy on my shoulders.

Chapter Three

The morning light sliced through the blinds into my skull. I groaned as I burrowed deeper into the pillow, willing the hangover away. My stomach churned with shame and unprocessed whiskey, and my mouth tasted like I'd filled it with dryer lint before going to bed.

I was getting too old to drink more than a cocktail or two, and certainly too old to swig Jack Daniel's straight from the bottle.

Memories from the night before leaked into my mind. My cheeks heated as the humiliation and emotional hangover burned through me. I'd lost my shit at the bonfire and then tried to drunkenly seduce Merrick.

"What was I thinking?" I groaned. My hoarse voice echoed off the walls of the empty bedroom where I'd yet to hang a single painting or picture. I stared at the stack of half-unpacked boxes in the corner as I prayed the night before had been just a bad dream.

The anniversary of Alec's death hung over me like a storm cloud every year, and Merrick had sat with me in the dark as I unraveled— not trying to fix or dismiss it. He just let it be. And for the first time, I saw the man behind the stoic mask with his own unguarded grief, and it was like looking into a mirror. He knew what it was to live life carrying a broken heart and a ghost on your back.

It'd been three years, and I still hadn't been on a real date. Hell, I couldn't even talk to Alec's sweet mom on the phone. The grief was a dam, and I couldn't dare let it breach. The regret would drown me. So I just kept stacking sandbags—work, hard liquor, and my dark humor—to keep the water at bay. To keep myself from drowning.

I needed to apologize. To both of them. My grief and guilt weren't burdens I liked to share.

I fumbled for my phone with clumsy hands, gripping it as I tried to decide who to text first. Both situations left my face feeling hot and my hands clammy.

ME:

Hey. I'm sorry about last night.

Merrick's response came before I could set my phone down.

MERRICK:

Don't stress, I understand better than anyone.

Right. Don't stress. I just threw myself at you last night like the club groupies Eva told me about—sweetbutts. Ugh.

One apology down, one to go. Might as well finish my tour before my coffee. Rip it like a Band-Aid.

ME:

Hey, sorry I overreacted last night.

Hope you'll still be my friend after my little menty-b.

I rolled onto my back and stared at the ceiling. Maybe the shame and embarrassment would evaporate through my pores with the whiskey. My phone chirped as his response came through.

HATCHET:

Good morning, doll. Eva explained
everything. Wanna grab brunch? I can
swing by and pick you up in 30.

I smiled. His easy-going nature filled the hollow emptiness in my chest with warmth.

ME:

I would love that, but make it an hour. I
smell like bad decisions.

HATCHET:

My favorite scent on a woman.

I dragged my aching body to the bathroom. While the water warmed, I studied myself in the mirror. God, I was a mess. I stared at my bloodshot eyes, smudged eyeliner, and tangled hair for a moment before pulling the shirt I'd worn yesterday over my head. I breathed in the scent of bonfire before dropping it to the floor and stepping under the spray.

I let the water scald my skin as I tried to scrub away the memory of Merrick's gentle rejection. He'd done the right thing, but it didn't make it any less mortifying.

I didn't feel much better about how I'd left things with Hatchet. He couldn't have known that the combination of his unexpected touch and the mention of Taylor Swift would rip a memory to the surface that gutted me. A tear slipped down my cheek as I pressed Alec from my mind into that box of feelings I couldn't deal with.

I stepped out of the shower and sighed.

Standing before my closet, I sought the most aggressively platonic outfit I could find. High-rise black jeans, a faded Good Charlotte concert tee from high school, and battered running shoes. I swiped on mascara and slipped on my glasses, hoping to hide the circles under my eyes that left me looking like a delirious raccoon.

I heard a honk, and my phone pinged with a text that let me

know Hatchet waited outside. I threw my wet hair in a high ponytail and grabbed my purse before rushing out the door.

Hatchet leaned against the side of his truck, the morning sunlight catching on the sandy stubble along his jaw. His easy-going grin melted the tension in my shoulders.

Brunch with Hatchet might just be the hangover cure I needed.

Chapter Four

The women I picked up for dates usually strutted out to my truck with big hair, high heels, and enough tits and ass on display to make a preacher stare.

Kenna bounced down her front steps looking like the heroine at the start of every romcom—an unassuming beauty in basic clothes. Her red hair was pulled back, showing her high cheekbones and the flush on her freckled cheeks. She'd hidden her eyes behind glasses with dark-green frames.

I should've been bored. Instead, I was half hard and wondering what she looked like under the oversized T-shirt cinched at her waist in a knot.

I leaned against the passenger door as she approached. Her pink lips parted in surprise as I handed her a hot cinnamon vanilla latte— her favorite order from Maisie's, according to Eva.

"Hey, doll. Thought you might need some caffeine."

She took the cup and brought it to her nose, closing her eyes and breathing in the sweet scent. "You're the best. I might survive today after all."

I opened the door like the gentleman I wasn't and jogged to the other side to get behind the wheel. I toggled to the Spotify app on the dash. "As agreed upon in our terms of this friendship, you get to pick the music. Anything you want." I made a show of surrendering control.

Kenna giggled. "I'm willing to compromise. I pick the music on the way to brunch, and you can on the way back."

She selected a song and pressed play, and Theory of a Deadman filled the cab.

My eyebrows shot up. "Didn't peg you as a hard rock chick."

She grinned and rolled down the window. "I like country and pop, too. I'll even listen to orchestral music sometimes."

"Don't know what the fuck orchestral music is. Is that, like, flutes and violins and shit?"

Kenna laughed harder. "I used to play the violin. Some of my favorite rock songs sound amazing in an orchestra. But we'll ease into that playlist, biker boy. Wouldn't want to overwhelm you."

I chuckled at the nickname. She'd called me that last night, too. Right before she fell apart. "How are you feeling this morning?" I asked carefully—leaving the question open to interpretation on whether it was about the hangover or her emotional state.

"I'm fine." She glanced at me with a grimace, exhaustion etched into her expression. "OK, I feel like shit. I really am sorry about last night. Sometimes I just—"

"You don't owe me an explanation," I interrupted. "I know enough from what Eva told me last night, and I've seen enough loss with my brothers to know that not everyone wants to talk about it. But, if you ever want to, I'm here."

She offered me a sad half smile. "You're a good friend."

"I aim to please. Now, are you ready for the best breakfast tacos in Texas?" I put the truck in park.

Kenna glanced at the food truck outside her window. She narrowed her eyes as she took in its peeling paint and the barely legible handwritten menu on a tattered poster board. "Um, are you sure? Because I think I've got hepatitis just from looking at it."

I laughed. "Trust me. The sketchier the truck, the better the tacos. It's science. Let me get your door."

Kenna bit her lip as she watched me circle the truck to help her out. I led her to a battered picnic table and offered to order. She sipped her latte, watching me with suspicion. After a few minutes, I returned with a buffet of my favorites.

Her eyes widened as she took in the ten tacos I set before her. "Is the entire club joining us?"

I scoffed. "As if I'd share with those assholes. I'll eat whatever you can't."

Kenna unwrapped one and took a cautious first bite. "God, that's so good," she moaned.

I nearly dropped my own breakfast at the sound. I cleared my throat and shifted in my seat, glad the table hid my now-hardened dick. "So you'll trust me next time?"

She licked salsa from her thumb and smirked. "Maybe. Being right one time doesn't mean you're right all the time."

"Hmm." I pretended to contemplate. "You're wrong, but I'll let it slide for now. You'll see on our next date."

She tensed. "Date?"

"Yeah, I picked you up from your house, surprised you with coffee, and introduced you to the best breakfast tacos in Texas. A brunch date. What more could you ask for on a Saturday morning?"

She offered a strained smile and clenched her fingers around her latte as she stared at the table. "Hatchet, I really like you. But I don't know that I'm in a good space to date right now. I'm a mess."

I brushed a hand over her fist and squeezed gently. "Then this is a friend date. Just promise I'll be the first to know when you're ready for more."

She met my gaze and offered a small smile. "Deal."

* * *

My phone pinged as an email from Linc landed in my inbox, the notification echoing through my room above the clubhouse like a warning shot. I opened the attachment and started scrolling. Phone logs, credit card records, security cam footage. Time-stamped details of our daily lives ready for dissection. Every beer tab and drunken text message. And more dick pics than I cared to see, including my own. It was a goddamn digital autopsy.

I drummed my fingers on the battered dresser. I hated this part. The waiting. The overthinking. We should have been dragging every Maverick to the junkyard for a *friendly* conversation, not skimming through PDFs and spreadsheets like we were fucking accountants. My hatchet at a throat was often the only motivation someone needed to spill.

Merrick and his fucking protocols. His concerns for maintaining club unity would be our downfall. I cracked my knuckles. Every second we wasted with this methodical bullshit gave the rat a chance to cover his tracks, or worse, spill club business to the feds that would land us in prison. If it were up to me, we'd already have answers by now.

I stared at the file of evidence and wondered which of my brothers was the rat.

Who would betray us?

The urge to break something—someone—itched under my skin. All we needed was one mistake, one slip-up. Then I could trade these spreadsheets for sharp steel, and the real fun would begin.

Chapter Five

An eerie silence blanketed the clubhouse, and the air hung thick with the scent of lemon cleaner layered over stale beer and smoke. Thane slid a cardboard box across the scarred oak table, its edges frayed.

"This is our club history," he said as he rustled through the pile of papers, rolled-up posters, and news clips.

He handed Eva an old photograph of a group of men with grease-stained jeans and wolfish grins. They straddled their motorcycles in front of a rundown bar, their expressions a mix of fuck-the-world defiance and brotherhood. I leaned in for a closer look. One sported a black eye, and all of them wore the same swagger I'd come to expect in the short time I'd spent around the Mavericks.

"The club was founded by these three—Maxwell Morris, Don Prout, and Tobias Grove."

"Morris?" Eva asked. "Any relation to Merrick?"

Thane nodded. "His old man. Died a few years ago. You can't outride lung cancer."

He lit a cigarette, taking in a drag before blowing the smoke away from us. The irony of reminiscing about your friend's lung cancer while smoking struck me. Eva poked me under the table, as if my face betrayed every thought. I fought to control my expression, but Thane's smirk told me he hadn't missed it.

"Tobias is dead, too. His son, Tyler, is a prospect right now. Don's the last founder not yet in the dirt."

Eva stood and rustled through the contents of the box. "I'm meeting with Maisie this week to talk about PR for her booth at the market, so I can get some background from Don. I'm sure he can give me some context. I want Kenna to create a video about the club's history, and this is a great starting point."

Dust motes swirled in the sunlight as her fingers brushed over the faded flyers and Polaroids.

I tucked a strand of auburn hair behind my ear. "I can talk to Merrick about what it was like to grow up a part of the club," I offered, trying to sound casual.

Eva arched a brow at me. I ignored the heat creeping up my neck.

"I owe him a drink for driving my drunk ass home the other night," I explained. "So I can kill two birds."

I pulled out my phone, thumbs hovering for a moment before I typed. I pushed away the unnecessary guilt that crashed through me.

ME:

> When are you free for dinner? I'm helping Eva with the 50th anniversary planning. Thane shared that your dad was a founding member. I want to talk to you about growing up in the club … and thank you for the ride home again.

I watched the three dots below my text as Merrick keyed in his response. My heart leapt in my throat when my phone pinged.

MERRICK:

Sure. I'm free tonight or Thursday.

ME:

> Let's do tonight at 6. Do you like lamb chops and risotto?

MERRICK:

Sounds great. Can I bring anything?

ME:

If you have any photos from growing up in the club, bring them. Otherwise, just bring an appetite.

Thane guided Eva and me from his office to a wall of photos in the hallway. Just as he was pointing out another picture of the founders, a clean-cut man with a boyish expression and glasses slipped through the front door.

"Tyler," Thane boomed across the open space, his voice sharp and commanding.

Tyler jumped. He adjusted his glasses with a nervous flick of his fingers, then squared his shoulders. "Prez, how's it going?"

"I don't know if you've met Kenna yet," Thane said, gesturing to me. "She and Eva need to talk to you about your dad."

"My dad?"

I offered a smile. "I want to learn more about his role as a co-founder and what it was like for you to grow up with the club. Why you became a prospect."

"Tyler's going to be a hot-shot lawyer. Once he passes the bar, he'll be just as valuable as his dad. Hope you're studying, boy."

The set of his jaw was his only show of irritation at Thane's comment. He brushed his fingers over his prospect patch unconsciously. "Yeah, working on it. This is my dad's legacy. Wouldn't want to let him down."

"It was nice to meet you," I offered, breaking the tension. "I'll reach out to set up a time for us to chat." I extended my hand.

Tyler hesitated, just a heartbeat, before reaching out. His fingers brushed the back of my hand for a split second before his grip firmed up.

Eva and I said our goodbyes and headed outside. The sun cast long shadows across the gravel lot. Eva leaned against her Jeep, crossing her arms with a smirk. "So, inviting Merrick over for dinner, huh?"

I rolled my eyes and dug out my keys. "He's one of like, three friends I have here in Texas. I can't have dinner with you and Reaper every night."

"Sure you can. We love having you over."

I opened the door and tossed my bag onto the passenger seat. "Sorry, but there's only so long I can stomach my dinner while you two make suggestive comments. How often do you end up fucking at the dinner table before you finish your meal when I'm not there?"

Eva grinned. "Oh, meals get finished."

I grimaced. "That is exactly what I'm talking about. I'm glad you found love. But sometimes I'd like to eat a meal without feeling like I'm intruding on your foreplay."

Eva laughed, tossing her hair back. "Fair. In that case, I need to go buy some whipped cream for dessert."

I groaned, slamming my car door a little harder than necessary. "You're the worst."

She winked and climbed into her Jeep. "You're just jealous."

I grinned at her, shaking my head, but my smile fell from my face as soon as she turned away.

Maybe I was a little envious. I wanted that kind of certainty. That sense of belonging. I'd had it before, with Alec, and the pain of losing him nearly killed me. I couldn't imagine putting myself back through that kind of heartbreak again.

As the clubhouse faded in the rearview mirror, my thoughts drifted to my dinner plans with Merrick. There was something about him—an intensity and foreboding, like standing at the edge of a storm. The promise of electricity raged in the air around him.

Hatchet, though ... he was different. Fun, light, full of warmth. When I was with him, for just a moment, I could forget the shadows. He made me laugh, feel seen, and for the first time in a long time, like I could breathe. The way he looked at me made my heart skip, and when he smiled, the sun broke through the clouds.

I sighed, my fingers tightening on the steering wheel. It was a moot point. I wasn't ready for anything beyond friendship. Not with Hatchet, not with Merrick, not with anyone. For now, I just needed to keep moving forward, one day at a time, and hope that someday, I'd find the courage to let myself love again.

* * *

With a few hours to spare before Merrick arrived, I found myself sorting through the barrage of emails that had filled the general inbox for Lioness Communications, the PR and marketing consultancy Eva and I ran.

It was typically filled with cold outreach from vendors we'd never work with and a handful of media inquiries related to our clients. I clicked into an email from an investigative reporter for the Houston Chronicle. I skimmed it before picking up the phone to call Thane. It rang twice before he answered.

"Hello? Hey, knock that shit off; I'm on the phone."

"Thane?" I asked. "I'm sorry to bother you, but—"

"No bother, darlin'. What's going on?"

"I have a reporter asking for an interview with you about your relationship with the Riot."

"No."

I stifled a laugh at his sharp response. "No, you don't know what the Riot is? Or, no, you don't want to talk about your relationship with them?"

"Did they give a source? What makes them think we're connected to the Riot?"

"The reporter didn't say. And we shouldn't ask if we don't plan to offer an interview. It's not something she's obligated to share with us."

"And I'm not obligated to interview with her."

"You're right. You're not. But she'll write the story either way. Do you want to tell me what the Riot is? And why you don't want to talk about it?"

Thane said nothing.

"I can't help manage media for the club if you don't tell me. I signed the NDA. I'll manage this the best I can, but leaving me in the dark won't work."

Thane grumbled under his breath before speaking. "The Red Rock Riot Motorcycle Club. They're in New Mexico."

"And?"

"We do business with them. Club business. Shit I can't tell you about."

"Is this club business legal?"

Thane stayed mute, his silence spelling out the answer I needed.

"OK, so this is definitely not something we should acknowledge. I'll respond and let her know that you don't do interviews regarding other clubs, and she should direct any questions she has about the Riot to their president. If you have a good relationship with the guy, you should give him a heads-up. The reporter might pretend she has an interview with you to get him to talk to her."

"Goddamn it. Just what I fucking need is to piss off Serpent and Jag."

"And they are?"

"Serpent is the president. Jaguar is the VP. And they're both fucking unhinged."

"Got it."

I had more questions, but I was certain Thane wouldn't answer a single one.

* * *

Merrick knocked on my door at six on the dot. The sound echoed through my still-half-unpacked home.

I wiped my palms on my jeans and kicked my running shoes out of the way. My heart thumped as I opened the door to see him standing on my stoop, wearing his cut with a zinfandel blend in one hand and a small bouquet in the other. A canvas bag hung from his arm.

"I, uh, thought of you when I saw these at the store," he stammered as he handed me the wildflowers. And Reaper swears this is the wine you're supposed to have with lamb, but ... hell, I'm just taking his word for it." The words tumbled out of him, more uncertain question than confident statement.

A flush crept across my cheeks. "Thank you. Please, come inside. Don't mind the mess. I'm still unpacking." I turned away, hoping to mask how his awkward charm made my heart race.

Merrick's boots thudded behind me as he stepped inside. His gaze swept across the room as I fussed with the flowers, placing them in a mason jar at the center of my small table.

"What's in the bag?"

"A photo album. Some club stuff my dad saved and a few photos I've added over the years." He pulled the items from the bag and stacked them neatly on the counter. "Can I help you with anything?"

"No, please, just sit. The lamb's in the oven and the risotto's done." I opened the wine and poured him a glass. I bit back a laugh as the gruff, scarred biker carefully took the long-stemmed glass into his large hands. "You don't strike me as a wine guy."

He grinned. "I'm not. Beer and whiskey, mostly. This is the first home-cooked meal I've had in a while. I live off cold pizza and sandwiches."

I smiled, pouring a glass for myself. "Well, I love to cook, so you're welcome to join me anytime. I always make too much and have leftovers for days."

The timer beeped, and I pulled the sizzling cast-iron pan with two racks of lamb from the oven. The scent of rosemary and garlic filled the kitchen. With practiced precision, I carefully cut and plated the chops atop a bed of risotto, trying not to notice how Merrick watched my every move.

"This is impressive," he said as I placed a plate before him.

"A thank you and an apology."

Merrick raised a brow at me in question.

"I screwed up the other night, and while I'd like to blame whiskey, it was my fault."

He shook his head. "You don't owe me an apology."

The memory burned hot and sharp as a flush crawled up my neck. "I just ... I want to be friends, and throwing myself at you like that isn't a great start."

He shrugged. "You were pretty drunk. Liquor makes us do things we would never do otherwise."

I stayed quiet at that. He was right. I'd never wanted to be with a man like Merrick, and I'd certainly never had a one-night stand. I pushed away the errant thoughts about him that left me curious, left heat pooling in my belly.

Merrick took a bite of the lamb, and his eyes widened. "This is so good. It might be one of the top ten dinners I've ever had in my life."

I laughed, and the tension in my shoulders eased. "Well, you set the bar pretty low with cold pizza."

"True, but I've eaten at Reaper's a few times. He's like Gordon Ramsay with a gun."

I nodded, having benefited from his chef skills several times in the past week.

Merrick swallowed a gulp of wine. "So, what do you want to know?"

"What was it like, growing up?"

Merrick tilted his head, chewing on another bite of lamb before responding. "The club was different then. Rougher."

I tried not to smirk. Merrick would be a tough interview. He didn't say more than was necessary. I'd either have to get him drunk or use the interviewing skills I'd built during my stint as a broadcast reporter. "Thane said your dad was one of the founders?"

"Yeah, he'd grown up seeing clubs in Nevada. When he moved to Texas to be with my mom, he met Don and Tobias. They didn't like the Rangers and what they represented. So, they started the Mavericks out of an abandoned bar Tobias bought with his inheritance."

"The nice clubhouse hasn't always been there?"

"Fuck no. The first one was falling apart. They made just enough improvements to get it insured, and then it mysteriously burned to the ground."

"Mysteriously?"

Merrick shrugged. "I was old enough to know the circumstances were suspicious. I knew better than to ask questions."

"What about your dad? What was he like?"

"Probably hits every stereotype when you think about a biker in the 1970s. He was a chain-smoking, whiskey-drinking, fist-fighting son-of-a-bitch. He taught me everything I know about working on old bikes. He died a few years ago. Lung cancer."

"I'm sorry." I bit my lip. "My dad died about seventeen years ago. He was a smoker, too, but now"—I gesture to the urn sitting atop a shelf—"he's all ash."

Merrick choked on the sip of wine he'd just swallowed.

I laughed. "Sorry. I always forget that dead dad jokes make people uncomfortable."

He cleared his throat. "Not uncomfortable. You just surprised me."

We chatted for a few about our fathers, swapping stories and memories.

As we quieted, Merrick stood, grabbing our empty plates and taking them to the sink.

I watched in curiosity at this rough man being so ... clean. Domesticated. He rinsed our plates and put them in the dishwasher.

"What?" he asked, noticing the expression on my face.

"Nothing. I just didn't expect a biker to be so housetrained."

Merrick leaned his head back and laughed, his entire body shaking. "My mother ingrained it in me. The person who cooks doesn't do the dishes. Don't expect this behavior from my brothers, though. I let Hatchet stay with me once, and it was like living with a deranged spider monkey."

I stood to pour us each another glass of wine. Merrick grabbed the photo album, and we moved to the couch, our knees nearly brushing together as we sat. He flipped open to the front page.

A young boy stood beside a tall, bearded man in front of a bar with a hand-painted Mavericks sign. He pointed to the photo. "This is my dad and me in front of the original clubhouse."

He flipped to another page, where a younger girl sat at the bar with books and papers spread before her. "This is Merci, my little sister."

I glanced at a photo of a dark-haired woman pouring a row of shots behind the bar. Her intense gaze featured the same warm brown eyes staring back at me.

"Is that your mom?"

Merrick nodded. "During the day, she taught art classes at the university. At night, she was the club bartender."

"Is your mom still involved with the club? Is Merci?"

Merrick shook his head. "After my dad died, my mom moved in with her sister in Georgia. We all did our best to keep Merci away from the club once she hit high school. She's too smart for this life."

Merrick pulled out his phone and showed me a picture of him beside a tall woman with raven hair. She wore a long white coat and a bright smile. "Merci just graduated from med school. She's an intern at a hospital in the city." She was the spitting image of their mother.

"Wow. So, what about you? When did you decide to join the Mavericks?"

Merrick flipped forward a few pages and pointed to a photo of his younger self wearing a prospect patch beside his father. "I always knew I'd be a Maverick. I became a prospect when I got home after my last deployment to Afghanistan. Dad wanted me to carry on his legacy."

"But what do you do for, like, a job?"

Merrick chuckled. "When I was younger, I made most of my money fixing bikes and fighting in underground clubs. Then I spent four years in the Army. Now my job is the club. As sergeant-at-arms,

I get a salary. There's a house at the back of the club property where I live, so my expenses are pretty low."

"But what do you actually do?"

He shrugged. "A little this, a little that. I keep club members and their old ladies safe. Keep an eye on the businesses. Manage our private security business. Make sure the Rangers stay out of town."

"Eva said you saved her life."

Merrick looked surprised. "She told you about that?"

"Not really. She said she couldn't tell me much, but that I could trust you and the other guys."

He nodded. "Reaper is our brother, and that makes Eva a part of our family." He looked at me curiously. "What about you? I've told you all about my family, but you haven't mentioned yours beyond your dad."

I released a big sigh. "That's because I'm the black sheep. I have three younger siblings. Everest is thirty. He's a CFO in Boston. Logan is twenty-eight. Lawyer. And Kendall is the baby. She's twenty. She's becoming a psychiatrist."

"Why are you the black sheep?"

I swallowed the last of my wine. "Because I double majored in broadcasting and PR, and I quit my job to move here. I don't work for a Fortune 500 like my brothers. I'm not getting a doctorate like my sister. My choices don't make for great conversation at the country club."

"Country club?"

"Yeah, my family's kind of rich."

Merrick didn't seem surprised at the admission.

"Can I keep these photos for now? I want to scan them in. Maybe use them for the video."

Merrick nodded. "The album's been in my attic for years, so no rush to get it back."

We stared at each other for a moment, and I bit my lip as I wondered what it would be like to kiss him. I shook the thought from my mind. Maybe I was more buzzed than I realized. I needed to stop before making an ass out of myself. Again.

Merrick stood. "I should get going. Thanks for dinner."

"You're welcome. We'll have to do this again. I don't have many friends here yet, and it was nice to have someone to eat with for once."

After Merrick left, I flipped through the album of photos. His energy seemed different as a child. Lighter and brighter, with a scar-free face, a big smile, and positive energy. I wondered if the club life had changed that about him.

I flipped to the end of the album, and the last photo was Merrick standing beside a beautiful woman with jet-black hair. He was kissing the top of her head. The front of her cut had a patch of a red rose.

The only thing that followed was empty slots.

Chapter Six

My vision began to swim, the letters on the pages blurring into a muddy haze. My back ached from hunching over the table the night before. I'd slept for only a few hours before waking again and posting all the evidence on my wall with pins—a puzzle of brothers and broken loyalty.

My front door flew open, slamming the wall behind it. "Knock knock, motherfucker." Hatchet strode in with a steaming coffee and a pink box from Maisie's. The scent of fresh donuts and cinnamon rolls wafted through the room.

Reaper followed close behind with two coffees. He handed me one as his eyes skimmed the wall. "Fuck me, Merrick. You look like you've been up all night."

Hatchet snorted. "Told you he'd have a wall like he's on *CSI*."

Reaper shrugged. "*CSI: Outlaws*. I'd watch it."

I took a long sip of coffee, the heat searing my tongue, before walking them through everything I'd discovered: inconsistencies, suspicious credit card charges, phone calls, and text messages to unknown numbers. The evidence was scattered.

"Everyone's still a suspect at this point," I admitted, rubbing my temples. "But I'm narrowing it down."

Hatchet flipped open the box, the scent of sugar and fried dough filling the room. He grabbed a glazed donut, devouring half of it in one bite.

"So, what's next?"

"I had Linc pull records for anyone who's been a failed prospect or hangaround for the past five years. He also pulled together information on the sweetbutts, but they don't have access to enough dirt to be a valuable CI."

Reaper nodded. "Good thinking."

I pointed to a picture of a former prospect. "I'm sure you remember Danny. After we stripped him of his patch, he was arrested. Assault charges, among a few other things. He did a little time, but he's already been released. That's exactly when the feds like to swoop in and make a deal."

Hatchet smirked. "Danny in the clubhouse with the candlestick. You might just win this game of Clue after all."

Reaper tilted his head. "Considering the beating you two gave him after he touched Eva, I'd think he'd want as much separation from the Mavericks as he can get."

"Or he's pissed enough to want to bring our entire club down. Maybe he wants payback. He bitched to his buddies that he got kicked out of the club because of a woman."

Reaper rubbed his jaw. "You think he knows enough to hurt us?"

"Not as much as a fully patched brother, but enough. He went on a few runs. And if he's working with the cops or feds, they could be feeding him info. Using him to build a bigger case."

"Maybe," Reaper mused. "Let's grab him today and take him to the junkyard. If I remember right, he works third shift at the factory off Bowles. He should be off within the hour."

I grabbed my cut and keys. "Let's go."

Hatchet grinned as he cracked his knuckles. "It's going to be a great morning."

* * *

A few hours later, my tools lay spread before me, gleaming under the dim junkyard warehouse light. Pliers, a blowtorch, a bone saw, and my favorite blade. I ran a finger down the flat side, the textured metal cool beneath my touch.

Danny strained against the zip ties securing him to the wobbly metal chair. The duct tape over his mouth muffled his pleas. At first, he'd claimed innocence—even after a few punches to the face left blood pouring from his nostrils.

"Let's try this again," I said, peeling the tape back just enough to reveal his split lip. "Who are you talking to? Is it the Texas Rangers? Or the FBI?"

He spat blood onto the concrete. "I told you; I don't know anything about—"

Hatchet's fist cracked into his nose before he finished. Cartilage crunched, and crimson blood streamed down his chin. "We won't ask again."

Still, Danny clung to his lie, his eyes tight with anger and defiance.

Hatchet's phone rang, and he grinned as he silenced it.

I reached for the blade, its polished surface glinting under the dim light. I traced the flat edge along Danny's cheek before gripping his wrist and positioning the knife above his hands.

"Going to be hard to work at a factory without any fingers." I slowly pressed the sharp edge onto his skin. He shrieked as flesh and bone gave way.

"We're going to repeat this nine more times before I move on to your ears."

"Feds!" Danny choked. "They cornered me after my arrest. Let me out in exchange for information."

I left the pinky finger hanging from his hand by a shred of skin and stepped back, wiping his blood off the blade on my jeans. "What'd you give 'em?"

"Runs I rode on. Hangouts. Some supplier names. The warehouse location."

"Which warehouse?"

"The one off 3083."

Reaper let out a slow, controlled breath, his shoulders relaxing slightly. That one was full of fenced vehicles picked up in the Woodlands—hot bikes and cars that could be broken down and sold quickly. But the real prize, the warehouse on County Line Road, still stocked stolen military-grade weapons.

Thankfully, the prospects weren't privy to that location.

"That's all?" I asked, my tone sharp.

"That's all, I swear," Danny whimpered. "They wanted more, but I didn't have anything else to give. They asked if I could get back in the club, but once I explained why I was kicked out, they cut me loose."

A sudden ring cut through the thick silence. My phone, perched among the tools of my trade, lit up with Kenna's name.

Hatchet's eyes shifted to mine. "She just called me, too. Maybe something's wrong."

I glanced at my blood-spattered hands. "Answer it," I gruffed. I didn't like that she'd called Hatchet before me.

"Hello?" Hatchet said, pressing the phone to his ear.

I couldn't make out all the words, but the hysteria in Kenna's voice was unmistakable. Hatchet's brow furrowed as he toggled the phone to speaker.

"... can't get a hold of Eva because she's in a meeting, and I can't get home because my keys were in my purse. I need someone to get the spare set from my house so I can drive."

"Slow down. What happened? Where are you?" Hatchet asked.

"I'm in downtown Houston at the police station. Wait, Hatchet? Is that you? I thought I called Merrick."

"Merrick couldn't answer, so I picked up his phone. He's standing right here. You're on speakerphone."

"What happened?" I growled, my tone rough.

Kenna's voice trembled. "I was mugged. The guy ran off with my purse. I'm sorry. If you guys are busy, I can wait for Eva to get out of her meeting later this afternoon."

"No," Hatchet said. "I'm on my way right now to pick you up. I'll be there in thirty."

"OK," she said, her voice breaking as Hatchet ended the call and set the phone back on the table.

He gave my blood-spattered clothes a once-over. "I think it's better if you finish this. I'll go pick her up."

I nodded. "I'll meet you at the clubhouse later." I drew my silenced Sig Sauer, ignoring Danny's pleas. "Are the feds getting information from anyone else?"

"I think they have someone in the club," he stuttered, "but I swear, I don't know who. No one talks to me since I got kicked out."

I tilted my head, hearing the truth in his tone. "Then we're done here."

I squeezed the trigger, and the gunshot blasted through Danny's skull.

Chapter Seven

HATCHET

I barely remembered tearing out of the junkyard on my Harley.

My mind raced ahead of my body as I thought about Kenna at the police station, clearly shaken. The thought twisted my gut, mixing fury with a fierce protectiveness. I needed to see her, to touch her, to know she was safe.

I hit over a hundred and ten on the highway, the wind screaming in my ears and suffocating my lungs. I took the downtown exit at a reckless speed, weaving through traffic with practiced ease, and skidded to a stop in front of the police station, parking my bike right on the sidewalk, ticket be damned.

Inside, the station smelled of burnt coffee and sweat. The fluorescent lights buzzed overhead. I'd been here before, cuffed in a corner, staring at the scuffed linoleum for hours before the club lawyer sprung me.

I ignored the stares my cut drew as I scanned the room for Kenna. I found her huddled in the corner, her fiery red hair a beacon in the drab space with lines of evaporating fear still etched across her face. Without a word, I crossed the room and pulled her into my arms.

"Hey, are you OK?" I asked, looking into her eyes.

She nodded, tears rimming her lashes. "Yeah," she said in a shaky voice.

My gaze grazed across her body. Red, hand-shaped marks covered one arm. Scabs peppered her palms. Her dress slacks were torn and bloody at the knees. I tipped her chin up, noticing a bruise forming under her jaw.

"He fucking hit you?"

Tears broke free and streamed down her cheeks. "I tried to fight back when he grabbed my purse. He punched me and then pushed me to the ground."

My jaw flexed as I tamped down the fury inside me. I kept my arm around her, pulling her close as I looked across the room. Then I spotted Detective Rodriguez—a burly man with a bike of his own, who'd brought it to Bones once for new pipes. He'd always treated us fairly, not judging the Mavericks or assuming we were criminals. He'd even occasionally given us information that proved helpful.

"Detective Rodriguez," I called, my voice steady despite the rage inside me.

He glanced up, recognition flashing across his face. His eyes flicked between Kenna and me, understanding dawning as he realized she was associated with the club.

"Hatchet, it's good to see you." He extended a meaty hand.

I shook it. "Do you have any leads on this?"

The detective shook his head. "Not my case. But I suspect it was a street gang."

"Was anything caught on camera?"

He shrugged. "No city cameras. Maybe a local business. Don't hold your breath, though. You know how it is. People get mugged every day down here. The case will get buried in days."

I grabbed a scrap of paper from a nearby desk and scribbled my number. "Call me if you hear anything. We can't have thugs beating our women up downtown. If PD isn't going to handle this, the Mavericks will."

· · ·

The detective stared at me for a moment, his dark-brown eyes calculating. "I'm sure you've heard about the increase in violent crime over the past month?"

I nodded. It was all the news anchors talked about every morning.

"There's a new gang in the Third Ward," Rodriguez continued. "They call themselves the Jackals. They're young and stupid. Reckless. Based on the colors Ms. Walsh described, that's who you're looking for."

"Thanks." I clapped the detective on the shoulder. "Bring your bike back in soon. The next upgrade's on us."

Once we stepped into the sun, I took another look at Kenna. Her skin was pale, her eyes still watery. I brushed a thumb over her cheek, wiping away a tear. The light caught the fine dusting of freckles across her nose, making her look younger and more vulnerable.

"Let's get you home," I murmured.

She blinked up at me. "Did you bring my keys?"

I shook my head. "We'll get a prospect to pick it up later. You shouldn't be driving." I straddled my bike and handed her a helmet from the saddlebag. "Get on."

I clenched my jaw as I watched her shaky fingers fumble with the helmet strap.

"Here," I said, pulling her hands away from the clasp. "Let me."

She took a deep breath, steadying herself. I clipped it, and she swung a leg over behind me. The engine roared to life beneath us, and the vibration thrummed through my body and into hers. I took her hands and wrapped her arms around my waist, holding them there for a moment.

"Hang on," I yelled over the roar of the engine.

She pressed against my back, her grip tightening as we pulled away from the curb and merged onto the highway.

After a short drive, I stopped at a diner outside of town. "I think you need a milkshake and a piece of cake," I said as I helped Kenna off my bike.

She managed a small smile. "Can they add vodka to the milkshake?"

I laughed. "Probably not here, but we'll get you a drink at the clubhouse."

Kenna settled into the booth and scanned the menu. I ordered before she decided on a strawberry milkshake and a slice of chocolate cake. As soon as the waitress left, I excused myself and stepped outside to call Merrick.

"How is she?" he asked without even uttering a hello.

I scrubbed a hand over my short beard. "Shaken and bruised. She downplayed it. She was punched and thrown to the ground. Scratched the fuck out of her hands, and I'm betting she's got more bruises I can't see."

"Fuck," Merrick growled. "What's PD doing about it?"

"Rodriguez was there. Not his case, but he thinks it was a new gang. Says it'll get buried. See if Linc can get hold of the police report and find any camera footage from the local businesses."

"I'll get him on it."

"We'll stop and get her keys on the way to the clubhouse after we leave the diner. I didn't want her to drive. We'll get a prospect to fetch her car tonight."

"Bayou is here. We can have him grab it."

I slipped my phone back into the pocket of my cut and walked back into the diner just as the waitress brought our milkshakes to the table. Kenna offered me a bite of her cake. I shook my head.

"Thank you for dropping everything to come get me," she said in a soft voice. She paused as she considered her next words. "What did you mean when you told the detective that the Mavericks would handle it?"

I sucked down my chocolate milkshake. The cold smoothness soothed my hoarse throat. "You should be able to walk down the street during the middle of the day without being afraid."

She chewed on her straw for a moment. "Nice evasion. I probably don't want to know, do I?"

I smirked. "Probably not."

"And you wouldn't tell me, would you?"

I chuckled. "Definitely not."

"Because it falls under 'club business,' I assume?"

I huffed a laugh at her air quotes. "Sassy. Almost back to your normal self." She rolled her eyes, and I watched as she took another bite of cake. I waved down the waitress as I took in the darkening bruise below her jaw. "Can we get a bag of ice?"

The waitress shot me a glare. Her eyes flicked between Kenna's bruises and the split skin on my knuckles, as if I were the one who'd hurt her. She left without a word, returning with a quart-sized bag of crushed ice wrapped in a paper towel.

"You good, hon? Need me to call anyone?"

I appreciated the waitress's concern, though I hated the assumption that was clear in her eyes.

"Don't worry," Kenna said, reading into her look. "He's not the one who did this."

The waitress nodded, skeptical relief flickering across her face before she bustled off to another table.

We finished our shakes in comfortable silence. The hum of the diner and the clink of silverware filled the space between us. Afterward, we stopped by Kenna's house for her spare keys. I followed her in, peering into the mostly unpacked boxes sitting in the corner as she changed her clothes. I wondered if she'd ever get the chance to settle, or if the chaos of this start to her life in Texas would chase her away.

When we pulled up to the clubhouse, the sun cast a sharp reflection across the chrome and polished paint on the bikes lined up outside. I helped Kenna off my Harley, my hand lingering on her elbow, steadying her as she found her footing. She was still a little shaky, and I wanted to make sure she was ready to face the group of concerned Mavericks waiting inside.

The clubhouse door creaked open as we stepped through. Linc, Reaper, and Merrick sat at the bar, their conversation halting as they turned to take us in.

"What do you want to drink?" I brushed her lower back, pressing her to the bar.

She sank onto a stool. "Tequila. On the rocks."

I moved behind the bar, watching as Merrick's eyes darkened at the sight of her scrapes and bruises. I filled a fresh bag of ice and pressed it to her bruised jaw before turning to pour a triple shot of tequila into a crystal glass.

"Linc got some video from a bodega," Merrick offered softly. "We have his face. We'll find him."

Kenna gave him a rueful smile. "Hatchet says you'll 'take care of it.'" She used air quotes with a tight laugh.

"We will," Merrick promised, his tone serious.

Kenna bit her lip. "I know I should be worried. But honestly? I'm not." She let out a shaky laugh, half defiance, half confession. "It's messed up, right? I keep telling myself that violence isn't the answer, but I want him to be afraid. I want him to know what it's like to feel powerless."

"Atta, girl. That's the Maverick spirit," I said, pressing the drink into her hand.

She whispered a thank you and closed her eyes as she took a long sip. The overwhelming, simmering male protectiveness in the room seemed to settle her nerves. There wasn't a safer place for her right now.

Merrick brushed a hand on her shoulder. "There isn't a solid line between right and wrong. People like to pretend it's a painted stripe down the middle of the highway. It's not. The road's full of potholes and detours. We do what we have to do to take care of our own, even if it means crossing the line."

She swirled the tequila in her glass and took a long sip. Her lips quirked into a wry smile. "Guess I'm more like the Mavericks than I thought."

That so-called line between right and wrong? It stopped meaning shit to me a long time ago. And when it came to protecting Kenna, there wasn't a line I wouldn't ignore, erase, or drag someone across.

The clubhouse door flew open as Eva rushed in. "Kenna," she said with relief. "Reaper told me what happened. You should have called me. I would have left."

Kenna shook her head. "It's fine. Hatchet picked me up."

Reaper wrapped an arm around Eva, kissing the top of her head before looking at Kenna. "We don't want either of you downtown without one of us right now. Hell, I don't want either of you going for a run out here without a prospect trailing you. The Jackals are becoming more violent by the day."

Eva rolled her eyes before glancing at Kenna. "Lucky us. The Mavericks' personal bodyguard service is a special experience."

Kenna glanced between Merrick and me, realizing Reaper was completely serious.

"I have to take one of you with me every time I need to go downtown?"

"Until we get this taken care of, yes," Merrick said as his eyes bore into hers. "They're violent. A woman was killed yesterday in a carjacking. You could have been hurt much worse today. I won't allow that to happen."

"You realize I have meetings downtown almost every day? Shadowing us is going to be a full-time job. And I can't have bikers sitting in. No offense."

I wrapped an arm around her. "Don't worry. We'll stay outside. Just make sure you leave a window cracked for me."

The room erupted in laughter, easing the tension for a moment. Kenna leaned into me, her body warm and solid against my side.

My eyes met Merrick's, and I caught the subtle shift in his expression. His face was usually a mask of cool detachment, but now his lips pressed into a thin line and his dark eyes flickered with a simmering anger. He wasn't just pissed. He was haunted by the sight of Kenna's bruises, by the same helplessness I felt about not being there to stop it.

Merrick cared, maybe more than he'd ever admit. I knew him better than most. I'd ridden with him through hell and back. Since losing Rose, he'd locked away a part of himself—the part that let him care deeply about anyone outside the club. He'd buried his heart with her, and none of us had ever seen him come close to digging it up. His budding friendship with Kenna was the first flicker I'd seen in years of the Merrick I once knew.

Chapter Eight

Tension hummed in the clubhouse air as men trickled in for Church.

Reaper leaned forward. "Fuck me. I have a bad feeling that shit's about to get real. I'm not sure these Jackals play by our outlaw rules."

Through Linc's sleuthing, we'd identified the gang member who'd attacked Kenna. His laptop sat open on the table with a grainy image of the man frozen on the screen. Young, cocky, and stupid enough to think he was untouchable.

He'd be in the ground by midnight.

"Why haven't we heard of these guys before?" I asked my brothers.

Linc typed on his keyboard for a moment, then spun the screen to face us. "They're a spin-off of Los Guerreros. Houston PD only recently tagged them as an organized crew."

"I asked around. Don saw two guys wearing their colors near the bakery the other day," Thane gruffed as he rubbed his goatee. "He pulled his piece when he caught them trying to break into a customer's car. Pussies ran away."

"Archer saw a few scouting in the Woodlands this week, too," Hatchet added. "One looked about twelve."

"Great. Baby gang bangers," Reaper grumbled. "Just what fucking Houston needs. Why now? Why are they escalating this quickly?"

"Interesting." Linc hummed at his screen, tapping a line of code.

"What?" I growled.

"Remember Diego Pérez from my high school football team?" he asked, looking at Reaper. "He graduated a few years before me. Damn good hacker. He's their vice president. Rap sheet says he just got out of prison after hacking the security of a jewelry store. Only got caught because a cop walked by when he was inside."

"He always was a greedy bastard. One of the best pickpockets I'd ever watched in action," Reaper acknowledged. "Sounds like he's escalated. This might bring in a few more clients to Maverick Security."

I glanced between Reaper and Thane and drummed my fingers on my thigh. "I think we should bring Fuse back into the fold. We could use another enforcer with all this shit going on. And if more of the town's businesses want Maverick protection, we'll need extra muscle."

A grin split on Hatchet's face as he pounded his fist on the table. "Hell yeah."

Thane nodded. "Agreed. Call him today and brief him on the situation."

"Good." I hesitated before continuing, knowing full well I'd get pushback. "I also want someone on Kenna's house every night until further notice."

Everyone's eyes shifted to me.

Thane's brow furrowed. "She's not a part of the club. She's not an old lady or on track to become one. She's a consultant."

I flexed my jaw. "That didn't stop us from protecting Eva when she was in danger. I'm asking for a prospect to watch her house at night for a week or so, just to make sure the fucker who stole her purse and keys doesn't come back looking for a second payday. She drives a Range Rover, for fuck's sake. That set of wheels easily costs $100,000."

Reaper watched me, his expression curious. His sharp eyes assessed me before he responded carefully to Thane. "You're right. She's not technically a part of the club. But she's Eva's best friend, and her work is important to the club's reputation. She's the one who flagged that someone was digging into our business with the Riot. If you hadn't given Serpent a heads-up, he'd have shown up and put a bullet in your head."

Thane waved a hand. "Fine. Have Coast watch her house for the next few nights."

I sipped my coffee, the bitter warmth grounding me as I shifted the subject before Thane could change his mind. "The Jackals have made a lot of enemies across the city. They're infringing on territories. Our best bet right now is to hope one of the other crews takes them out."

Hatchet leaned forward. His eyes sparkled, undoubtedly with bad ideas and recklessness. "What if we set them up? Make it seem like they're fucking with the cartel's business. They won't last a month once they have that target on their back."

I grimaced. "I'd like us to stay as far away from those motherfuckers as we can. Engaging with the cartel in any way is a last fucking resort."

Thane and Reaper nodded in agreement.

After the meeting broke, I strode out of the clubhouse. The heavy door thudded shut behind me, and I breathed in the humid morning air, the scent of gasoline mixing with damp earth. I rolled my shoulders, trying to release the restless energy coiled in my chest.

"Hold up," Reaper called from behind me.

I turned to face him. "What?"

Reaper crossed his arms. "The fuck is going on?"

I shrugged. "With what?" I feigned ignorance, though I could already see where this was heading.

"You, motherfucker. What's up with you and Kenna?"

"Nothing." I turned to walk away, but Reaper grabbed my arm and yanked me back to face him. I squared off, ready to punch him in the face.

"Nothing? I seem to remember you being completely opposed to me protecting Eva when she first started working with the club. Now you're outside Kenna's house all night?"

I narrowed my eyes but kept my mouth shut.

"Yeah, I know you were there last night," Reaper continued. "I saw your truck. I drove by, too. Eva was worried, so I offered to check up on her. Color me surprised when I saw you standing guard."

"Kenna's a friend of the club, and we need to watch her back. It's that simple."

Reaper raised a brow at me skeptically. "That's it? She's a friend of the club? That's the only reason we're putting club resources on her?"

"She's Eva's best friend. Eva is your old lady. It's no different from when you protected Eva when she was only Rhetta's best friend to you." My tone grew irritated.

Reaper huffed a laugh. "I see the way you watch her when she's on Hatchet's arm. If you two let a woman get between you—"

"Enough," I snapped. "I'm not debating this with you. Kenna's a friend. If she wants to be with Hatchet, I won't stop her." I let out a bitter laugh. "Not that it would last long."

Reaper flexed his jaw. He stared at me before releasing a long sigh. "If you say so."

He clapped me on the shoulder, his grip tightening for a second before he let go. The unspoken warning hung heavy in the air between us.

Don't let this get messy.

Don't let a woman get between Hatchet and me, and tear the club apart.

Chapter Nine

The nights following my downtown mugging blurred by in a fit of restless dreams and panicked awakenings. I tossed and turned all night, tangling my sheets around my legs. My body tensed at every creak as the house settled around me, and the echo of imagined footsteps made my heart race. In the dark, shadows seemed to shift in the corners into the shapes of men and monsters.

My mind replayed the moment over and over. The stranger's grip on my purse, the punch to my jaw, the sharp sting of my palms scraping across the pavement. The paralyzing helplessness.

Eva and I met up at a local trail to go for an easy run with Hawk. The morning air was already thick, and the scent of dewy grass and wildflowers tickled my nose. Mockingbirds chirped in the trees, and the distant hum of traffic was a reminder that life drove forward despite my nightmares.

We slowed to a walk after a mile or so to give Hawk a rest. "You look tired," Eva commented as she took in the dark circles around my eyes.

My instinct was to make a joke, to turn this bruised, haunted sleeplessness into something lighter for Eva's sake. But I knew she'd see right through it.

I sighed. "Every little noise wakes me up. I don't know why. It's not like anything happened at home. But they have my purse, which means they have my driver's license. They have my address."

Eva handed me Hawk's leash so she could rustle around in her purse. With a rubber band, she pulled her hair off her sweaty neck and into a ponytail.

"Maybe you should get a dog. A big one. The shelter's always looking for fosters."

I laughed as Hawk caught sight of a squirrel and pulled at the leash, jerking me forward. He let out a small yip in frustration.

"Maybe. It would be nice not to be alone at night."

Eva bumped my shoulder. "I can think of other ways to solve that problem, based on the looks I see Hatchet throwing your way."

I laughed, but it was hollow. "We're friends. That's all. I'm not ready for more. I told him that."

"Sorry I keep pushing," Eva said with a sad smile. "I know you and Alec were together for a long time. But he wouldn't want you to be alone. You know that, right?"

I glanced away, pressing the emotion down and swallowing the lump in my throat. "I know. But I'm not ready to move on. I'm not over it."

Eva squeezed my arm. "I don't know that you'll ever get over it. You can make space for someone else without losing what you had with Alec."

Her words settled over me. But the thought of opening my heart again, of letting someone in, was terrifying. The mugging had only made it worse—reminding me how fragile my safety was. I stayed silent for a beat before shifting the topic. "Maybe we should take a self-defense class or something."

Eva scoffed. "As if our personal bodyguards will let anyone get close enough for us to need to use it."

It was true. Zen, a new prospect, trailed us from a respectful distance, far enough away that he couldn't eavesdrop, but close enough that he could protect us if needed. Sweat streamed down his brow, and for a moment I felt bad making the poor guy jog behind us in his boots.

I stopped as an idea tickled my mind. "What if the club hosted a self-defense class for women?" Hawk pressed against his collar again, and I handed his leash to Eva.

She raised a brow. "Good idea. Not every woman in Houston has bikers shadowing their every move." She glanced back at Zen with a grin.

"Exactly. And the guys know how to fight. Merrick told me that's how he used to make money."

Eva raised a brow but didn't comment on this revelation. "I bet there would be a lot of interest with the uptick in crime downtown. I'll run it by Thane tonight when he and Rhetta come over for dinner."

I smiled as a flicker of hope sparked in my chest.

I couldn't control the world, but I could do something to help others—and maybe, in the process, ignite strength within myself.

* * *

Within hours of submitting my adoption application to the shelter, my phone rang.

"Good afternoon. This is Jolene from the animal shelter. The dog you were interested in just got adopted, but we have another that's about the same age and size. Would you like to meet him?"

I jolted to attention. "Yeah, of course. I'm definitely interested."

"He's a lovely Dutch Shepherd. About nine months old. This breed doesn't do well in shelters, so we'd like to place him as soon as possible. He doesn't seem to have any behavioral issues. The owner surrendered him because the new place she's moving to doesn't allow dogs."

"I can be there in about an hour."

I hung up the phone and rushed to my vehicle with a grin. The idea of not being alone at night, of having a dog to keep the nightmares at bay, eased my anxiety and filled my heart with hope.

After a quick stop at the pet store—where I filled a cart with plush toys, treats, and a soft bed—I pulled into the shelter parking lot. Barking echoed from inside the building, and I could smell the faint scent of industrial cleaner mixed with an undercurrent of wet fur and feces.

The disinterested receptionist barely looked up at me as I walked in. "Are you here to adopt or surrender?"

"Adopt. I just spoke to Jolene."

"Take a seat. She'll be out shortly."

I waited on the edge of a plastic chair, flipping through pamphlets about kennel cough and the importance of crate training.

Finally, the door swung open, and a leggy brindle-coated dog bounded toward me with a wagging tail.

"You must be Kenna," the petite blonde said. "I'm Jolene, and this is the dog we just got in. We haven't even named him yet."

I ran my hands over his thin, wiggling body. He tried to lick me and then nibbled on my arm.

"He's a big boy. Is he going to grow more?" I asked, laughing as he pawed at my knee.

Jolene chuckled. "He'll probably fill out a bit more as he matures, but he shouldn't get much bigger. If he does, you might need to name him Clifford." She handed me a clipboard. "Once you fill out this paperwork, you can spend a bit of time with him in the yard to make sure he's a good fit. Then you're good to take him home."

As I signed the forms, Jolene explained what to expect with a shelter dog. "The first three days, he'll need space and time to decompress. During the first three weeks, you'll want to focus on building a routine and starting basic training. And it could take up to three months for him to trust you and feel fully comfortable in your home."

I nodded. The responsibility felt daunting but also exhilarating. I'd never had a dog. My mother had insisted that their claws would destroy her furniture. And, before moving to Texas, I'd spent too much time at the office to have a pet at home.

On the drive, my dog lay on the back seat like a gentleman. He rested his head on his paws as he watched the world go by and then supervised me as I assembled his crate in the living room. His ears perked up at every sound, but he'd yet to bark. When I handed him a squeaky toy, he took it gently before flopping onto his new bed.

As I watched him, a sense of calm settled over me. For the first time, the house didn't feel empty. Maybe I wouldn't be so afraid of the dark anymore.

I snapped a picture of him flopped on his back, paws in the air, inviting belly rubs. I sent it to Eva.

ME:

What should I name him?

EVA:

Well, that escalated quickly. He's a beast.

ME:

I think I'll call him Brisket. A Texas name for a Texas dog.

EVA:

You cannot name a dog after your favorite BBQ dish.

ME:

Brisket says keep your judgment to yourself.

EVA:

I'm happy you have a new running buddy. It's getting too hot for me to go through that torture with you.

The deafening silence of my home was replaced with the gentle click of Brisket's claws on the hardwood, the rustle of him settling into his bed, and the occasional contented sigh. My heart brimmed with happiness as I played with him through the evening. As the night deepened, Brisket curled up beside me on the couch. His warm body pressed against my leg, and the sound of his steady breathing filled the room with a sense of safety and companionship.

Instead of putting him in his crate, I let him sleep beside me in bed.

And for the first time in days, I slept through the night.

* * *

The music pulsed throughout the yard as I pulled up to the Mavericks clubhouse, mingling with the distant laughter and the clicking of cooling engines. The air smelled of grilled meat and beer.

I'd hoped to arrive before the real party began, to capture video interviews to show the history of the club, but the lot was already filled with bikes.

I pulled my bag from the back of my Range Rover and slung it over my shoulder. A gruff voice sounded behind me.

"Need a hand?" Merrick reached for the tripod, lights, and boom mic before I had a chance to respond.

"Thanks," I said with a smile.

"You're not going to make me be on camera, are you?"

I chuckled. "I'm pretty sure I can't *make* you do anything. But I will ask nicely." I batted my eyelashes at him.

"Are you open to negotiation?"

I arched my brow. "Maybe."

"Another home-cooked dinner?" Merrick asked with a hopeful note in his voice.

"Deal. But only if you help me wrangle the others before they're too drunk for an interview. And you convince them to take it seriously."

He nodded. "If anyone gives you problems, point them toward me."

I glanced around the yard, looking for a location to set up. The chrome-coated bikes and activity in the background would add character to the backdrop, and the evening light would cast a golden glow on each member.

"This spot is perfect," I said, setting my camera bag on the ground.

Warmth flooded me as Merrick handed me the tripod, his hand brushing mine. I set up the equipment with practiced ease, despite the nervous flutter in my stomach.

"Stand here," I directed.

"Fuck. You were serious," Merrick lamented.

"I'll keep the suffering to a minimum. Because of everything you told me the other night, I already know what soundbites I need. I'll ask a few easy questions, and then you're free to terrorize the others into coming over here. I'll throw in my famous carrot cake and a dozen chocolate chip cookies for your cooperation."

The surest way to get a bachelor to do anything was to speak to their stomach or their cock, and I wasn't ready for the latter. Still, the brief thought of Merrick in that way sent a flutter through my belly, followed by a flicker of guilt.

"You're not putting this on social media, are you?" Merrick asked, shifting uncomfortably.

I giggled. "You don't like social media?"

He shook his head. "I'm too old for that shit."

"How about this: I'll check with you first if there's any part of this interview I want to use on the Mavericks' Instagram?"

He begrudgingly agreed.

Keeping to my promise, I asked Merrick a handful of questions about his dad and his experience growing up in the club.

"How long have you been the sergeant-at-arms?" I asked, getting into things that we hadn't yet discussed.

"Since 2020."

"I need you to restate the question in your answer," I reminded him. "And elaborate with details when you can."

Merrick rolled his shoulders and took a deep breath before rumbling his response. "I've served as the Mavericks' sergeant-at-arms since 2020. I was promoted when Reaper became the VP. Before that, I was an enforcer."

I smiled. "See, that wasn't so hard."

I continued my line of layered, open-ended questioning, choosing ones that would draw out the history, emotion, and honesty I'd observed through the club. After a few, Merrick began to relax, answering my questions with ease. I skimmed through my notes to find the dates I'd jotted down during my research. "You came in as a prospect when your father was serving as president and Tobias Grove was VP. Thane was sergeant-at-arms. What was it like to join when the founders were still a part of the club?"

"Look at you, digging up the details," he murmured.

I smirked and raised my brows as I waited for his answer.

"I joined as a prospect after I was honorably discharged from the U.S. Army. I never questioned whether I would join. The Lone Star Mavericks Motorcycle Club runs in my blood. It's a part of my soul."

Giddiness ran through me. That final quote would be a perfect highlight in the video.

"Is there anything else you'd like to add?"

Merrick scoffed. "No, I think my special on *60 Minutes* is over."

I approached him, angling my head to gaze up into his eyes. "I know you hated every second of that, but I appreciate it. And that final soundbite earned you *two* home-cooked dinners."

He smiled at me for a moment, making my breath catch in my throat. "Appreciate you making it worth my time."

The Texas night pressed warm and thick against my skin, the air barely cooling despite the setting sun. Merrick fell into my role as a camera assistant—always so careful, so respectful, like he was afraid I'd combust if he got too close. He followed my direction, moving lights and positioning the old folding chair that had seen better days.

He herded other men to stand before my camera. Some acted like they'd been waiting their whole lives for this moment, grinning wide and hamming it up for the lens. Others only did it because Merrick hovered behind me, arms crossed, looking like he'd personally drag them to hell if they objected.

I noticed the way his eyes softened when he thought I wasn't looking, how his mouth twitched at my sarcastic comments. He was stoic, sure, but not cold. There was a current under all that stillness. I wondered what it would be like if he ever let go of all that control. If, just once, he forgot to be the club's steady hand and let himself be reckless—with me. The thought made my cheeks go hot, and I pretended to fiddle with the camera settings just to give myself something to do. I watched him wrangle another biker my way, and I tried not to think too hard about the way my heart stuttered every time he looked at me.

Chapter Ten

Having Kenna's attention on me the night before—her camera lens fixed, her questions sharp—left me more rattled than I cared to admit. I'd faced down rival clubs, the barrel of more guns than I could count, and my own demons, but sitting in that ring of light exposed me in a different way.

Her skill as an interviewer caught me off guard. With her gaze pinning me in place, every question felt like a scalpel slicing through layers to expose the real me.

I was used to threats I could see. Fists, bullets, inattentive drivers. Those I know how to handle. You braced, you fought, you counter-maneuvered. Order, control, routine. That kept you safe. You didn't let anyone close enough to see the cracks in your armor, because once they did, they knew where to press.

Now, standing on Kenna's porch, I rolled my shoulders and tried to shake off the nerves. Part of me wondered if I should walk away now before things got too complicated. Before being drawn into this life put her own in danger. But as much as I knew I should walk away, I wanted whatever scrap of her I could have—even if it were just a friendship.

Loud, exuberant barking greeted me after a quick knock. The oak door swung open, and there she was—red hair wild, cheeks flushed, barely hanging on as a brindle-colored dog the size of a small bear tried to drag her through the screen.

"Come in. He's friendly," she said with a grin. "Brisket, sit!" The dog hovered his butt above the ground in a half sit, like it was a negotiable request.

"When the fuck did you get a dog?" I asked as I opened the screen door.

"A few days ago."

She tossed me a treat. "I'm going to let him go. When he gets to you, make him sit. Ignore him if he jumps on you. We're working on manners."

Kenna released Brisket, and he skidded in front of me. As she predicted, he leaped up and planted his paws square on my chest. If I were a smaller man, he would have knocked me flat on my ass.

"Sit," I commanded in a deep voice.

Brisket immediately plopped his butt to the ground and waited patiently for the treat. "Jesus, Kenna. This dog would be taller than you if he stood on two legs."

She beamed. "I know! Isn't he perfect? I don't think anyone will break into my house at night with him on guard."

I paused, searching her face. There were shadows under her eyes, hidden under a layer of makeup. Something in my chest tightened. "Have you been worried about that?"

She bit her lip. "Logically, I know it's not likely to happen. But yeah. I've been feeling anxious, especially at night. Having Brisket in the house has helped."

I scrubbed the five o'clock shadow on my face. "You don't need to worry. I've had a prospect watch your house every night since the mugging, just in case they noted your address on your driver's license."

She laughed as if I were joking and then turned serious when she realized I wasn't.

"Wait. What? You have someone watching me?"

I shrugged. "Just at night."

"You can't have a prospect sit outside my house just in case someone tries to break in. And you should have asked me first. I don't like the idea of someone watching me without me knowing about it."

"The prospect isn't watching you. He's watching the traffic and your house, just in case—until we get the Jackal situation resolved."

Her cheeks flushed, and for a second, I let myself admire her. I wanted to close the space between us and lean into her heat.

She cleared her throat, breaking the spell. "Well, come in. And this time, I've got whiskey and beer, so you don't have to pretend you like wine."

I chuckled as I followed her inside. "A beer would be great."

* * *

"You heard from Dixon?" Thane asked, a web of smoke surrounding him from his spot at the bar.

I waved to Leah and pointed at the row of whiskeys on the wall. She smiled and nodded a silent promise to bring me a drink. I'd serve myself, but I knew it pissed her off to no end when we did that.

"No, but he should be on the road already. I didn't tell him about the rat, but I asked him to be careful because we had concerns the feds could be watching."

Thane lit another smoke. "Fucker's always broke. You think it could be him?"

I rubbed the stubble on my jaw. "Honestly, I hadn't considered him as a serious suspect. He's always been loyal. And his role with the club would implicate him for enough crimes that he'd spend more time in prison than the rest of us."

"Unless he cut a deal," Thane gruffed.

I shook my head. "I'll ask Linc to check his location. I wouldn't be surprised if he made a pit stop at a casino on the way back, considering the payout from this contract."

Thane crushed a cigarette into the ashtray before lighting another. "Serpent called. He's pissed we're delaying the deal."

"Better him pissed than us in prison. If the feds get wind of that mother lode of weapons, we're fucked."

Thane ground his teeth. "I know. Don't want to tell him we have a rat, but I might have to tell him something so he knows why we need to lie low for just a little bit longer."

"What came of the reporter that Kenna spoke to?"

Thane shrugged. "No word, no story, nothing. Kenna did her job. Shut that shit down. Probably helps that when the reporter dug up Jag's phone number, he told her he only had one thing to say on the record, and that was she could go fuck herself."

I chuckled. As insane as Serpent and Jag were, I liked them. "Sure that went over well."

"Sure it did. Hoity-toity reporter didn't know how to respond. Run that quote in your goddamn newspaper. Hiring a PR consultant was a damn good move for us. Kenna and Eva have kept our shit out of the headlines—except when they're featuring some good deed they seem to think is gold."

I nodded. "They bringing reporters to the anniversary party?"

"Maybe. It's a public event. Everyone has to be on their best behavior, at least until the afterparty. Kenna mentioned offering an exclusive to one of the beat reporters who likes to write about Texas history. Eva backed her on the idea. Thinks it's another way to put us and the club businesses in a positive light."

"You going to do it?"

Thane shrugged. "Kenna told the reporter she needs to review the questions first. Apparently, that's not something they're fond of, so they're at an impasse. But I'm the fucking president, and the reporter won't want to run the story without talking to me. No questions, no interview."

I rubbed the back of my neck, needing to move the subject away from Kenna. Thane was too observant and would start digging into what was happening between us if given the chance. "You see the headlines about the Jackals this morning? They pulled a woman from her car. Kid was still strapped in the back seat when they took off."

"I heard on the radio that a girl was robbed at the grocery store last week," Hatchet added.

"The business line's been ringing off the hook. And not just businesses. Got a call for security at a goddamn family reunion. People are scared."

Thane's jaw tightened. "Fuck. I'm going to greenlight Kenna's little self-defense class idea. You and a few other guys can teach the basics."

I blinked, caught off guard. "You serious?"

He nodded, eyes hard. "Yeah. Shit's getting worse out there. If the cops can't keep up, we do what we can for our own. Kenna's right—women need to know how to fight back, or at least buy themselves a few seconds. They should be able to go to the store in the middle of the day without worrying."

"Fine," I said, trying to keep my voice even. "I'll talk to the guys and work with Kenna and Eva to set something up. "

Inside, my thoughts spun like tires in black clay. The city was changing, and not for the better. The Jackals became more bold and unpredictable by the day. The random violence creeping into the corners of our city served as a reminder that not every outlaw revered loyalty or honor, and they certainly didn't value women.

If this gang didn't stop soon, I'd be taking matters into my own hands.

Chapter Eleven

HATCHET

When Kenna texted the group saying she needed to visit downtown for an appointment, I volunteered first to shadow her. Of course, part of it was pure selfishness. I wanted her attention, and the thought of one of the other guys spending the day with her shot a pang of jealousy through my gut.

I'd never been the settling-down type. Never thought I'd want to be. But Kenna? She'd made me wonder if I could one day be the type of guy who committed for more than a night.

On top of it all, I was cursed with a competitive streak. Every man in the club looked at Kenna like she was the grand prize. I wanted her to choose me, even if I didn't know what the hell I'd do if she actually did.

Kenna walked out of her house in a sundress as I pulled up on my Harley, twirling keys in her hand. "We're taking my car."

Disappointment coursed through me at missing the heat of her body pressed against mine on the back of my bike. "Will you at least let me drive?"

She considered it for a moment. "Nope," she said, popping the P. "We have to pick up some kids' games for the party."

I shrugged off my cut and folded it, gently placing it in the back seat before jumping in shotgun. Kenna settled in the driver's seat and started the engine.

I knew from the file Linc pulled together before she started working for the club that she'd never worried about scraping together enough money to pay for rent or groceries. Her trust fund meant she'd never need to work a day in her life. It was a parachute she could pull at any time if things got too rough.

Me? I'd been free-falling my whole life. No safety net, no backup plan. Just a fucked-up life fueled by hustle and desperation, always one bad call from losing it all. Part of me wanted to resent her for it. For having everything handed to her. For never having to fight for a damn thing. But she never acted better than any of us. If anything, it seemed like she was searching for connection in all the chaos.

"Where are we headed?" I asked, toggling through her playlists on the screen.

"First, I need to pick out paper for the invites, and then the best part of the day—cake tasting." Contagious excitement rolled off Kenna in waves.

I raised a brow. "This feels oddly like wedding planning. I'm going to regret volunteering for this, aren't I?"

Kenna giggled. "I'm surprised you've ever thought about planning a wedding."

"I haven't, but I've heard about when some of the old ladies planned theirs." I fake shuddered.

Kenna stayed quiet for a beat. "Do you think you'll ever settle down?"

Her loaded question gave me pause. "Maybe the right woman will come along. Become my old lady."

She wrinkled her nose. I reached across and I tapped it with my finger.

"What's that look for?"

"The old lady thing. I don't get it."

"Well, when a man and a woman love each other very, very much—"

She smacked me on the arm and laughed. "Seriously. Do you really believe a woman is property?"

"Ah, so it's not the old lady thing that bothers you. It's the property patch."

"Yeah, it's not the early 1900s. We have rights now, you know?"

I rubbed a hand over the back of my neck. "I've never had an old lady, so I'm speaking purely from an outsider's perspective. I've watched my brothers meet theirs, and they've never seen them as property in the sense you're thinking."

She glanced at me curiously as I continued.

"Look at Reaper. Have you ever once seen him treat Eva in a way that made you cringe?"

She considered it for a moment. "No, Reaper is head over heels in love with her."

"Right. The guys don't treat their old ladies like they're less-than. The property patch is a commitment, just like an engagement ring. By giving them the title and a cut, they're telling the world that they're committed to making sure she's safe, secure, and happy."

Kenna chewed on her lip as she contemplated. "Do you want that? Someday?"

I shrugged. "Maybe, but I'm not in a rush. Waiting for the right girl, I guess."

Kenna blushed. I reached across casually to intertwine my fingers with hers as she drove. I didn't let go until Kenna pulled into the parking lot of her first stop. The attendant strolled out as she popped the back hatch, ready to load up the backyard games.

"The kids are going to lose their goddamn minds," I commented, looking at the slip-n-slide.

Kenna ripped open a nondescript cardboard box and tipped it toward me. Squirt guns in every color and size filled it.

I picked up a large super-soaker in neon green. "I call this one."

Kenna giggled. "Why do I have a feeling I am going to regret this decision?"

"Because you will." I slung the strap over my shoulder like it was a rifle. "There will be no safe zones. Anyone entering this party signs an unspoken waiver."

She arched her brow. "Even me?"

"Especially you. No one escapes the purge."

"Great. Remind me to pick up some waterproof mascara."

"You think the makeup's going to save you? You're target number one."

She jabbed a finger into my chest. "Bring it, biker boy. I had one of these as a kid, and my aim was deadly."

Kenna shut the hatch, wiped her hands on her dress, and we got back into the Range Rover. A few blocks later, she parked in front of a boutique window, and I began to laugh.

"What?" she asked.

"I didn't know there was even a place that only sold paper."

"They have an antique gold paper that will be perfect for the invitations. And it's not just paper. They sell gifts, too."

I gave her a skeptical glance as we walked in, my hand brushing her back as I ushered her through the door.

"I'll be back at the paper bar. It shouldn't take long if you want to browse."

An entire goddamn store for paper. Journals, cards, and crafts. Shit I'd never imagined, like measuring spoons in the shape of tulips and cat-themed coasters. I listened as she and another woman debated different weights of paper and whether she should go with the cotton or shimmer, whatever that meant.

I picked up a small plush fox. Its red fur reminded me of Kenna's vibrant auburn hair. I carried it to the cashier, pulling out my wallet.

"I don't need a bag," I said as I ripped off the tag and held the small toy behind my back.

Kenna approached with a stack of wrapped paper. "Ready to go?"

"Yeah, I wasn't able to find the perfect journal to write all my feelings in," I joked. "Too bad."

She laughed as I followed her back to the parking lot. Once she settled in the driver's seat, I grinned at her. "I have a surprise for you."

Her eyes widened as I pulled the small fox from behind my back.

"It's so cute!" Her voice heightened as she took the plush toy into her hand. "Thank you."

"It reminded me of you. Small. Clever. Red fur."

"I do not have fur."

I raised a brow suggestively. "Good to know."

She giggled as she set the fox in the corner of her dash. She opened her purse, fishing out a small pill packet, and popped one into her mouth.

"You OK?" I asked.

She grimaced. "Yeah, I can just feel a migraine trying to break through. I get them about once a month. I'm fine, though. This should stop it." Kenna punched the address to the bakery into her GPS and pulled away from the paper store.

"Why aren't we having Maisie bake the cakes for the party?"

"Maisie is bringing cinnamon rolls and donuts, but she doesn't make custom cakes. And this cake is going to make a statement."

"What does that even mean?" I groaned.

Kenna laughed. "To be honest, I don't know. The baker is going to show us what she came up with today."

She parked outside a bakery, pausing to pat the toy fox on its head. "Should I leave the window cracked for him?"

I chuckled. "Probably best you don't. Not with the Jackals slinking around. And if my cut gets stolen, Thane will skin me alive."

"Sorry, little guy." She apologized to the toy before glancing at me. "Could I get a tiny fox-sized cut for him? He could be the little Mavericks mascot."

"We'll have to check with Rhetta on that one. She handles the orders for cuts and patches."

The bell clanged as we walked through the bakery door. A wall of cool air hit us, countering the midday Texas heat.

A tall brunette came around the corner, wearing a white apron streaked with colored frosting. "Are you two here for a wedding cake tasting?"

I wrapped an arm around Kenna. "When is our wedding, doll?"

Kenna smacked my arm and laughed. "We're here for the Mavericks Motorcycle Club appointment."

"Ah, yes," the woman said. "Please, take a seat. My name is Maria. I'll bring the samples and sketches out."

Kenna and I sat at a small table in the corner as Maria brought out fifteen mini cupcakes, labels placed below them to indicate the flavor. She set a fork and a plate in front of each of us.

"Here are a few sketches that you can look through as you taste. Because the fiftieth anniversary is the golden milestone, I'm proposing a three-tiered cake with buttercream and gold leaf. The gold motorcycle you showed me would look great on top. You can pick a flavor for each tier. We could add sheet cakes as well, depending on how many guests you'll have. I'll be back to check on you in a bit."

Kenna carefully cut a cupcake in half. "Let's start with the lighter flavors, and then we'll eat the chocolate ones last."

"We'll be heading back to the clubhouse with paper and diabetes," I joked.

We tasted each flavor, each better than the last. Kenna released a sexy moan when she tried the final one—a rich espresso fudge cake with a whipped cream topping. "This is definitely my favorite. It might be better than sex."

I laughed. "You must not be having the right type of sex."

She snickered as she reached to wipe a crumb from my beard. "To be fair, it's been a long time, and cake is all I have right now."

I caught her hand and held it for a moment before Maria cleared her throat. Kenna pulled her hand away as she looked up at the baker.

"Any thoughts on the sketches? Have you chosen the flavors?"

Kenna smiled. "They look great. The tiered cake can be the chocolate whiskey, salted caramel, and the orange chocolate flavors. And then we can have sheet cakes of vanilla, lemon, and the espresso fudge. To be honest, the espresso fudge might not get served. I'll take it home and eat it for a week."

"You should get Funfetti, too," I suggested. "Kids love that shit."

"I knew you were here for more than just eye candy."

"After all that cake, I don't think either of us needs any candy," I muttered.

We left the bakery with the windows down, the air thick with sticky Texas heat and the lingering smell of buttercream. Kenna hummed under her breath, tapping her fingers on the steering wheel. I'd never seen anyone take dessert so seriously, and I had to admit, she had good taste.

I spotted the parts store as she headed back toward her house. "Hey, can you swing in there?" I asked, pointing to the next turn. "Need to grab a clutch cable."

We pulled into the lot, gravel crunching under the tires. "Be right back," I told her, already halfway out the door.

She hummed in agreement and turned up the music.

The store was quiet, just a baseball game playing on a small TV near the register and the faint hum of a fan. I found what I needed in two minutes flat.

That's when I heard the yelling.

I glanced out the window, and my stomach dropped. A skinny man wearing a green bandanna stood at Kenna's window, shouting through the glass. Fear shone on her face from across the lot.

I threw cash on the counter, grabbed the part, and hit the door at a run. My hand went straight to my holster, fingers closing around the grip of my Beretta.

He didn't spot me until I was almost at his back. "Hey!" I barked.

The man turned, startled, and I realized he couldn't be older than sixteen. He wore the same colors as the bastard who'd attacked

Kenna downtown. My blood went cold. He might be a child, but he was clearly a member of the Jackals.

"Back. Off," I growled, every word slow and clear. He squared his shoulders and tried to look tough as I leveled the gun at his chest.

"Get away from her. Now. I have no problem putting a bullet hole or two in you."

His eyes darted from me to the gun, then to Kenna. Her eyes shone with relief. For a second, I thought he might do something stupid. But then he bolted, stumbling over his own feet as he took off across the lot. I lowered my weapon after he disappeared behind a row of battered trucks.

I holstered the pistol and knocked on the window. Kenna gripped the wheel, still frozen with fear. "Unlock the door," I commanded.

I heard the click and opened the door, taking in the pale sheen of sweat across her forehead.

"You OK?" I asked, voice softer now.

She nodded, but her eyes were glassy and her breath short. I wanted to say something to make her feel safer, but words felt useless. I reached for her hand and squeezed it.

"Let's get you home."

Chapter Twelve

Hatchet was annoying on a good day. All hopped up on sugar after spending the afternoon with Kenna? Irritating as fuck. I bristled as he babbled about their little downtown excursion and espresso chocolate cake she'd said was better than sex. The way he grinned made me want to put my fist through a wall.

What pissed me off more was that he'd left her alone in that parking lot. I could barely keep my voice level as I snapped, "You were there to protect her."

Hatchet just rolled his eyes. "Jesus, Merrick. I was like, ten feet away. I was there with my gun in his face within seconds."

"Both of you, shut the fuck up," Reaper cut in. "You bicker like an old married couple. We need to figure out what the hell we're doing about this situation before someone gets hurt."

He wasn't wrong. The city was getting dangerous—more desperate people without jobs, choosing crime as a way to fill their wallets. Not that we weren't criminals, but we didn't go after women.

"They're escalating," I growled. "It's not just our women who are in danger. It's every woman who drives into the city."

Reaper raised a brow when I referred to "our women" but let it slide without comment. He leaned back and folded his arms across his chest. "The ladies have been planning their self-defense class. I know a few of you have been volun-told to help teach it."

I grunted. "It's a start. But I don't want anyone going into the city by themselves. Or being left alone in a car so we can run personal errands."

Hatchet shot me a look, but for once, he didn't argue. Maybe he finally understood. Or perhaps he was just tired of hearing me bitch.

"It's a solid PR move, too," Thane said, rubbing a hand over his graying goatee. "Eva's good at making us look like the good guys."

"We keep the prospect on Kenna's house, too. My gut says she's a target. They're looking for the payday they think she'll be. All they had to do was Google the name on her driver's license to see who her family is."

Thane waved a hand dismissively, like he didn't want to continue the debate. "Sure. Whatever you want. Linc, any update on the rat situation?"

Linc leaned forward, pulling up a file on his laptop. "System flagged that the CI met with their handler yesterday. Danny's dead, so it wasn't him."

Thane slammed his fist on the table. "We need to figure out who's fucking us over. Did you check into Dixon?"

Linc shook his head. "The meeting took place in Houston. I pinged his phone. He beelined for the Empire City Casino right after finishing up his contract, and he's been there ever since."

Reaper studied the names on Linc's screen. "What about Tyler's buddy, Roger? He's been sniffing around. Asking a lot of questions."

"Maybe. You think Roger's borrowing Tyler's credibility to get closer to all of us?" Reaper asked.

I rolled my shoulders, attempting to release the building tension. "Let's keep an eye on him. Maybe feed him some false intel about a deal."

Reaper nodded. "Roger just started working for me. I'll let him overhear a phone call. I'll make something up, maybe mention the warehouse on the east side. It's empty, so no big deal if the feds raid it."

As the room emptied, I lingered. I rubbed my temples, a headache brewing. I let my gaze linger on the faded club patches lining the wall. Each one represented a brother who'd bled for the club.

Trust was the foundation of everything we built, and loyalty was the Maverick's currency.

If I didn't find the rat soon, we'd all pay the price.

* * *

An early morning text from Kenna drew me away from scheduling out the next month's shifts for Maverick Security.

KENNA:

Can we meet today to plan the next self-defense class?

ME:

I'm free right now. Breakfast?

KENNA:

Brisket and I are about to go for a run. Join us if you think you can keep up.

ME:

Be there in 15.

I grabbed my gym bag and fired up my Harley to head to Kenna's house.

She greeted me at the door, hair up in a high ponytail, sports bra and shorts leaving little to the imagination. "You won't be able to keep up with me wearing that," she jeered, lips quirking into a challenge as she pulled Brisket away from her door.

I held up the bag, and Brisket balanced on two paws as he sniffed it like he searched for contraband. "Just need to change. I wasn't about to ride my bike in shorts."

She giggled, the sound quick and bright, and I felt something shift in my chest.

As I changed into a pair of gray gym shorts and a moisture-wicking shirt, I found myself checking the mirror—something I hadn't bothered with in years. Tight jaw. Scar on my temple. Thin lines around my brown eyes reminding me I neared mid-life, if I was lucky to outlive this lifestyle.

"You ready yet?" she yelled impatiently.

I opened the door to see her stretching in the kitchen, her high ponytail swinging. My gut tightened at the sight of her long, bare legs on display.

"You're pretty eager to be left in the dust," I said with a smirk as I tied my running shoes.

Kenna flashed a cocky grin over her shoulder. "It's on."

We set out on the trail, the early light glinting off dew-soaked grass. She and Brisket immediately sped ahead, a competitive streak I didn't know she had beginning to show.

"Is this a race I didn't sign up for?" I called after her as I closed the gap.

"Only if I win." Her laugh drifted through the humid air. Brisket barked once, like he was in on her joke.

I let her keep the lead for a moment, admiring the curve of her ass, and then picked up the pace, falling in easily beside her. My eyes scanned the trees and benches, automatically cataloguing potential threats and routes.

"So how long have you been a runner?"

She sidestepped a tree root and glanced at me. "Since high school. I volunteered at a center for women and girls. They had a running club. My mom thought it would be a good extracurricular for college applications. Those women had been through hell—abuse, trafficking, shit I didn't think happened to people in my world. I loved how running gave them control. Something to do as they rebuilt their lives."

"But it sounds like it was more than just a résumé builder."

She upped her pace. "After my dad died, my mom married this lawyer. Things got ugly fast. It showed me how easy it is for everything to fall apart."

I glanced at her, waiting. She didn't look back, eyes fixed forward on the trail ahead.

"I started running races and marathons to raise money for victims of domestic violence and human trafficking."

I strode beside her, admiring her compassion.

"What about you?" she asked. "You seem to be keeping up just fine."

I huffed a short laugh. "I haven't run much since getting out of the Army," I admitted, a bit more breathless than I'd expected. "Did enough miles to last a lifetime back then. I usually spend my time in the boxing ring instead. Sometimes it feels good to smash Hatchet in his pretty face."

She snorted, shaking her head, but her stride faltered. I noticed then how her lips pressed flat, a flash of discomfort tightening her jaw.

"You all right?" I slowed with her, tamping down the urge to reach out.

"I'm fine," she said, a little too fast, picking up her pace again before wavering, breath catching.

"Kenna."

She let out a frustrated sigh, turning her face away. "It's just— cramping. Really bad, out of nowhere."

"Maybe we should have eased into it," I offered, running down the list of potential injuries in my head.

She huffed out a laugh, humor thin but grateful. "Not those kinds of cramps."

"Oh," I said, understanding finally dawning as I gave her a sidelong nod. "Got it. You want to head back?"

She blew out a breath. "Yeah. Since you're here, do you mind going into town with me? I have a couple of errands I need to run."

We circled back to hers at a slower pace, the morning sun

breaking hot through the trees. She unlocked the door and gestured toward the hallway. Brisket flopped onto the cool tile, tongue lolling.

"You can shower first. Towels are in the top cupboard."

I muttered a thanks, closed the door behind me, and stripped off my sweat-soaked shirt. The water pounded against my neck and back as I tried not to think about Kenna. A hot desire I hadn't felt in years stirred inside me.

Every inch of me strained, hard and wanting. I glanced down, biting back a curse. I stroked my cock once, letting out a ragged breath. Spending time with Kenna was sweet, yet wildly frustrating. It wasn't just her looks getting to me. It was how she was equal parts steel and wildflowers, sharp yet sweet.

The more I pictured her—the swell of her breasts straining against her sports bra, her hips, her sweet lips—the faster I moved, desperate for relief and hoping the water muffled the sound of my strokes.

I groaned quietly, but my release left me unsatisfied, amplifying my craving for her.

I stood for a moment, letting the hot spray wash away my guilt. This wasn't supposed to happen—not here, not now—but Kenna had a way of getting under my skin that I couldn't shake.

"Hey, do you want a smoothie?" Kenna yelled through the door, voice bright and oblivious, cutting hard through the thick air inside the shower.

I cleared my throat, scrubbed a hand over my face, and called back, "Yeah, sure. Sounds good."

"Strawberry or blueberry?" she asked.

I turned off the water. "Surprise me."

Her laugh echoed faintly down the hallway.

I toweled off fast, heart still drumming beneath my ribs, and yanked on my clothes, determined to look less rattled than I felt. When I walked into the kitchen, Kenna was already pouring a pink smoothie into a tall glass. She shoved it across the island toward me.

I took a long, cold gulp, letting it tamp down the fire still burning under my skin. "Thanks. Go grab your shower. I'll clean up in here."

She lingered, pushing a sweaty strand of red hair behind her ear, eyes glinting with something playful. "Should I wear jeans? So we can take your bike?"

I cleared my throat. "Yeah," I said, trying not to picture exactly how her legs would look poured into tight denim.

When she emerged ten minutes later in tight, dark-wash jeans and a black tank top edged with lace, I almost choked on the last of my smoothie. My cock thickened instantly, straining against my zipper. I turned away, attempting to distract myself from the rush of desire coiling in my gut. "Almost done loading the dishwasher for you."

"Thanks," she chirped, oblivious to my turmoil. She kissed her dog on top of his head. "Be a good boy. No parties while we're out."

I smirked, shaking my head at how she spoke to her dog like he was a small child.

Outside, I shrugged on my cut and tossed her a helmet before swinging my leg over the bike. She climbed on and pressed her chest to my back, arms circling tight.

"Where we heading?" I asked.

"Library first. Then the pharmacy."

I slammed my visor down as I revved the engine, feeling the warm line of her body—every shift, every press, every damn curve—fuse with me through leather and denim. The ride was short but every stoplight felt like torture. Halfway there, I reached back, brushing my knuckles along her thigh, a quick check to make sure she was settled. Her fingers squeezed my side, a silent answer that nearly undid my control.

At the library, she slid off behind me. "Do you read for fun, or just stick to motorcycle manuals?"

I chuckled. "I read. Mostly war biographies, old history stuff."

She wrinkled her nose in mock disgust. "You sound like my grandpa."

I nudged her shoulder playfully. "Careful. I was already building my first bike when you were just learning how to read."

She rolled her eyes and shoved me gently as we walked inside. She made a beeline for the true crime section, fingers trailing over the spines.

I lingered nearby, arms crossed. "What is it with women and true crime?" I asked curiously, voice low enough not to get shushed.

She pulled out a thick paperback with a bloody cover. "Morbid curiosity. Why do some people cross the line?"

"Sometimes they have no other choice." The answer slipped out, heavier than intended.

Her head tilted, curiosity flickering in her eyes. "Sounds like you speak from experience."

I met her sharp gaze. "Life experience teaches you a lot about the line. Where it is, how easy it is to blur, and how fast things get complicated after."

Kenna tucked the book under her arm, studying me. "So, hypothetically speaking, what would make you cross it?"

I shrugged, glancing down the row of battered paperbacks. "Depends on what's at stake. Some things are worth the consequences. Saving someone you love. Protecting the innocent. Retribution."

A beat of charged silence stretched between us. Then she smirked, stepping close enough to bump her shoulder into mine. "Something tells me you've got stories that'd fit right in on this shelf."

"Some stories are best kept off the record."

Chapter Thirteen

Nerves twisted in my stomach as I paced the edge of the park. I scanned the parking lot for women brave enough to show up for the self-defense class we'd worked so hard to organize. What if no one came? What if the club's reputation scared them off? I wiped my palms on my jeans, forcing myself to breathe.

Rhetta manned the registration table like a Southern debutante in leather.

"Look over there, sugar," she said, gesturing to two blond sorority girls heading our way. "Told you we'd have takers."

My heart leaped as more women trickled in. Three women in their forties with sunny energy signed the waivers. "This is our weekly ritual," one of them announced with a grin. "Last week was goat yoga. This week? Biker boot camp. We try something new every Saturday." I couldn't help but laugh.

A nervous brunette in her early thirties hovered at the edge, arms crossed tight across her chest. Her eyes darted everywhere but at the men. I knew that look. It was one worn by a woman who'd felt power-less at some point. One who knew "not all men"—but had maybe judged wrong once or twice, leaving her trust in others tattered and torn. I made a mental note to keep an eye on her and to step in if it seemed like anyone made her uncomfortable.

A boisterous pack of twenty-somethings rolled up just as we were about to begin. By the time Eva nudged me forward, there were eleven women in total lined up before us.

I grabbed Hatchet's arm before I could lose my nerve. He blinked at me in surprise but didn't pull away. He stepped forward as I sucked in a shaky breath.

"Good morning, ladies. I'm Kenna. A few weeks ago, I was mugged downtown. I felt helpless and scared. More recently, I was nearly carjacked in a parking lot. Both times, I was lucky enough to have my friend, Hatchet, come to the rescue."

Hatchet gave a dramatic bow, earning a ripple of laughter.

I rolled my eyes. "But here's the thing—I don't want to rely on luck or anyone else to keep me safe. We need to be able to defend ourselves. We will not be victims. That's why we put together this free class for anyone interested in learning about self-defense."

I stepped aside as Rhetta moved forward to speak. "Thanks, sugar. I'm Rhetta, and my husband is the president of the Mavericks Motorcycle Club. I'd like to introduce you to the Mavericks who'll be teaching this class today. You've already met Hatchet. We're also going to learn from Fuse, Merrick, Archer, and Coast."

I watched the crowd as she spoke. Some women looked nervous, some curious, and one looked seconds away from ripping her clothes off and throwing herself at the guys to fulfill a "why choose" fantasy.

Eva shot me a sly glance, and I had to bite my lip to keep from laughing. She'd insisted on picking only the Mavericks who were single to help teach this class, mainly to keep Reaper out of the crosshairs of flirty newcomers.

"We're splitting into groups of two, with one group of three," Rhetta continued. "Kenna, Eva, and I will float around to help demonstrate the moves."

The sorority girls rushed for Hatchet, who turned up the charm immediately. The forties crew clustered around Fuse. The loud twenty-somethings split between Archer and Coast, leaving the nervous brunette and one straggler with Merrick. I drifted toward them, determined to help the woman who looked like she might bolt at any second feel more comfortable.

I brushed my hand gently against her arm, and she flinched. "Sorry, didn't mean to scare you. What's your name?"

She managed a tight smile. "Callie."

"You picked the best group, Callie," I whispered, nodding toward Merrick. "He's basically the beast from *Beauty and the Beast*. Looks like he's a brute that could break you in half, but he's actually the kind of guy who brings you flowers."

Callie's lips twitched, showing just a hint of a genuine smile.

Merrick stepped forward. "All right, ladies," he rumbled. "First, we're going to learn how to break someone's grip if they grab your wrist. Kenna, come here."

I stepped up, heart thumping, but trusting him completely. He wrapped his hand around my wrist—gentle, but firm enough to show the move. "If someone grabs you like this, don't panic." He demonstrated, guiding me in twisting my body to show the group how I could break free.

He looked down at me with a grin. "Good. Show them again. This time faster and with a bit more force."

As Merrick walked our group through more techniques, I glanced over at Hatchet's corner of the park. The two sorority girls giggled as he wooed them. A flare of annoyance sparked in my chest. This was supposed to be about empowerment, not a live-action dating app. I caught Hatchet's eye and shot him a glare sharp enough to slice through his charisma. He blinked, straightened, and immediately dialed back the flirting, his tone suddenly all business.

Satisfied, I drifted over to Fuse's group, where the trio of forty-something women peppered him with questions. Fuse stood tall, tattooed arms folded. The man was the picture of confidence and command. He surveyed his group like he was about to lead them into battle, not a self-defense drill.

"Kenna, help me out," he ordered.

I stepped forward, earning a round of applause from the women.

"It's a situation that nearly every woman has been in. It's dark, and you're alone, and someone is coming up behind you. Are you prepared if they put their hands on you?"

Fuse adjusted my position with a businesslike touch.

"Don't second-guess. Don't hesitate. As soon as they make their move, you make yours. An elbow strike will do in this situation. It's simple, effective, and you don't need to be a bodybuilder to make it hurt. Kenna's small, but she has sharp elbows. Kenna, I want you to hit as hard as you can as soon as I touch your side."

I felt the brush of Fuse's hand across my side before I moved exactly as he'd shown, hammering my elbow back into his ribs. Fuse grunted and staggered, making the group laugh. "See? She's fierce. That's what I want from all of you. Never hesitate. Never apologize."

The women echoed his energy as they practiced the strike. Fuse moved among them, correcting stances and offering encouragement.

"You're stronger than you think," he told one woman. "Trust yourself."

He caught my eye and winked.

"Confidence is half the battle," Fuse continued. "The other half is making sure your attacker regrets ever picking you. I want you to leave me with bruises. Make sure I remember you tonight with every breath."

I couldn't help but smile. Fuse made sure everyone in his group felt powerful—and maybe even a little dangerous.

I made my way over to Archer's group, where the energy felt instantly lighter. Where Fuse taught like a commander of armies, Archer acted like a big brother.

"Perfect! That's exactly it," Archer said as a petite woman with a pixie cut nailed a move.

I snapped a few photos on my phone, framing the shot as Archer gently corrected another woman's posture, his hand hovering just above her shoulder to guide her without ever making her uncomfortable. He caught me taking pictures and flashed a wide grin, then turned to the group.

I caught a candid shot of the group mid-laugh, Archer in the center, arms outstretched. It was perfect for the Mavericks' social feed—community, strength, and a little bit of joy in the middle of all the seriousness.

I grinned, feeling the warm, encouraging energy ripple out from Archer's group.

I wandered over to Coast, where things were quieter compared to the others. He listened intently as one of the women shared a story about an experience she'd had walking home from the bar one night.

"That sounds terrifying," he said, voice carrying a genuine weight. "My daughter's nineteen now, and the stories she's told me … same shit. I shouldn't have to ask her to text me when she gets home safe, but I do every time because I've seen what some men are capable of."

He demonstrated a simple escape move, letting the women try it on him as I captured snapshots with my phone.

When one woman struggled to break his grip, Coast never looked frustrated. "Let's make it smaller. It's less about strength, more about leverage. My daughter's barely a hundred pounds, and she can use this move to take me down."

On her second try, the woman slipped free and grinned wide. "Hell yes, that's it. Any fight at all is more than most guys expect."

I snapped another quick photo, catching the way Coast offered a reassuring fist bump after each woman attempted the move.

As I watched each group, a surprising sense of calm settled over me. The coiled tension in my chest started to loosen.

After two hours, sweat and laughter hung in the air as Rhetta clapped her hands to get everyone's attention. "All right, ladies! Thank you for coming out today. We'll be back next month. Same time, same place. Bring your friends."

A chorus of thank-yous rippled through the group as women gathered their things. Some lingered, chatting with the Mavericks, their faces flushed with excitement and pride. One of the forties crew gave Fuse a bear hug, and Archer was surrounded by his group, exchanging high-fives. Then, of course, there was Hatchet. One of the sorority girls sidled up to him, slipped a piece of paper into his hand, and whispered something that made him grin. I rolled my eyes. Eva caught my expression and nudged me with her elbow, smirking.

"That's just Hatchet for you," she whispered. "He's a magnet."

I shook my head. "Next time, we'll pair him with the cougars. Maybe we'll invite a senior citizens' home to participate, and I'll have him work with some old biddies."

Eva cocked a brow. "Jealous?"

I scoffed. "Of course not. I just want the women to walk away with skill, not a phone number."

As the women drifted away, I gathered the guys near the picnic tables. I brushed a stray curl from my face as I tried to find the right words. "Seriously, thank you. You made a real difference today. Some of those women walked in scared and left looking like they could take on the world."

Hatchet, Fuse, and Archer walked toward their bikes while Coast helped Rhetta break down the registration table.

"Nice work today," Merrick said, his voice low and warm.

"Thanks," I said with a grin. "I just wish I could do more. I was worried about one of them."

"Callie?"

"Yeah." I frowned. "Something was off. She seemed ready to bolt. I don't think you caught it, but she flinched when you moved too fast—like she expected to get hit."

His eyes darkened. "I saw," he said solemnly. "Maybe next time you can bring Maisie. She volunteers at the women's shelter."

"Maybe. Our community needs more than a shelter. A place to sleep isn't enough. They need a place to heal, physically and emotionally. I don't think there's anything like that here."

"So build it," he said simply, as if it were as easy as opening a door.

I scoffed. "Do you have any idea how much it would cost? Equipment, technology, a website, marketing. Not to mention the security you need for a facility that serves victims of domestic violence."

He grinned. "I know a good marketer," he said, an eyebrow raised.

I rolled my eyes. "Funny. I'm a great marketer," I said with a laugh. "But I don't know a damn thing about running a nonprofit or fundraising."

"The club would back it," he said softly. "We raise money for causes all the time. And Maverick Security could post someone there daily. I happen to know the guy in charge."

"Would the club really support it?"

Merrick nodded once. "You should talk to Thane and Reaper about it. They'd get behind it. Reaper's mom is a domestic violence survivor. Mavericks have always stood to protect women and children."

"Well," I said, clearing my throat. "Guess I have some homework to do."

* * *

My stomach dropped as I skimmed through the news on my phone while sipping my morning coffee.

Fucking fuck.

I took a screenshot of the headline and sent it to Eva.

"Motorcycle Club With Violent History Teaches Women's Self-Defense Class"

My pulse pounded in my ears as I skimmed the article. Some of the facts sounded plausible, the story supported by police reports. It detailed instances of missing prospects, drug dealing, and highway shoot-outs. But the sentence that made my blood boil lay right below Fuse's prison headshot.

"One instructor, Flint 'Fuse' Wood, served seven years in H.H. Coffield correctional facility on charges of assault and attempted murder of a single mother."

Red-hot fury coated my gaze. I'd told Eva we should be more worried about the prison biker. But she'd urged me to trust her. To trust them.

My heart raced as I hopped in my Range Rover and peeled out of the driveway. I glanced at the clock. I'd arrive just before their weekly Church meeting. Good. I wanted them all in one place.

When I reached the clubhouse, I stormed through to Thane's office without knocking. The scent of cigars hit me in a wave as I threw open the door. The men were already seated around the round table in the corner, their faces turning toward me in surprise. I shoved my phone in Thane's face, the Chronicle article on screen. He glanced at the phone, then to me, his expression unreadable.

"Did I fucking invite you?" Thane snarled. "Get the fuck out."

"How much of this is true?" I demanded, my voice shaking. I glanced around the table, my gaze landing on each face—Reaper, Hatchet, Linc, and Fuse. I showed my phone to each of them, my hands trembling. "I need to know what I'm defending—or if I even can defend all of you. Rangers bleeding out on the highway. Prospects going missing. Probably buried in a swamp. You're selling cocaine to kids? And Fuse beat a woman nearly to death? Is this the kind of club you are? Is this the kind of men you are? You're no better than the Jackals."

Thane narrowed his eyes at me.

"Disrespect me or my club again, little girl, and *you* might just go missing."

My jaw dropped at the threat. I felt a tug on my arm and glanced back to see Merrick, his stoic expression betrayed by the storm in his eyes.

"Come with me," he commanded in a voice that left no room for debate. A voice he'd never used on me. He tugged on my arm again, half dragging me from Thane's office into another small room with a sofa and two large filing cabinets. An assortment of guns hung on the wall.

"You can't speak to our president like that," he said, his voice tight.

"He's not my president. You're criminals." My voice cracked.

Merrick's jaw flexed. "We never claimed to be Boy Scouts."

I clenched my fists. "I can't represent a club that allows men to beat up women."

Merrick pressed his fingers to the bridge of his nose and exhaled sharply before turning to open the filing cabinet. He dug through the folders before pulling one out. He opened it, rifling through the pages before bringing one to the top and handing it to me.

It was a doctor's report—cold, clinical, detached. A seven-year-old female with poorly healed breaks and a recent head injury, all indicative of child abuse. I flipped through the papers to read a Child Protective Services report. I flipped to another page. Despite the clear abuse, the state granted the mother custody again. Then a police report, two months later. Of all of them, this one was the worst. Unspeakable.

Tears glistened in my eyes as I glanced up at Merrick.

"She's Bayou's daughter," he explained. "He has custody now. But the shit the girl's mother and her boyfriend put the kid through will haunt her for the rest of her life. When Bayou found out, Fuse was there. He made the call to make the guy pay, and then the goddamn woman attacked them with a shovel. She was more concerned about her deadbeat boyfriend than the hell the man was putting her child through. Fuse took the fall so Bayou wouldn't go to prison. Gracie needed someone to raise her."

I swallowed hard. My anger dissipated like a tornado sucked back into the clouds.

"Sometimes the truth isn't in the headlines," Merrick said quietly.

The pages trembled in my hands. "What about the other reports? The missing prospects? The Rangers? The drugs?"

Merrick's expression remained unreadable. "I can't explain it all.

But we have a reason for everything we do. Sometimes prospects leave on their own. Sometimes we make them. And sometimes we have to defend ourselves. We don't go around looking for trouble, but sometimes it finds us. The drugs, though, were the Rangers. And we put a stop to that a few weeks ago."

"How?"

Merrick's eyes hardened as he stared into mine. "If I tell you, I can't take it back. It becomes your secret to keep, too. We don't share club business lightly."

"I want to know," I insisted. "I need to know. Besides, I signed the NDA, and I can't protect the club's reputation if I don't know what's happening."

Merrick paused for a beat before relenting. "We went to Austin a few weeks ago and told the Rangers they needed to stay out of our territory. Stop dealing. Their president pulled a gun on Reaper and shot him in the leg. So, Reaper shot him in the chest. The new president agreed to a truce."

"And the missing prospects?"

"Usually, they skip town if we kick them out. Easier to live life if we aren't the monsters in the dark. We only make them disappear if they've done something unforgivable or that puts the rest of us at risk."

"Like what?"

"Feeding information to law enforcement."

"And by making them disappear, you mean ..." I trailed off, uncertain I wanted to hear the answer.

Merrick only gazed at me, his silence giving me the confirmation I needed.

I stared at the report until the words blurred. It would be so much easier if the world were simple—bad guys, good guys. No gray, no in-between.

My phone pinged with a group text from Eva. I tilted it so Merrick could also read the messages.

EVA:

> Looked up the reporter's name. It was one of the girls in Hatchet's group at the self-defense class. She's an intern at the paper.

HATCHET:

> I went out with her, but I didn't tell her shit.

EVA:

> I'll text the editor. He asked for an exclusive for the anniversary, and then he let this shit fly? She didn't disclose that she was a reporter, and she never called us for comment.

> And really, Hatchet? A college student?

I grimaced at the message. Hatchet was single. He wasn't obligated to any sort of exclusivity with me. I'd told him I wasn't ready to date. But it still stung that he'd gone out with one of the flirtatious sorority girls from the self-defense class I coordinated.

"You should go," Merrick said, breaking me out of thought.

"How fucked am I with Thane?"

He rubbed his jaw, considering. "Give him a few days to cool down. Maybe let Eva handle the Mavericks business for a bit."

"And what about you?" I asked, my voice small. "Do you think I was wrong?"

Merrick sighed. "I think you care. That's not a bad thing. But you can't storm in here like that. Thane's only going to give you a pass once. He's not the forgiving type. And if you'd pulled that shit in front of the entire club, I'm not sure I could have stopped him."

"Stopped him from what?" I asked, my voice rising.

"You don't want to know. I don't want to even think about it. Just ... don't trust everything you read about us. There's always more to the story."

"It's hard to trust this club when I find out shit like this from a newspaper, not you guys."

He nodded. "Fair. You want answers, ask me next time."

I swallowed, my anger deflating. "I just want to do the right thing. Be on the right side of the story."

Merrick's expression softened, just a fraction of a second. "So do we. In our own way."

"Thanks. For showing me the file. For answering my questions. And for not letting Thane kill me."

He gave a slight shrug. "Go home, Kenna. Try to stay out of trouble for a few days."

I managed a weak smile. "No promises."

Merrick's lips twitched.

I drove home in silence, no music or true crime podcasts. Just the hum of the engine and the echo of Merrick's words. *There's always more to the story.*

Merrick hadn't given me the whole account, but he'd trusted me with pieces of it so I could understand.

In a twisted way, it was almost comical how the Mavericks could be so gentle and so brutal in the same breath. They were the kind of guys who'd change your tire in the rain. And yet, I'd also seen the violence simmering just beneath the surface.

The Mavericks weren't saints—not even close. The headline painted them as monsters, but the truth was messier. Sometimes the violence was their way of serving justice in a world that failed to offer it.

And at least they were honest about who they were. They wore their sins like tattoos. Visible. Real.

The people I grew up with would stab you in the back over a petty slight, all while pretending to be your best friend. At least the Mavericks owned it. They'd stab you in the front, and then tell you why.

Maybe that's why I liked them. Because here, in this brutal, broken world, there was a kind of honesty and honor among the Mavericks I hadn't found anywhere else.

But it scared me, too. Every step closer felt like shedding another layer of who I used to be. I wasn't sure where the line was anymore—between right and wrong, between justice and revenge, between being an outsider and becoming one of them.

Chapter Fourteen

I slipped on my cut and snuck through the hallway. The apartment was quiet except for the hum of the air conditioning and muffled snores from the bedroom.

I snagged a banana from the counter as I tried to remember her name. Allie? Ellie? Shit. It didn't matter. I'd never see her again anyway. She lived in the Woodlands, a bougie planned community with green spaces and little shops. I'd probably be her first and last walk on the wild side. She'd become someone's suburban trophy wife in a few years and regale her mommy group with the story of how she fucked a Maverick. I was more than happy to oblige with her fantasy for rough sex with a biker, though I'd hesitated when she asked me to choke her. That wasn't really my thing.

The morning haze promised a scorching day. I ducked into a coffee shop below her apartment to order a cappuccino that cost more than I'd spent at the bar the night before. The barista watched me with curiosity, so I shot her a wink, earning a blush and a stammer as she handed me my drink with her phone number written on the sleeve.

With street parking scarce, I'd left my bike a few blocks away.

Between the security cameras and well-lit streets, I'd had little concern about anyone—Jackals included—stealing my bike overnight. As I cut through the park, I spotted Tyler slouched on a bench, shoulders hunched, staring at his phone.

My hand tightened around the coffee cup. Alarm bells rang through my mind. I couldn't recall where Tyler lived, but it sure as fuck wasn't the Woodlands. He worked for Reaper, and that meant sunrise starts on construction sites, not leisurely park strolls in the morning.

I checked my phone for the time. Yeah, this wasn't right. I moved to the shade, letting a group of joggers pass. Tyler kept glancing around, like he was waiting for someone.

A woman in a navy suit appeared moments later, her stride purposeful as she approached. She slid onto the bench beside him. My pulse ticked up. I ducked behind a tree, pretending to check my phone, but my gaze stayed locked on the pair. Tyler's hands moved restlessly, rubbing his palms on his jeans, nodding too quickly at whatever she was saying. He kept scanning the park.

Something was off. Way fucking off.

I waited until the woman stood and snapped a photo of her face as she turned my way, zooming in to capture a close-up of her sharp features. Tyler stayed put for five minutes, checking his phone and fiddling with his wallet before standing.

I'd waited, hoping it was just his doppelganger. But it was Tyler.

I shot a group text to Thane, Reaper, Merrick, Linc, and Fuse.

ME:

Where's Tyler supposed to be this morning?

REAPER:

Coming in late. Dentist appt. Why?

ME:

Looks more like a meeting with his handler.

I attached a few photos, one with the woman's face clear enough for a search.

REAPER:

Fuck me. Linc, see if you can find out who
she is.

ME:

I'll grab the fucker and bring him in.

MERRICK:

Stand down. Let's meet at the clubhouse
first. We need to handle this right.

Fucking Merrick.

* * *

I rolled up to the clubhouse. Inside, Merrick, Thane, and Reaper waited. Tension crackled between them like a live wire.

"He's a rat," Thane muttered, slamming his fist on the bar. "I knew something was off about him. He wasn't the same kid I knew after he got back from college."

Merrick just shook his head. "We don't know that yet. Linc will find out."

As if on cue, Linc walked in. He slid a file across the bar to Thane. "She's FBI. Safe Streets and Gang Unit. Tyler's meeting with a fucking fed."

"Shit," Merrick muttered. "We need to find out what he knows. What he's told her. Because of his dad, I'm sure we've all shared more than we would with any other prospect."

"I'll text him," Reaper said. "I can ask him to swing by and grab something from Thane after his 'dentist appointment.'"

"He won't need to worry about the dentist when I'm done with him," Merrick growled.

The bait was set. We waited, the air thick with anticipation. Then we heard two vehicles pull up—a bike and a car. My stomach tightened. Who else would drop by the clubhouse this early in the morning? We pulled our weapons, ready to snatch Tyler.

The door swung open, and in walked Kenna with Tyler trailing behind her. The tension ratcheted up another notch. Tyler took one look at us—guns drawn, faces grim—and knew he was made. Before anyone could move, he grabbed Kenna by the throat, squeezing hard enough that her lips parted as she gasped for air. He reached behind and pulled a gun from his waistband, pressing it to her head as she clawed at his wrist. She looked between us with a panicked expression, silently begging to be saved.

"Let me leave or I fucking kill her." His wild eyes darted between the weapons trained on his frantic movements as he used Kenna as a human shield.

Kenna's eyes met mine, wide with fear but still sharp. I wanted to shoot the bastard, but one wrong move and she was dead. His fingers dug into her throat, rough enough that they'd leave a hand mark for weeks.

Merrick's icy voice cut through the room. "You hurt her, you die. And it won't be quick."

Tyler laughed, but it was hollow. "Pretty sure I'm dead either way. You think I don't know you're going to kill me?"

Reaper stepped forward, hands up, voice steady. "You don't want to do this. You're not that guy. Your father wouldn't want this. You remember what he stood for—no hurting women, no hurting kids. He helped build this club on honor. Don't throw that away. Don't betray his legacy more than you already have."

Tyler's eyes flickered at the mention of his dad, his grip loosening just a fraction. Kenna coughed, sucking in a breath of air like she'd been held underwater. For a second, I saw the doubt and the guilt as he remembered the man who'd raised him.

That was all Kenna needed. She twisted suddenly, driving her elbow into Tyler's ribs in a move Fuse would have been proud of. She stomped hard on his foot, and he grunted, grip slipping, and Kenna tore herself free. She bolted straight for me, eyes wide with terror and adrenaline. I holstered my weapon, trusting the others to keep theirs trained on Tyler, and pulled her into my arms. I held her tight as she sobbed against my chest.

"You did so good," I murmured. "You're safe now. You were so brave. I've got you."

She clung to me, her entire body shaking, her breath racking through her in ragged gasps.

Tyler, realizing he was out of options, turned to run.

Merrick didn't hesitate. He fired a single shot.

Kenna screamed into my shoulder as the gunshot echoed through the space. Tyler went down with a cry, blood pouring between his fingers as he clutched his leg.

The clubhouse erupted into chaos—shouting, cursing, Reaper barking orders. But all I could focus on was Kenna, trembling in my arms.

Merrick strode toward Tyler, his face a mask of fury. He hauled him up by the collar, his fist slamming into Tyler's jaw with a sickening crack. Tyler's head snapped back, blood spraying from his mouth. Merrick hit him again, and again, each blow landing with brutal precision.

Kenna let out a squeak. I tightened my hold on her and yelled. "Merrick! Enough! Kenna's seen enough!"

Merrick barely glanced at me, checking his red-hot rage just enough to clock the fear on her face. His face twisted in a pained expression before he ripped Tyler up from the ground by his neck and dragged him toward the door.

"Reaper, call Eva," Merrick commanded. "Get her here now to take Kenna home, then meet me at the junkyard."

The door slammed shut behind them. The clubhouse suddenly seemed too quiet, except for Kenna's shaky breaths and the distant roar of a truck peeling from the parking lot.

Kenna trembled against me as we listened to Reaper make the call, giving Eva little detail.

"Eva's fifteen minutes out. Stay with Kenna until she's here," Reaper ordered as he followed Merrick.

I nodded once and guided Kenna to one of the corner sofas. I sat, pulling her into my lap and holding her tight. She trembled with the aftershocks of the adrenaline rush. I stroked her hair, murmuring soft reassurances. Her breath shuddered against my chest, but when she finally pulled back, her eyes blazed—not just with dissipating fear, but also fury.

"What are they going to do to Tyler?"

I hesitated. "Don't worry about that right now, doll. You did good. Real good."

"That's not an answer," she said, looking up at me. Her eyes were still wide and glassy, but there was a spark of defiance there, too.

I sighed. "It's not a question you want answered. Not right now."

She wiped her face with the back of her hand. "I know you're trying to protect me, but I'm not stupid. And I should be horrified about what I'm imagining. I should beg you all to show mercy. But maybe I'm not that good a person. Because right now, I want him to hurt. I want him to feel a fraction of the helplessness I just felt."

I pulled her close, kissing her forehead. "You didn't look helpless to me. You defended yourself. But it's not something you need to worry about. Tyler was already in trouble. His fate is sealed. But after that trick back there? Now we'll spend every last waking moment making him wish he was dead."

She looked like she wanted to ask a question, but then she just nodded, leaning into me again. I held her close, listening to her breathing slow.

Eva busted through the door, her face sharp with concern as she searched the room. Kenna stood as their eyes met.

"What happened?" Eva demanded.

I stood, guiding Kenna forward with my hand across her lower back. "Tyler used her as a human shield."

"Our Tyler? Why the fuck would he do that?"

"I can't explain right now. Just take her home and stay with her,

OK? It's going to be a late night. Reaper probably won't be home until morning."

"Let me guess: club business?" Eva muttered before wrapping an arm around Kenna's shoulders. "Come on. Let's get you out of here."

"Hatchet?" Eva called out to me.

"Yeah?"

Fire danced in her eyes. "Make him fucking pay."

I gave her a savage grin. "We will," I promised.

I looked forward to what Merrick had planned for Tyler, and I had a few ideas of my own to make sure he'd regret ever touching Kenna.

Chapter Fifteen

I took each corner a bit harder than I needed to, reveling at the sound of Tyler's body bouncing around in the bed of my truck like a sack of potatoes. But every jolt, every muffled groan from the back, did little to soothe the fury still boiling in my veins.

The image burned behind my eyes. Kenna's face pale with fear, her eyes wildly darting between me and Hatchet with a plea for one of us to save her. Her throat reddening under Tyler's grip. His fucking gun aimed at her temple.

I insisted for weeks—to myself and Reaper, when he pressed— that Kenna was just a friend. But watching Tyler threaten to end her? It wasn't rage I felt first. It was fear. Cold, gut-churning fear. In one horrible moment, I realized what I stood to lose.

I'd lied to myself since the moment I met Kenna. And when she ran to Hatchet, it stung. Not because I wanted her to run to me—OK, maybe a little—but because it reminded me how much Hatchet cared for her, too. And I'd seen the way she looked at him. The way she trusted him. The way her eyes lit up when he walked into a room.

But what stung worse was the way she'd looked at me after I'd beaten Tyler to a pulp. The flicker of horror in her eyes. I'd seen it before, in the faces of men who realized too late what I was capable of. But Kenna? She wasn't supposed to see that side of me. She wasn't supposed to know how deep the darkness went.

I gripped the steering wheel tighter.

If Hatchet hadn't yelled, if he hadn't pulled me back with her name, I might've killed Tyler right there. She'd have seen the monster I kept chained up.

She might not trust me for a long time. Hell, considering what she saw, that trust might already be shattered beyond repair.

The rusted junkyard gates loomed ahead. I killed the headlights and rolled into the shadows of the warehouse, the tires crunching over broken glass. Tyler's whimpering grated on my last nerve.

I threw the truck into park and stormed to the bed, yanking him out by his collar. He hit the ground hard, blood dripping from his busted face and the bullet wound in his leg onto the concrete.

The warehouse swallowed the sound, the air thick with the stink of decay. I stared down at him, my hands still trembling with adrenaline. Not from the violence—that was easy. From the truth I couldn't outrun anymore.

I was falling for Kenna, and I wasn't sure what that meant. For me or Hatchet. I'd seen the way he looked at her, and I wouldn't get between my brother and a girl—especially since she might be the only one who could get him to settle down. I'd have to bury my feelings for her beneath my loyalty to him and the club.

After seeing the monster within me, she'd never fall for me. No, she'd seen the truth—the violence, the dark rage, the part of me that could snap a man in half and not lose sleep.

I grabbed Tyler by the scruff of his neck and dragged him into the warehouse. My muscles strained against his dead weight. I grunted at the effort, but my heart was heavier. My mind steeled itself as I considered the girl I couldn't have, and the brother I wouldn't betray.

I sat Tyler in a heavy metal chair, leaning his upper body awkwardly against the back. He slumped, still knocked out from the rough ride over. I must have taken one of the turns hard enough that he hit his head. Chains clinked as I pulled them from the wall.

I could've used zip ties, but I liked the sound of metal links rattling and how the weight of them against a man's chest made the point clear: there was no escape.

I wrapped the chains around Tyler's wrists and ankles, securing him to the chair. I laid out my tools on a nearby table—bolt cutters, knives, pliers, a hammer, a blow torch, and a bone saw. I pulled my favorite blade from my hip, gripping the smooth rosewood handle and running a finger down the water-like patterns swirling along the edge.

The door creaked open, and Reaper stepped inside, his expression unreadable in the dim light. I glanced up, a question in my eyes.

"Eva's got Kenna. She'll text if anything's wrong. She's the right person to help her process what just happened. She knows how to answer the questions Kenna will have about how we'll handle this."

I nodded, my jaw tight. "Good."

Reaper hesitated, then crossed his arms. "You all right?"

I kept my eyes on the tools, my voice flat. "Fine."

Reaper didn't let up. "You sure? Because you looked ready to tear Tyler apart with your bare hands. And not just for the club. I know you and Kenna—"

I slammed a fist down on the table, the sound echoing through the warehouse. "There is no me and Kenna. Got it? I'm not about to let some woman compromise the club."

Reaper opened his mouth like he wanted to say more, but before he could, the door swung open again. Hatchet walked in, his face grim, his eyes scanning the scene. I shot Reaper a glare—a "shut your fucking mouth"—and he gave a barely perceptible nod.

At that moment, Tyler began to stir, his head lolling as he came to. His eyes fluttered open, confusion quickly giving way to fear as he took in the chains, the tools, and the three of us standing over him.

I leaned in close, my voice a low growl. "Welcome back, asshole. We've got questions."

Hatchet leaned against the table beside me.

Tyler looked like hell. Blood poured from his busted face, and his leg bled where I'd shot him. I'd half-assed a tourniquet around the wound to slow the bleeding earlier, but his skin had already ashened from the blood loss. He tried to shift, but the chains held him tight.

I crouched down, getting right in his face. "Why were you meeting with a fed this morning?"

He swallowed hard, throat bobbing. "I didn't have a choice."

I snorted, shaking my head. "Bullshit. Hatchet?"

My best friend grinned and pulled his hatchet from his belt loop. He threw it in the air and caught it by the handle. I rolled my eyes. Fucking dramatics every time.

"How about your trigger finger?" Hatchet said as he admired the sharp edge of his weapon. "After all, you were going to shoot my girl."

Tyler screamed as Hatchet held his hand against the arm of the chair and sliced his pointer finger clean off. In his haste, he hit part of Tyler's middle finger, leaving it dangling by a thread of skin.

"We have all fucking night, but I have shit to do," I said in a bored tone, pressing down the anxious knot in my gut as I worried about what Kenna would think about what we were about to do. "From now on, you answer questions in detail, or I'll cut every finger off with a dull spoon before moving to your toes."

Tyler gasped, pain making his voice shaky. "I've been meeting the feds for months. They recruited me after I failed the bar. Said my ties to the club made me valuable. Said I could be an agent, go undercover—"

"How long? How long have you been a rat?"

"Since I moved back," he whispered. "It's why I took the job with Reaper and became a prospect. She promised a letter of recommendation that would guarantee me a shot at Quantico."

I stared at him. Disgust curled in my chest. Our fathers had founded this club together. The Lone Star Mavericks Motorcycle Club stood because of their blood and sweat. Tyler had betrayed their legacy for a shot at a fucking badge.

Hatchet picked up the pliers, clicking them together with a menacing sound that made Tyler flinch. "What have you told them?"

Tyler shook his head, and panic flashed in his eyes. Hatchet didn't waste time with threats. He gripped Tyler's hand and pried one nail up. Tyler howled, blood pooling under the jagged nail bed.

"You feel like talking yet?" Hatchet asked. "Want to tell us what you told the feds?"

"Nothing that would put anyone away, I swear! Just little things. Routines, names, that kind of thing. They wanted dirt on Reaper. They think he's using his construction business to launder money."

I clenched my fists. The urge to end him was strong. But I knew what killing a fed's informant would mean. The FBI would come down on us like a sledgehammer, and the club would pay.

I turned back to Tyler, my voice low. "You risked all of us for a badge? Your brothers? Their fucking families?"

He looked at me, desperation in his eyes. "I wanted out. I wanted more than this fucking club. When my dad died, it was all he had. He left everything to the club. The FBI offered me a chance to get a real job, a life."

Reaper laughed. The dark, humorless sound echoed across the bare walls. "Your dad is rolling in his grave. The man was a loyal Maverick, through and through. He'd be ashamed of what you've become."

Fury twisted Tyler's face. "You all talk of loyalty. But where was that when my dad was passed over for president after Maxwell died? He was the VP. He co-founded the club. He should have been next. Instead, you fuckers voted in Thane."

I stepped closer. "You were a fucking child. You don't know what it was like back then. The club was living in the past. We needed Thane's leadership to change our direction, or the club would have crumbled. Your dad knew that. He respected the vote."

Tyler's jaw worked. "You're going to kill me." Resignation sounded through his voice.

"Right now, we're going to let you sit," Reaper said. "No food, no water. The officers will meet and decide what happens next. Hatchet, get a prospect here to keep an eye on him. I'll call Church."

Hatchet nodded, shoving the table of tools aside. "You're lucky, Tyler. If it were my call, you'd already be in pieces."

I locked eyes with Tyler, letting him see the promise in my gaze. "You better hope the club is feeling merciful. Because if it were up to me, you wouldn't see another sunrise."

I turned away, leaving Tyler chained in the darkness.

Chapter Sixteen

Brisket pressed his warm weight against me on the sofa as if he could sense my racing thoughts. My throat still ached where Tyler's fingers had dug in.

Eva handed me a steaming-hot porcelain mug. I sipped the coffee and let the hot bitterness anchor me.

"What did Tyler do?" I rasped, brushing my hand across the spot on my neck that still pulsed with pain. "What would make him crazy enough to hold a gun to my head?"

Eva sank into the armchair across from me. "I don't know much, other than Tyler was caught meeting with an FBI agent."

"What kind of information could he have that is worth my life?"

She shrugged. "Listen, there's a lot even I don't know. For good reason. Women are kept separate from club business to protect us."

I scoffed. "To protect? Or to control?" The words slipped out before I could stop them.

Eva rolled her eyes. I'd promised a long time ago to stop bickering with her over the motorcycle club's patriarchal culture—a vow I frequently failed to keep, especially with how raw and confused I felt about their vigilante style of justice.

"What do you think they'll do to Tyler?"

Eva glanced away, her jaw flexing. "I don't think you want to know that."

"I do." My voice rose, startling Brisket. He nosed my hand, and I scratched his ears absently. "After the first time I visited the clubhouse, I spent all night reading articles about what motorcycle clubs like this do. What men like Reaper do for those clubs. Merrick told me a little bit about what happened with the Rangers. And he explained why Fuse went to prison. But doesn't that bother you? I think Merrick would've beaten Tyler to death if Hatchet hadn't told him to stop."

Eva nodded. "I think Tyler might deserve that."

My eyes widened in shock. "You—what?"

Eva leaned forward. "Tyler held a gun to your head. Your neck is bruised. You had to practically break his ribs to get away. He betrayed the club—men who'd take a bullet for him. You think he deserves sympathy? You think he deserves mercy?"

I huffed in response, my chest tight with conflicting emotions. Anger and guilt tangled in my gut. "But do we get to decide who lives and who dies?"

"He's willing to give away information that could land the guys in prison. I won't lose any sleep if they bury his body tonight."

I stared at her. This wasn't the Eva I knew—the perfectionistic high achiever with a moral compass. Her relationship with Reaper and the club had changed her.

Or maybe this ruthlessness had always been there, simmering beneath her polished exterior.

The thought unsettled me, but so did the realization that part of me understood her anger. Part of me wanted Tyler to pay, too.

I slumped back, exhaustion weighing heavier than my fury. My mind kept replaying the scene—the cold press of the gun at my temple, the wild desperation in Tyler's eyes, the sickening sound of Merrick's fists battering flesh. I remembered the way Merrick looked at me, his eyes dark with rage, protectiveness, and maybe even fear.

"Doesn't it bother you?" I asked, my voice barely above a whisper. "That the man you love is capable of that level of violence?"

She stilled. "Reaper's capable of worse. So is Hatchet. Honestly, so am I."

I opened my mouth in surprise, but my phone rang, the screen lighting up with Hatchet's name.

"Hello?" I answered.

"Hey, doll. How are you feeling?" Hatchet asked, his tone soft and concerned.

"Sore, but fine." I rubbed my neck.

Eva's phone jingled, and she stepped out of the room before I continued. "What's happening? What are you going to do about Tyler?"

"Don't worry about it."

"Tell me," I insisted, my voice cracking. "I was the one with a gun to the head. I deserve to know."

Hatchet sighed. "We don't even know yet. We're heading back to the clubhouse for Church. This whole situation is fucked. I just wanted to make sure you're OK."

"I'm OK. How's Merrick?"

Hatchet hesitated. "He's fine."

"Really?"

Hatchet huffed out a laugh, but there was no real humor in it. "I haven't seen him lose control like that before. Listen, I have to go. Take care of yourself. Doc should be there in a few to look at that wrist."

Eva stepped back into the room, slipping her phone back in her pocket. "They're meeting for Church to discuss what to do. My guess is Tyler being an informant makes things complicated. If he disappears, the feds will have more reason to knock at our doors."

I bit my lip, my mind racing with possibilities—none of them good. "So what does that mean? They just let him go?"

"If they do, it won't be because they want to."

I swallowed hard, my throat still aching and my wrist throbbing.

The thought of what might happen next—what these men were capable of—settled like a stone in my stomach. Yesterday, I'd been furious at Thane, horrified by Fuse's past, and ready to walk away. But after the attack, after seeing Merrick's rage and Eva's cold resolve, I was left feeling lost. I wanted to believe in justice, in mercy, in doing the right thing. But in this world, the lines were blurred, and I wasn't sure I knew what side to stand on.

Brisket nudged my hand again, and I buried my fingers in his fur, seeking comfort. I needed to figure out what I believed in—and whether I was strong enough to stand behind a club that believed violence and loyalty were two sides of the same coin.

Chapter Seventeen

Thane slammed the gavel. The murmurs in the room came to a quiet, and he threw me a look that said the floor was mine. Around the table, every officer watched me, knowing a bomb was about to drop.

I cleared my throat. "A few weeks ago, Linc found evidence of a rat in the club."

The room erupted with curses. I let it ride for a beat, then raised my hand for silence.

"A few of us have known for weeks, which is why we paused a lot of business. Not that we didn't trust all of you, but we had to keep our mouths shut while we looked into everyone."

"Who the fuck is it?" Don demanded. His soft, grandfatherly look was gone, and in place was the fierce biker who'd helped start this club.

"It's Tyler." Ripples of shock ran through the room. "We have him. He's chained up in the warehouse right now."

Jack slammed a fist onto the table. "You're telling me that little shit's been feeding info to the feds under our noses? How long?" His Southern drawl softened the harshness of anger in his expression.

"Since he moved back," I said. "The FBI recruited him after he failed the bar. They promised him a letter of recommendation for Quantico if he played ball. He's been meeting with a handler for months, feeding her information."

Archer leaned forward. "What's he actually given her? Anything that could put us away?"

I shrugged. "According to him, nothing that would stick. But he's compromised our security. And today, when we confronted him, he grabbed Kenna. Put a goddamn gun to her head. If she hadn't fought back, we'd be talking about a body, not a betrayal."

"Two bodies, because he'd be dead the moment he put a bullet through her head, and then I'd tear apart his body with my bare hands," Hatchet growled. "He used Kenna as a fucking shield. For me, that alone is enough to take him out. He's a rat and a coward."

Reaper's jaw clenched. "He's a liability."

Fuse shook his head, voice calm but edged with steel. "We kill him, the feds will be on us before the body's cold. They'll know it was us. We're already on their radar, but nothing's stuck. If they had anything solid, we'd all be in the pen. Killing Tyler gives the feds something real."

Thane steepled his fingers, his eyes cold and sharp. "Tyler's not worth burning my club to the ground. If we kill him, we risk everything."

Hatchet leaned in, voice raw. "So we just let him walk? Let him keep breathing after what he did to Kenna? If it were Rhetta, you'd have already dug the hole."

Thane narrowed his eyes. "Kenna's not an old lady. Different standard. Unless you're planning to settle down, kid, know your fucking place."

For a beat, a tense silence stretched across the room.

Archer broke the tension. "We need a plan," he said, his tone measured and thoughtful. "Something that doesn't lead back here. Or we find another way to neutralize him—something that keeps the club safe and off the FBI's radar."

Don shook his head. "That's just passing the problem down the line. He knows too much."

"Whatever we do, it needs to be unanimous," Reaper cut in. "No blood unless we all agree."

Linc grinned. "I have a solution. We don't kill him. Not directly. But we make sure everyone knows exactly what he is. And then we let the wolves do the rest."

I raised a brow. "The floor is yours."

Linc explained his plan, and I'd admit, it was smart. He would hack together evidence—messages, emails, and deepfake voice notes—to make it look like Tyler had been spying on the Rangers. We'd dump Tyler on the outskirts of Austin, alive and conscious. Linc would anonymously send evidence to Poe, the Rangers' president, and Tyler's handler.

"If the Rangers find Tyler first, he's a dead man," I mused. "And if the feds get to him first, he's compromised, exposed, and useless. It's smart."

"Either way, Tyler's fate is sealed," Fuse added. "He's out on front street. A marked man. He'll either be dead, abandoned by the feds, or end up in WITSEC. Our hands stay clean."

Thane whistled. "Smart."

I nodded. "It's probably the best way to minimize risk to the club. All in favor, say aye."

The officers unanimously agreed.

"Then it's settled. Linc, get started on your part. I'm heading back to the junkyard. We might be leaving Tyler alive, but he's not getting out unmarked."

Hatchet raised a brow. "I don't know what you have in mind, but count me in."

Our engines snarled as we rolled out from the clubhouse. Hatchet rode beside me with a grin that promised bloodshed. The club had spoken, and we'd deliver justice, Maverick-style.

When we reached the junkyard, the place was silent except for the distant buzz of cicadas. Hatchet and I pushed through the door, our boots echoing on the oil-stained concrete.

Tyler, still chained to the chair, looked up in resignation. He must've thought the vote would end him tonight. He wasn't entirely wrong.

Hatchet leaned in, voice low and cold. "You're not dying yet. But you'll fucking wish you were."

I pulled the knife from my belt, the steel catching the light. "You're never going to Quantico," I said, my voice flat as I admired the beautiful curve of the blade. "You're never going undercover for anyone. Not after tonight."

Hatchet grabbed Tyler's arm, pinning it to the chair. I pressed the blade to his skin, just below the elbow, and started to carve. The word "RAT" bloomed in angry, jagged letters across his forearm. Tyler screamed, the sound bouncing off the walls.

Hatchet held him steady in an ironclad grip. "You brought this on yourself, you little shit. You think the FBI will want you now?"

When I finished, Tyler's blood ran down his arm and pooled on the concrete. I wiped the blade clean on his shirt.

Hatchet grabbed a rag and wrapped it tightly around Tyler's arm. "Wouldn't want you to pass out from blood loss. I want to make sure you see who finds you first. Does your handler check her email at night? You better hope she does. Before Poe finds you."

I slipped a bag over Tyler's head and zip-tied his wrists before tossing him into the back of a van. We drove for nearly two hours before we dumped him in a field and emailed the evidence Linc had cooked up.

By dawn, Tyler would be a ghost.

Chapter Eighteen

A sharp rap at my door startled me. Brisket, curled at my feet, lifted his head with a low growl. I hesitated, my pulse racing as I padded across the floor and peered through the peephole.

Merrick stood on my porch, his dark hair damp, the scent of soap and leather wafting through the door. He wore a clean black T-shirt and jeans, but his jaw was set in a way that made my stomach tighten.

I opened the door, and his gaze went straight to my neck. My hand flew to cover the bruises. His expression darkened, fury flickering in his eyes before he schooled his features into neutrality.

I stepped aside to let him enter. He moved past me, filling the small space with his presence. Brisket sniffed his boots, tail wagging. Merrick scratched the dog's ears absently, his eyes never leaving my face.

"You OK?" he asked, voice low.

I shrugged, hugging my arms around myself. "I'm alive. Thanks to the self-defense you guys helped teach me."

He tipped my chin up, looking at the hand-shaped imprint on my neck. "You did good. You got away. That's more than most people. But it should have never happened in the first place."

I swallowed hard, my throat aching. "What happened to Tyler?"

Merrick's jaw tightened. "He's alive. For now."

"Will you—?"

"No," he cut in, sharp. "We won't kill him."

I let out a breath I hadn't realized I was holding. "So what'll happen to him?"

He hesitated, eyes flickering to the bruises again. "We exposed him. Left him for another club to deal with, if his handler doesn't get to him first. He's not our problem anymore."

I bit my lip, questions burning on my tongue. "Will they kill him?"

Merrick sighed. "Maybe. Probably. But it won't be by our hands."

I wanted to ask more, but the look in Merrick's eyes told me he wouldn't answer.

He stepped closer. "I just wanted to make sure you were OK."

I nodded and swallowed, my throat tight. "I am."

He reached out, fingers brushing lightly over my bruised skin. "I'm sorry you got hurt."

I looked up at him. "It's not your fault."

He shook his head. "It is. It's my responsibility to keep the club safe. To keep our women safe. I failed."

The ache in my throat grew sharper. "You didn't fail. No one could've known Tyler would do that."

Guilt and anger swirled in his expression. "I should've known. Should've seen it coming. That's the job. That's what I'm supposed to do."

I wanted to argue, but the look on his face stopped me. He wasn't just angry. He was haunted. Like he'd let down more than just the club.

I took a breath, forcing a small smile. "Well, it'll heal. The bruises will be gone by the party next week, I'm sure."

Surprise flickered across his face. "You're still coming?"

I raised an eyebrow. "Of course. You think a little bruise and a gun to my head is enough to scare me off?"

Merrick stared at me, his expression unreadable. "I thought after today you'd want to be as far from the club as possible."

I shrugged. "I'm not going to let one bad guy keep me away from my friends. Besides, I worked hard on the opening video, and I want to see your reaction." I offered a small smile, trying to prove that I was OK.

There was a moment of silence between us. I could see the conflict in his eyes.

"Kenna," he said. And in that one word, I heard the relief in his voice. Merrick stepped closer, and the tension in the room ratcheted up a notch.

Just then, the door swung open without a knock, and Hatchet's grinning face appeared. Brisket bounded over, weaving between his legs and nearly tripping him. Hatchet strode to me, arms already outstretched for a hug. "There's my girl! You look better than I expected," he teased, pulling me close and kissing the top of my head.

Merrick's expression flickered before he schooled it back to neutral.

"You OK?" Hatchet asked, rubbing my back before pulling away.

"I'm fine," I said, smiling despite myself. "The bruises look worse than they feel."

Hatchet held up a pink bakery box. "Good, 'cause I come bearing gifts. Maisie's donuts, fresh from the oven. Figured you could use a sugar fix." He opened the box to show colorful sprinkled donuts.

I laughed, grabbing a donut with pink frosting. "You're the best."

Hatchet winked. "Damn right." He glanced at Merrick, then back at me. "Sorry, am I interrupting?"

Merrick cleared his throat. "No. I was just leaving." He gave me a slight nod. "Take care of yourself."

I nodded, and my chest tightened as I watched Merrick's broad back disappear out the door.

* * *

The brutal Texas sun beat down on my bare shoulders as I helped Eva set up for the club's fiftieth anniversary party. The bruises around my neck had faded to a faint yellow easily hidden by a bit of makeup, but today, my head was the real problem. I slipped a migraine pill from my purse and swallowed it dry.

"You OK?" Eva asked

"Fine," I insisted, forcing a smile. "Just a headache."

Her eyes narrowed as I slipped on my dark sunglasses.

Even under the shade of the tent, sweat trickled down my back, and the throbbing in my temples pulsed in time with my heartbeat. To make matters worse, Aunt Flo had decided to crash the party. My cramps, worse than usual, sent sharp pains through my center, and the cysts that liked to make my life hell every few cycles pulsed within me.

I gritted my teeth and kept working, helping Eva arrange tables and chairs, but every movement sent a fresh wave of pain through my abdomen.

As we tested the video to make sure the audio and visual equipment worked, I hunched over and gripped the edge of the table as a vicious cramp took my breath away.

"What's wrong?"

I tried to straighten, but my hand stayed pressed to my stomach. "It's nothing. Just ... my period. Cramps. The migraine isn't helping."

Eva's expression softened. "You should go home and rest. I can put the prospects on setup. You can come back later if you're feeling better."

I shook my head, even though the movement made my temples throb. "I don't want to bail on you."

Eva crossed her arms. "You're not bailing. You're taking care of yourself. Go. Lie down. If you feel better, come back. If not, stay home. No one will blame you."

I hesitated, but another piercing pain twisted through me, and I knew she was right. "OK. Thanks."

She gave me a quick hug. "Take care of yourself. I'll text you pictures if you don't make it."

I managed a weak smile before grabbing my bag and heading for my car, the sunglasses still shielding my eyes from the unforgiving sun.

Chapter Nineteen

The yard vibrated with energy as the long-awaited anniversary party drew in club members, supporters, and curious neighbors alike. A large banner hung off the side of the clubhouse with a timeline of the club's history, complete with blown-up versions of the photos I'd given Kenna. Another banner honored the men we'd lost over the years—on the road, in wars, and to their own personal demons.

Rhetta kicked off the event from a stage in front of the clubhouse. I watched the crowd from my spot near the back, scanning for threats out of habit.

"Welcome and thank you for coming to celebrate the Lone Star Mavericks Motorcycle Club's fiftieth anniversary. I'm Rhetta Blackwell, tonight's emcee and the wife of our fearless leader. Before we break for dinner, drinks, and a damn good time tonight"—she paused to allow the loud cheers from the crowd—"we have a short video to share about our history and community impact."

She stepped aside as a video projected on a white screen. It told the story of our club through brief interview clips, photos, and videos. It wove in the ways we'd helped the community—from a playground built by Reaper's construction company in a local park to the run that raised tens of thousands of dollars for the women's shelter. I'd known Kenna was a talented interviewer, but the way she stitched together the past, present, and future told our story better than I'd ever imagined.

I tensed when my voice filled the air: "The Lone Star Mavericks Motorcycle Club runs in my blood. It's a part of my soul." The screen faded to black with a childhood photo of me standing beside my father in front of the original rundown building.

Hatchet smacked me on the back, and Eva glanced at me with a grin.

"Sorry. I know you hate the attention, but Kenna insisted that this was the perfect way to end the video," Eva said.

"Where is Kenna?" Hatchet asked, glancing around.

Eva frowned. "I had to send her home halfway through setup."

My brow furrowed. "Why?"

Eva hesitated. "She's not feeling well."

"She's sick?"

Eva patted my arm. "Not exactly. Her day started with a migraine, and then she got hit with cramps. I sent her home. She'll be fine. She's been texting me all afternoon. The woman doesn't know how to rest."

"That's too bad. All she's been talking about is this party and the damn cake," Hatchet said, wandering away to the bar.

I hated the idea of Kenna in pain, home alone while we enjoyed the party she'd planned without her. The thought gnawed at me as I made an impulsive decision. I snuck to the back kitchen, cutting off a large piece of the espresso chocolate cake and carefully enclosing it in a plastic container.

"What do you think you're doing?" Maisie said as she stormed up to me. "I expect this thievery from Dixon, but not you."

"Calm down. I'm taking a piece to Kenna, since she's missing out. Eva sent her home. Migraine and cramps."

Maisie tilted her head. "Well, isn't that sweet? Let me put together a goody bag for her before the heathens eat all the cinnamon rolls and donuts. How about I grab a to-go box from the buffet, too?"

I smiled. "Thanks, Mais."

"Stop by the coffee shop and ask Lenora to make her a raspberry iced tea. Raspberry leaf helps with cramping. You might grab her some Advil and a heating pad from the drugstore next door while you're at it."

I raised my brows. "You sure that's not too much?"

She smiled sweetly and patted my chest. "Not for someone you care about, dear."

I nixed the plan to take my bike, carrying the canvas bag filled with sweet treats and a generous sampling of the buffet to my truck. Gravel crunched behind me, and I turned to see Fuse.

"Calling it a night already?" he asked.

"Just taking some dinner and cake to Kenna. She had to leave early. Knocked down by a migraine and cramps, according to Eva."

A slow smile spread across Fuse's face. "That woman is exactly what you need."

I scowled. "She's a friend."

"Pretend all you want. I've known you for a long time, brother. I've seen you with her. You don't look at anyone else the way you look at Kenna. Not even Rose."

I ground my teeth. I pressed my palms to the back of my neck and sighed.

"Fuck. I know. She's not ready, though."

"You won't know unless you make a move. Decide and act, before someone else does."

"Hatchet likes her," I argued weakly.

Fuse gave a clipped, dismissive laugh. "Hatchet likes anything with a pair of tits. He'll never settle down. Don't lose a good woman because you're too chickenshit to commit."

I didn't respond as I got into my truck, ignoring Fuse's ripple of laughter at my blatant dismissal. But his words rumbled through my mind on my way first to the coffee shop for the iced tea and then to

Kenna's house. I hesitated for a moment outside, worried she'd see this as an overstep. Before I could change my mind, I shot her a text.

ME:

What are you doing? Are you dressed?

KENNA:

Yes? That's a bizarre question to ask. I'm just watching TV.

ME:

Stay on the couch. I'm coming in.

KENNA:

Wait? What?

I keyed in the front door code and opened the door to see a shocked Kenna covered with a blanket. Brisket let out a deep woof before dancing on his paws before me with a wagging tail.

The chilly room sent goose bumps across my bare arms as I stepped inside. "Jesus, Kenna. You must have the air set at sixty degrees."

"What are you doing here?"

I handed her the raspberry tea and wiped my damp hand on my jeans. "How's your migraine?"

"It's mostly gone. But, again, what are you doing here?"

I strolled to the kitchen counter, pushed aside a stack of dog-eared true crime books, and began to pull containers from the bag. Brisket sniffed the air and let out a low, hopeful whine. "I thought you might want dinner, and I know you want this." I pulled the cake container from the bag and opened it. The sweet scent of chocolate espresso floated through the room.

Kenna moaned. "Is that the cake? You brought me cake?"

"You couldn't stop talking about it. And we both know there won't be a crumb left once it leaves the clubhouse kitchen. I have donuts and cinnamon rolls, too. How are your cramps?"

Kenna cringed, wrinkling her nose. "Eva told you about that?"

I pulled a heating pad, a bottle of Advil, and a bag of lavender Epsom salts from the bag. "A hot bath might help. Or the heating pad. Wanted to make sure you had something for the pain, too. Wasn't sure if you had everything you needed, since you just moved here."

"Who are you? What happened to my tough biker friend?"

I shrugged. "It's not a big deal. I didn't want you to miss out on the best part of the party."

She smirked. "You mean you didn't think the video was the best part?"

I laughed. "I can't believe you ended it on me."

"I can't help that I'm such a great interviewer that you gave me a golden soundbite."

I rolled my eyes. "Do you want me to start a hot bath for you?"

"Can I eat the cake in the bath?"

I grinned. "Only if you save me a bite."

She shook her head. "I hope you brought two slices, because I'm not sharing. I should eat some real food first, though. I was too sick to eat earlier. "

She slowly stood, trying to shield the grimace of pain on her face.

"Sit," I commanded. "I'll bring a dish to you. Would you like the heating pad?"

"That would be great."

I plugged in the small heating pad and handed it to her.

"Thanks. Usually, I'm not in this much pain, but I have some cysts that have flared up, and I can barely stand," she explained, looking a little embarrassed.

I nodded. "My sister lived with me when she was in high school. I know how it can be."

I busied myself in the kitchen, trying to ignore how her gaze followed my every move as I made us each a plate and nuked them in the microwave. Brisket followed hot on my heels, hoping for crumbs. We ate in comfortable silence with the dog staring us down.

"I can fill the tub for you and get out of your hair," I offered, as I took her empty plate to the counter.

"This heating pad is helping. Do you want to stay and watch a movie instead?"

"Sure. Do you want your cake now?"

She fiddled with the remote. "God, yes."

I grabbed the cake and a fork from the kitchen before settling beside her on the couch. The space between us was small, and I could feel the warmth of her body. She released a breathy moan after the first bite.

"Just as mind-blowing as I remembered it. Try a bite." She offered a forkful of the decadent cake to me, and I raised a brow.

"You sure? I thought you weren't into sharing."

"It's the least I can do, considering what I'm about to make you watch."

I leaned in to take a bite. Our eyes locked for a beat. For a second, my world narrowed to just her—her lips, her eyes, the way her breath hitched as I moved closer. I could have kissed her then. I wanted to. But I pulled back and grabbed the remote instead.

She shrieked. "Give that back!"

"Not until you tell me what movie you're going to make me watch."

I held the remote high enough that her adorably short arms couldn't reach it.

"I was going to introduce you to *Twilight*."

"Absolutely not. My brothers would never let me live that down."

She giggled. "They never have to know. I promise."

"Liar. You'll tell Hatchet the first chance you get. And he'll tell everyone."

She threw her head back and laughed. "I need to know if you're Team Edward or Team Jacob."

"I can answer that without watching the movie. Team Jacob."

Kenna gasped dramatically, holding her hand over her heart. "Why?"

"Because a sparkling man is fucking ridiculous. And being a werewolf is way cooler. Now we've settled that, we can watch something else."

"Fine. What's your favorite movie?"

"*The Boondock Saints.*"

"Let's watch that, then."

I raised a brow at her. "It's dark and violent."

She rolled her eyes. "I can handle dark and violent. I might even *like* dark and violent."

Her words hung between us. I was dark. I could be violent.

I brushed the thoughts away as she pressed play.

Over the next hour and a half, Kenna moved closer. Halfway through the movie, she leaned against me and fell asleep. With her head resting on my shoulder, I breathed in her scent—a sweet and earthy floral mix, like she'd bathed in rose petals. I wanted to wrap my arms around her, to pull her closer and never let go.

But I didn't. She wasn't ready. That much was clear. Her heart still belonged to another man—a dead man. A ghost.

After the movie, I carefully carried her to bed and pulled the sheets over her petite body. Seeing her red hair spread across her pillow, her eyes peacefully closed in sleep, stirred something deep inside me. I clicked my tongue, calling the dog to follow me out of the room, and softly closed her door.

I stood outside with Brisket for a moment, breathing in the night air. A fire of desire for her coursed through my chest. But there was more to it. I felt a connection to Kenna. A balance. Her fire melted my frost.

I looked to the stars and wondered. Could a woman like Kenna love me? Understand me? Accept the darkness and violence that walked hand in hand with my life choices?

And, more importantly, was I willing to risk everything—my friendship with Hatchet, the club's unity—to find out?

Chapter Twenty

I followed the motions of the morning—filling the dog's bowl, brewing my coffee, microwaving a leftover cinnamon roll—but my mind was miles away, tangled in thoughts of Merrick.

He put me at ease in a way that left me feeling safe and unguarded. He'd shown up with cake and comfort, stayed to watch a movie, and let me lean on him when my body ached. He'd carried me to bed, tucked me in, and left without asking for anything in return. It was more thought and care than I'd gotten from anyone in a long time.

But Merrick hadn't shown interest in being more than a friend.

I sipped my coffee, staring out the kitchen window. My chest ached a little, disappointed that he hadn't made a move. There had been moments that made my heart race. But he hadn't acted on it. And he'd had plenty of chances.

He could have kissed me. He could have wrapped his arms around me on the couch while we watched the movie. He could have said something to let me know he wanted more.

But either he didn't feel that way about me, or he held his own reservations. Whatever the reason, it didn't matter. The truth was, we were just friends. And that had to be enough.

I bit into my cinnamon roll, letting the gooey sugar and warm dough crowd out my musings. I liked Merrick's friendship. He listened. He showed up when I needed him. I liked the man he was—stoic, loyal, and unexpectedly tender.

My phone rang, the shrill tone breaking me out of my thoughts. Annoyance coursed through me as I saw who it was.

"Hey, Mom," I said as cheerfully as I could muster.

"Kenna, dear. When are you coming home?"

No preamble. No "how are you?" Just demands.

"Texas is my home," I reminded her. "I don't know when I'll come for a visit. Maybe Thanksgiving."

My mother huffed at the inconvenience. "What about the annual picnic?"

I rolled my eyes. I despised the upscale barbecue event where she dragged me and my siblings around a ritzy country club, introducing us to her fake friends.

"I have a work event," I lied. "A client needs me."

"Oh? Who is this client?"

I grimaced. Shit. I couldn't exactly tell my mother I worked for a motorcycle club. She'd have a heart attack. "It's a private club. Very exclusive. Hard to get into. They're pretty secretive. I can't talk about 'club business.'" I laughed internally at my use of the term that generally annoyed me.

She hummed. "Maybe you'll find a nice husband at this club."

I held back a snort. "Yeah, you'd love these guys. They're very ... driven." On motorcycles, anyway.

"Well, I know you're busy with work, but I wanted to make sure you'd heard about Alec's memorial—"

I cut her off. "Sorry, a client's calling. Love you. Bye." I hung up the call and threw my phone down. It skittered across the countertop and immediately began to ring again. I glanced at the caller ID. It was Hatchet.

"Hey," I answered, relaxing against the kitchen counter.

"Good morning, doll. You, uh, feeling better?" Hatchet asked, his tone pitched just shy of squeamish, which made me smile.

Men and menstruation. I could practically hear him squirming across the line.

"Yeah, a lot better actually. And I didn't make anyone else bleed. Always a win when I make it through the first twenty-four hours without a murder."

He let out a chuckle. "Glad to hear it. Anyway, I'm calling for Thane. He wants you to swing by."

"Shit. Is he still mad at me for my ... outburst?"

Hatchet scoffed. "No, Merrick smoothed that over for you. You're forgiven. It's about the Riot. Serpent and Jag are in town. They want you and Eva on board for PR stuff. Can you do two?"

I pulled my phone away from my ear and flipped to my calendar app. "Yeah, that should be fine. Is Eva coming, or am I the sacrificial lamb?"

"She had some other client meeting, so Thane asked me to call you."

That probably meant Thane hadn't completely forgiven me, if Eva was still his first choice. "Guess I'll have to be OK with second place."

"You're always first in my book, doll. You want to go out tonight? Archer and I were going to hit up a new bar. There'll be dancing and plenty of free drinks."

I grinned. "You buying?"

"Always."

"Do you think we could get Eva to come?"

"You've met her, right? Eva would rather stay home with her books and her dog."

I giggled. "Yeah, you're right. I'm still going to invite her. I feel obligated to try. Statistically, every tenth invite works."

"Good luck with that. Pick you up at eight?"

I smiled. "Yeah, see you then."

"Wear a jacket. We're taking my bike."

Something fluttered low in my stomach—equal parts nerves and excitement. "Got it. Try not to kill us."

"You're always safe with me, doll. I'd never let anything happen to you."

* * *

What sounded like a herd of thundering mechanical buffalo pulled up to my house. I wobbled a bit in my heeled boots as I ran out the door. Archer and Fuse sat on their bikes as Hatchet swung his leg over, pulling a helmet from the saddlebags for me. Eva perched behind Reaper on his matte white Harley.

"You came!" I screeched, hugging Eva one-armed and sideways, careful to avoid the scorching-hot black pipes. She squeezed me back.

"I'm leaving early," she warned.

"We'll see about that, Grandma," I said as Hatchet handed me the helmet. I jammed it on, adjusting the strap below my chin, and swung my leg over the bike. Most of the guys didn't wear anything besides a backward ball cap or bandanna. But Hatchet seemed to intuitively know I'd be more comfortable with protection.

Inside, despite the long line curling around the block, Hatchet just nodded at the bouncer, who stepped aside and let us straight in.

"Are you a secret celebrity?" I asked him, trying to stay quiet but feeling like I had to shout above the pulsing crowd.

Hatchet shot me a sidelong grin. "I'm a fucking legend, doll."

I rolled my eyes. "Get us a drink," I ordered as I dragged Eva to the dance floor.

Our hips swayed to the bass, and we giggled as we danced in our own world, not worrying about what others thought. Because of her cut, most people gave Eva and me a wide berth.

I laughed and caught Eva's attention, pointing her gaze toward Hatchet, who was holding a tray of shots beside Reaper and Fuse, who were doing their best "security detail" impressions by the cocktail table. The table looked comically small before the brawny men. We wove through the crowd, the drinks calling for us.

"Did you giants steal this from a dollhouse?" I asked.

Hatchet didn't miss a beat, arching a brow as he handed me a shot.

"Girls always like to say size doesn't matter but then complain when it's not big enough," he joked.

I caught Eva's eye. She hated crowds and had only come for me. I'd be lucky if she lasted fifteen more minutes. "Last dance?" I mouthed. She nodded, and I dragged her back toward the pulsing blur of lights and bodies.

We threw ourselves into the music. Halfway through, an over-grown frat boy tried to grind up against Eva, wrapping a hand around her waist. She twisted away, but he leaned in, oblivious and determined.

Big mistake.

Before Eva could unleash her particular brand of mayhem, Reaper materialized. He tossed Eva—who squawked, sounding both outraged and delighted—over his shoulder before he reeled back and decked the guy, sending him flat on his back.

I pressed my hand over my mouth, eyes wide in gleeful shock. As the crowd shrieked at the spectacle, Fuse threw me a mock salute, following Reaper out the door.

My shoulders shook with laughter as Hatchet stepped up beside me. He slipped his arm around my waist, warm and casual, and before I could protest, he spun me onto the dance floor. Suddenly, it felt like the entire bar belonged to us.

Dancing with Hatchet was like willingly grabbing onto a live wire. He knew every beat, matching my moves. His hands found my hips, and I melted into the thrum of the music, feeling the beat in my chest and his body heat everywhere else.

God, I loved this. The floodlights, the strangers, the sticky floor, and the promise of bad decisions. For a second, I caught my reflection in one of the mirrored walls—a shock of wild red hair, flushed cheeks, and eyes so bright I almost didn't recognize myself.

Archer waved us over to the bar, where he slid us another pair of shots. Hatchet didn't miss a beat. He threw his back in one smooth move, his other arm locked around my waist as if claiming me, his hips swaying behind me like we'd never left the dance floor. He waved down the bartender for two glasses of water, and I leaned further into him, letting my head rest briefly against the hard plane of his chest.

Hatchet handed me a glass, and I downed the cool liquid gratefully. I wiped sweat from my brow, missing the ghost of his touch burning hot at my hips.

A girl with big hair and cherry-red lips started circling Hatchet, pressing her chest against him to try to whisper in his ear. Clearly a bit tipsy, her whisper came out as a shout.

"Save a horse, ride a biker. Want to dance?"

Hatchet blinked, rolled his eyes, and turned his attention back to me, deliberately ignoring the offer.

"Come on," the blonde said, running her hand down his back.

"Back off," I barked around Hatchet's shoulder.

Archer swooped in, taking the overly touchy woman's hand and leading her out to the dance floor. I raised my glass and mouthed a thank you to him.

Every nerve ending in me sparked the moment Hatchet's hands slid back to my waist. His thumbs traced tantalizing, deliberate circles on the bare skin exposed above my jeans, sending a shiver up my spine.

"You're dangerously beautiful tonight," he murmured in my ear.

My heart fluttered in my chest, but I kept my voice steady. "I thought you liked to live dangerously."

His fingers tightened the slightest bit. The unspoken promise in his grip made me catch my breath.

"I do. Trouble is, every time I'm near you, I forget where the line is."

I let myself linger in that heat, biting my lip to hide a smile. "Maybe tonight, we should see how close we can get without crossing it."

He dropped his head, letting his lips brush the shell of my ear—close enough I felt his breath, but not touching. "That sounds like a challenge, doll."

I turned to face him, laughing lightly. "Then accept it."

My pulse thundered at my throat, desperate for more, but I held the line. He grinned wickedly, eyes never leaving mine. Neither of us closed the distance, but the tension glittered sharp and heavy in the heat between us.

* * *

A golden haze leaked through my window as the sun rose only a few hours after landing in my bed. I buried my face deeper into the pillow. Brisket lay sprawled beside me. He thumped his tail as I woke, silently asking for a morning belly rub.

I hesitantly stretched my body, which ached from dancing and drinking until the bar closed. The ghost of Hatchet's touch still tingled across my body, the memory of his rough fingers causing my stomach to flip. He touched me like I was made of dynamite, careful yet confident with his trademark cockiness and desire for anything that gave him a rush of adrenaline.

Memories of him standing at my door after driving me home rushed back to me. We stood on my porch as he held my elbow, keeping me steady as I teetered in my heels. He stepped in, his palm grazing my arm lightly. I could feel in the gravity of the moment that he was going to kiss me.

And I panicked. Full system shutdown. I turned away and unlocked the door as I told him good night.

But Hatchet just grinned. He chuckled, low and warm, like I hadn't rejected him once again.

"I had a good time tonight, doll. Night," he'd said before swaggering off like he didn't have a single bruise on his ego. Like women who were a sure thing hadn't been throwing themselves at him all night long.

Rolling onto my back, I stared up at the ceiling fan spinning lazy circles above me. Why had I pulled away? I liked Hatchet. As Eva reminded me time and time again, Alec wouldn't expect me to stay loyal to his corpse. He'd want me to be happy. And I didn't have to jump into a long-term, committed relationship. I could choose casual. Fun.

I struggled to reprogram the muscle memory of heartbreak. Pushing people away was a reflex.

But after Hatchet left, the ache for Alec felt more distant. Not gone. Not by a long shot. But dulled at the edges, like a scar that had healed enough that you could trace it with your fingers without wincing.

I'd spent so much time buried under the weight of my grief, living in my old apartment, where the ghost of memories of my life before trailed my every step. Texas had given me a fresh start. A home with halls Alec had never walked. New friends who were becoming family. And a sweet, overgrown puppy that brought purpose to my day.

I closed my eyes, letting myself drift in the feeling of hope and happiness that filled my chest. Brisket whined, growing impatient as I lazed in bed.

"Fine, I'll get up. We'll go for a walk before the air feels like we're walking through hell," I said, as if the dog spoke English and could understand me. His warm, mocha eyes and excited yip told me he just might.

My phone pinged as a text came through.

EVA:

Don't forget that you're meeting with Thane and the Riot today.

ME:

> Yes, Mom. I won't be late.

EVA:

> Get there a few minutes early. And try not to piss off Thane again.

I rolled my eyes.

ME:

> He could try basic communication about what is actually happening in the club.

EVA:

> That is precisely the type of comment you need to keep in your head.

ME:

> I'll play nice today. Promise.

I strolled into the clubhouse five minutes before our meeting, having gotten a text from Merrick thirty minutes before reminding me that, from Thane's point of view, on time equaled late.

"Mornin', darlin'," Thane drawled. "This is Serpent. He's the president of the Red Rock Riot."

Thane gestured toward the man leaning against the pool table.

I nodded in hello. Serpent's presence made me stand up straighter. His black hair brushed his collar in wind-torn waves, like he hadn't bothered to run his fingers through it after a long, hard ride. A dark beard framed his mouth. His forearms, wrapped in tight cords of muscle, were a gallery of ink with snakes twisting through shadows and smoke. I recognized one piece as a Mayan deity from my brief stint in college as an archaeology student. The fact that this man carried that god on his skin made me wonder if he believed in what it stood for—power and sacrifice.

"And this is Jaguar. VP."

Jaguar straightened from where he'd been lounging in a chair. His slow movements were fluid, embodying the predatory grace of the large cat he was named for. He was leaner than Serpent, with the sleek build of an MMA fighter. His black hair was shaved close on the sides with a short, spiky mohawk running across the top of his head. A still-pink puckered scar cut through the side of his cheek.

I reached out a palm to shake with each of the men, their enormous hands swallowing my own.

"We're just waiting on Hatchet, and then we can head to the office to talk," Reaper explained.

A throaty laugh drifted from the hall. A stunning blonde with bright-blue eyes walked out from beside Hatchet.

A surge of jealousy coursed through me. I pursed my lips, reminding myself that Hatchet and I were not in a relationship.

Hatchet caught my gaze and pointedly stepped farther from the blonde as they entered the room.

"Kenna, this is Haven," Thane said. "She's Serpent and Jag's old lady."

Serpent AND Jag? My terrible poker face betrayed my curious thoughts as I heard the two men chuckle at my reaction.

"Did you pick one out that you liked, love?" Jaguar asked Haven, wrapping his arms around her. She pulled a small pistol from her purse, aiming the barrel at the ground as she handed it to him.

"The Springfield Hellcat," she said proudly. "Hatchet says it's the perfect size for me."

Jaguar admired the small weapon, looking down the barrel before carefully handing it back to Haven. "Nice. We'll do some target shooting when we get home to make sure you're comfortable with it."

"Let's head to my office to chat," Thane suggested. "Kenna's the one who alerted me to the reporters digging into your club. I think she can help you."

I trailed behind Thane, feeling Merrick close behind me and hearing the heavy bootsteps of the Riot men.

Once we sat down, I began to ask Serpent and Jaguar basic questions about their club and the reputational challenges they faced in their small community in New Mexico. A former member had made headlines—fighting in the grocery store, recklessly driving through a school zone, and—the last straw—assaulting an underage girl.

"Misconduct by one bad actor can tarnish an entire organization's image," I explained. "But this is repairable. You've already kicked him out. That shows you're not willing to accept that kind of behavior."

Serpent and Jag nodded, seemingly more open to my counsel than I'd have expected a month ago, before I'd found myself embedded in the motorcycle club world.

"Actions speak louder than words," I continued. "We don't need to tell the newspapers that your club is good. We need to show them. That's how Eva approached reputation repair with the Mavericks. She found the stories that showed the community who these guys really are."

Before I could say more, the unmistakable rat-tat-tat of gunfire sounded nearby, the shots ricocheting off the clubhouse steel siding.

The men were on their feet in a blur, hands finding pistols as easily as a normal man would find his phone. Jaguar, Thane, and Reaper rushed out as Merrick and Serpent reached for me and Haven.

"Get behind the desk," Merrick ordered. "Now."

I scrambled with Haven, dropping behind Thane's solid oak desk.

"Stay down. I'm locking the door behind us. Don't open it for anyone." Merrick waited for a beat as I stared at him, my heart thundering in my chest. "Words, Kenna. Use your words. Do you understand?"

"Yes," I squeaked. "Stay behind the desk. Don't open the door."

Serpent kneeled to kiss Haven and handed her the purse she'd left behind on the chair. "If anyone tries to get in here who isn't us, don't stop pulling the trigger until you're out of bullets," he added.

Haven's hand found mine, and the lock clicked behind the men as they left.

Deafening silence filled our ears. No more gunshots. No shouts. None of the chaos I'd expect in a firefight.

After ten minutes, heavy boots thudded down the hall. Haven

gripped the small pistol in her hand, peeking around the desk. The handle rattled as the person behind the door began to unlock it.

"You can come out," Merrick said as he opened the door. "You're safe."

Haven stood, running and throwing herself into Jaguar's arms.

"What happened?" I asked, my voice shakier than I'd expected.

Merrick's gaze skimmed over me before he shrugged. "Drive-by, but we're not sure yet who the target was. Hopefully, Linc can find out more from the camera."

He was so nonchalant, like drive-by shootings occurred every day.

"We're going to get on the road," Serpent said. "I don't want Haven caught in the crossfire. Thanks for meeting with us. We'll be in touch."

Chapter Twenty-One

HATCHET

Thane called Church at the ass-crack of dawn. I hauled ass on my bike to make it on time, regretting the five vodka and Redbulls I'd drunk the night before and the lumpy couch I'd crashed on.

"Glad you could roll out from under whatever blonde you found last night to join us," Merrick jabbed as he stared into my bloodshot eyes in Thane's office.

I shook my head but didn't respond. I'd gone out the night before, intending to do precisely what he'd suggested. But my heart just wasn't in it, and I found myself too buzzed to drive home, yet too distracted to fall into bed with anyone—though I'd had plenty of offers.

Chasing tits and ass, trading names I wouldn't remember, waking up in someone else's bed and sneaking out before she woke—it was all starting to feel hollow. Thirty-three shouldn't feel old, but something inside me was shifting. Maybe I was growing out of one-night stands. Or perhaps it was the pint-sized redhead who I couldn't get out of my mind.

Reaper strolled into the room with our president close behind.

Thane kicked the door shut, the impact vibrating the small display of souvenirs he'd picked up on the road over the years.

"So, we have no fucking idea who shot up the club," he roared.

Merrick flicked his gaze to Reaper, then to me. We all knew that tone. Thane's temper was legendary, and none of us wanted to draw attention until he calmed down.

Linc spoke up from the corner, spreading his hands open and speaking evenly like he approached a rabid rottweiler. "The evidence points to the Jackals. The shooter was on a street bike, not a Harley. So it's unlikely to be one of our rivals or the Riot's. The clubhouse is far enough from the road that we know it wasn't random. We're on to them, and they know it."

The air crackled for a breath, everyone watching to see who or what Thane would burn next. Instead, his rage dissipated as quickly as it appeared. He slid into his chair and lit a smoke, taking a deep drag before speaking.

"We should scale back the Memorial Day barbecue and take precautions moving forward," Thane said. "I don't want anyone here who you wouldn't personally vouch for. And I want men at the gates around the clock. Only members and old ladies get through. Anyone else needs approval from me."

I held back a groan. The club hadn't required guards in years. Rotating men at the gates twenty-four-seven was a duty that would fall to Merrick and me. It was a shit detail. We hardly had enough prospects to fill out the schedule. The fully patched members wouldn't want to volunteer as guards for the long, boring shifts, and those who did without complaint would be grouchy as hell after an all-nighter. And we'd be the bad guys for enforcing a fair rotation. Still, I kept my mouth shut and nodded.

As Merrick droned on about how he planned to divide up guard duty, my mind wandered to Kenna. I caught myself thinking about her at the oddest moments, and I started to wonder if it was a sign. I needed to make a move before it was too late. Before another man swooped in and I lost my chance. I'd been waiting, biding my time until she gave me some sort of indication she wanted more than friendship. But, if I was honest, what I was really waiting for was the feeling that I was ready to stop chasing after meaningless hookups and settle down with someone who wasn't afraid to call me on my bullshit. Someone like her.

Kenna was bright, fun, and goddamn it, she was beautiful. Sure, she had baggage, but who didn't? None of us was getting out of life without damaged edges. Since I'd met her nearly two months ago, I'd watched her shift. That sharp-edged sadness she wore around her eyes had faded. It still crept in sometimes, when she thought no one was watching, but more often she smiled and laughed now like she'd let go of some of that grief she'd wrapped around herself like a security blanket. And, the more time I spent with her, the more I realized I was shifting as well.

"Does that work for you?" Merrick asked, breaking me out of my thoughts. Shit, I'd zoned out.

"Sure," I said, having no idea what I'd agreed to.

Merrick narrowed his eyes. He knew I'd been in my head and would give me shit for it later, but never in front of Thane. His loyalty kept him from putting my neck on the chopping block when our president was in one of his moods.

"Then it's settled. Hatchet will cover the club while Thane, Reaper, and I handle the sitdown with Riot and the Fort Worth Mafia. We'll sort out the route to minimize the risk."

Damn it. I'd unknowingly volunteered to play guard dog while the guys rode through the desert.

Too late to counter now, though. I'd made my bed. But maybe it wouldn't be so bad if I could find a way to get Kenna in it too.

Chapter Twenty-Two

While a Memorial Day barbecue at the clubhouse had sounded fun, Eva and I had decided to skip out in favor of a movie marathon. We'd managed to talk Reaper into bringing us plates of pulled pork, smoked brisket, and baked beans while he and his brothers enjoyed a party without worrying about whether we'd find ourselves in the line of fire if another drive-by occurred.

In between laughing at the antics of our favorite characters, she grilled me about the apparent chemistry between me and Hatchet. And, despite my insistence that nothing was going on, she pressed on persistently.

Two bottles of wine and three movies later, Eva and Hawk crashed in my spare bedroom. They left before breakfast when Reaper honked on the horn at sunrise, picking them up. After a sleepy goodbye, Brisket and I curled back in bed, choosing to snooze for another few hours.

I stretched beneath the quilt, and Brisket groaned beside me, his long legs in the air as he insisted on belly rubs. My phone pinged, forcing me to fully open my eyes and acknowledge the morning.

HATCHET:

You missed a good time last night. Want to grab brunch? I can tell you all about how Archer got so drunk that he danced on the bar.

ME:

Please tell me you got video. Diner in an hour?

HATCHET:

See you then.

I walked Brisket before I showered, patiently allowing him to sniff the trail for chipmunks and Goldfish crackers dropped by toddlers. When we got back home, I barely had enough time to shower. I quickly dried my hair and swiped on mascara before slipping into a green and white polka dot sundress and lacing up my chunky black boots.

As I walked into the diner, the scent of bacon and coffee wrapped around me. Hatchet was already there, standing to greet me with a grin. He pulled me into a hug, his arms warm and strong.

"You look beautiful this morning."

I smiled up at him, letting myself enjoy the way his attention made me feel desired. Hatchet always made it clear he was attracted to me. He flirted easily, laughed often, and had that effortless charm that made it impossible not to like him. Maybe Eva was right. Even if he wasn't looking to settle down, Hatchet was the kind of man I could ease back into a relationship with. Maybe not forever, but at least for now. I could open myself up to something with him—something fun and light. Something that didn't demand more than I could give.

"Show me this video," I insisted as I slid into the booth beside him instead of across.

Hatchet pulled out his phone and played the video of a drunken Archer dancing on the bar like he was auditioning for *Coyote Ugly*. I laughed so hard that tears formed in the corners of my eyes.

Hatchet slipped his phone back into his pocket, and I started to slide away to move across from him, but he wrapped an arm around my hip to stop me.

"Stay," he whispered into my ear, his whiskers tickling my neck.

Goose bumps spread across my skin, and I leaned into him, noticing the envious look on the waitress's face as she took our order. We swapped stories, teased each other, and I laughed until my cheeks hurt. He made everything feel uncomplicated.

After we finished eating, Hatchet paid the bill and walked me to my Range Rover. His hand rested on my lower back, and the touch sent a flutter through my stomach.

"Thanks for brunch," I said, squinting in the sun as I gazed up at him.

Hatchet tipped my chin up with his thumb, his eyes searching mine. "It's always a pleasure." He paused and then leaned in, pressing his lips to mine.

I waited for the rush of feelings I'd expected. But as our lips met, I felt ... nothing. No spark, no racing heart, no longing.

All the underlying chemistry and attraction I'd thought I could feel for him fizzled away. I pulled back and looked up at him with furrowed brows, curious if he noticed how off it felt. But he only smiled. How could he not see that there was no fire in it? How could he not look at me with the same shock?

"Um, I need to go," I said suddenly. I needed space. Before Hatchet could respond, I jumped into my Range Rover and sped away. In the rearview mirror, I watched him stand in the dust, his expression mired in confusion.

As I drove, my mind raced. Was I broken? Maybe losing Alec had shattered a part of me irreparably. Maybe I couldn't love like that anymore.

Alec and I had been together since we were fifteen—high school, college, adulthood. I'd always believed he was my soulmate. Maybe every kiss, every moment would pale in comparison to what we had.

What about Merrick? The thought startled me. I'd pushed away any feelings that bubbled up in his presence because he'd never flirted like Hatchet. He was quiet, guarded, and respectful. He'd been there when I needed him, but he'd never crossed the line.

But the more I thought about it, the more it made sense that Merrick wouldn't show up that way. Like me, he'd experienced loss and grief in a way that changed a person.

Maybe that was why I felt so drawn to him—because he understood the shadows inside me, the parts that still ached and longed for the ghost of my past.

I gripped the steering wheel tighter. Maybe I wasn't broken. Maybe I just needed more than charm and laughter. Maybe I needed someone who could see me—scars and all—and still choose to stay.

I pulled into my driveway and put the vehicle in park. There was only one way to find out. To stop the spiraling. I opened my phone to send the text before I lost my nerve.

ME:

Can you come over?

I tapped the steering wheel impatiently. Merrick responded within seconds.

MERRICK:

What's going on?

ME:

Nothing serious. I just need to see you.

My gut churned as I considered how to broach this conversation now that I'd pulled the trigger.

MERRICK:

I'm close by. Be there in 10.

There was no backing out now. I paced by the door with a confused Brisket at my heels, wringing my hands in front of me. My stomach lurched as the distant rumble of a motorcycle grew louder, then cut off abruptly outside.

Was I really going to do this? Could I jeopardize our friendship in this wild experiment?

I opened the door to find Merrick jogging up to my house, concern etched across his face. The porch creaked as his heavy boots hit each step.

"What's wrong?" His eyes scanned my body, as if he were looking for bruises or marks.

I grabbed a fistful of his cut as he stepped through my door. "Kiss me," I demanded.

A faint crease pulled between his brows. "What?"

"Kiss. Me." I punctuated each word and tugged on the leather until he stood flush against my body.

For a heartbeat, he hesitated. "Kenna ..." He searched my face.

My stomach dropped as regret coursed through me. I loosened my grip on the leather as I began to step away.

"Fuck it," Merrick muttered, pressing into my body until he pinned me between the wall and the solid heat of his chest, one hand gripping my hip. He leaned down and brushed his lips against mine, his hand moving up to gently wrap around my neck. The kiss was tentative for a beat before it became hungry.

Sensation surged across my body, and my heart began to beat in my chest like a trapped hummingbird as his tongue swept across the seam of my mouth, coaxing me to open. He deepened the kiss, and I hummed in pleasure. I melted against him as he slowly consumed me.

Merrick pulled back and gazed at me, and my breath caught. He tucked a rogue curl behind my ear. "Not that I'm complaining, but why?"

I hesitated. I hadn't thought this part through. He stepped back, giving me space as he saw the uncertainty flit across my face.

I grimaced. "It's going to sound bad."

"Try me."

"I'm serious. It's horrible."

"Stop spiraling. Tell me," he said, his tone calm but insistent.

The words spilled out in a rush. "Hatchet kissed me after brunch, and I felt nothing. I was worried that maybe I was broken. Maybe I'd never feel this again because I'm dead inside. Numb. But then I started thinking about you. I wanted to kiss you to see how it felt." I stopped to catch my breath, bracing for anger or judgment to cross his face.

Merrick remained stoic. I shifted my gaze to the floor.

"Look at me," he commanded. Merrick tilted his head and raised a brow. "How did it feel when you kissed me?"

I swallowed hard as I searched for the words. "Like the world stopped turning and my heart started beating again."

A smile crept across his face.

"Um, what about you?" I bit my lip. "If you just want to be friends, I understand. I'm sorry if I crossed a line, I just—"

Merrick cut me off, crushing his lips to mine again before pulling back and cupping my face with his hands. "It feels like every moment I've spent with you, tinder has been added to a smoldering flame. When our lips touched, you ignited something inside me. Like a wildfire crossing the plains."

We stumbled to the couch, and I pressed him to sit down before straddling his lap. His hands moved down, cupping my ass as we kissed again.

I rolled my hips, and the move drew a low sound from his chest—half groan, half growl. His hands wrapped around my waist, guiding me as I moved slowly against him. He slid a palm under my shirt, the callouses of his hand scraping my skin and sending shivers through my entire body.

I moaned and pushed his cut over his shoulders before I pulled at his shirt, tugging it over his head and tossing it away. I ran my fingers over his pecs and arched my back as his hand began moving up my thigh. Then Merrick stilled.

I looked at him in question.

His forehead fell to mine and he sucked in a ragged breath. "If we take this any further, I won't have the control to stop."

"I don't want you to."

He squeezed his eyes shut like he fought to restrain his desire. "Neither do I, but does Hatchet know how you feel?"

I grimaced. "No, I don't think so. I was hoping he'd noticed the lack of heat as well, but he looked confused when I ran away."

Merrick laughed. "Hatchet doesn't do subtle. And he's a man. If we want to see where this goes, we tell him before anything happens. We owe him that much."

I sighed. I appreciated Merrick's loyalty. I really did. But at this particular moment, I wanted him enough not to care.

"Do you?" I asked, uncertainly. "You want to see if there's something real here?"

"I know there's something real. And I think life's too short to wait. But I don't know if you're ready."

I glanced away, knowing he meant Alec. "I want this. I think ..." I paused, gathering my thoughts. "I think I need you. I can't keep living like I'm buried next to Alec. And when I'm with you, I feel whole. But Hatchet ..." I hesitated, my chest tightening. "He's your best friend. He's one of my best friends. I don't want him thinking I've been playing games."

"We can tell him at the clubhouse tonight, Wildfire," Merrick insisted.

I blinked, caught off guard. "What did you just call me?"

He smirked. "Wildfire? It suits you. You're an unstoppable force."

I sighed. "Fine." I tried to shift off his lap, but he held me in place, stealing another kiss. I ground my hips against him, and he groaned.

"Wildfire," he warned.

"I know. Nothing can happen yet." My body ached for more.

Gripping my hips, Merrick gently pushed me off his lap. He stood, adjusting himself with a sheepish grin before leaning down for another kiss. "I have to go. I'll see you at the clubhouse. I'll talk to Hatchet."

A knot of anxiety twisted in my stomach. "Do you think he'll be mad? I don't want to come between you two."

Merrick shook his head, brushing his thumb over my cheek. "Don't worry about that."

He pulled his shirt over his head and gave me one last lingering look, then slipped out, leaving me breathless.

The door clicked shut. I pressed my back against the wall and brushed my fingertips across my lips, still tingling from his kiss.

What the hell had I just done? The couch was still warm where we'd tangled together, and I sank onto it, tucking my legs under me. Brisket hopped beside me and rested his chin on my leg.

Guilt crept in. For the man I'd once promised forever, whose ring still sat in my jewelry box. For the friend who'd looked at me in confusion as I fled following our kiss, who had shown me nothing but friendship and respect for my boundaries. And for Merrick, knowing the fire burning between us could destroy something between him and his best friend.

But beneath the nerves, there was a fierce certainty that I hadn't felt in a long, long time. I wasn't numb. I wasn't broken.

I was alive, and I wanted more.

* * *

A block of ice settled in my gut as I walked into the clubhouse a few hours later. I caught Hatchet's eye and gestured with my head to follow. I hadn't yet seen Merrick, but I couldn't pretend to be interested in more than friendship with Hatchet for a second longer.

His hand brushed my arm as he gazed into my eyes, the corners crinkling with concern. "Hey, doll. You ran off this morning. I'm sorry if I freaked you out. You good?"

I bit my lip. "We need to talk."

Hatchet raised his brows.

"Can we step outside?" I didn't wait for his response, turning and hoping he followed.

The clubhouse door closed behind us, echoing through the empty parking lot. I turned to face Hatchet and hesitated. I'd never had to reject someone I cared about before.

"I like you as a friend. But when you kissed me today, I realized that I just don't feel that way about you. I'm sorry."

Hurt flashed across his face before his expression shifted to a stony mask. "If that's how you feel." He shrugged, as if he didn't care.

"There's more I need to tell you."

His jaw worked silently, his lips thinning as he pressed his teeth together. He absently ran his fingers through his short beard.

"I think there's something between me and Merrick. I don't know what yet, but we didn't want to pursue it without telling you."

Hatchet scoffed. "So you're with Merrick?"

"I mean, I want to see where things could go with him. Is that OK? We don't want to hurt you." I reached for his arm, but he stepped away as he let out a sharp laugh.

"Does it matter what I think?"

I clenched my fists and pressed down the emotion bubbling in my chest. "Yeah, Hatchet, it does. I still care for you. And he does, too. He's your best friend, and I don't want to come between you."

"You know what? It's fine, Kenna," Hatchet said, letting out a clipped laugh with no real humor. "It really is. It just sucks that you led me on for so long."

Anger flared through me. "I didn't lead you on," I insisted. "I genuinely like you. I like hanging out with you. You're one of like, three friends I have here."

Irritation crinkled his face as he started to turn away.

I grabbed his arm, turning him back to face me. "I'm sorry. I really am."

"It's fine. We both knew I wasn't looking for anything serious, anyway."

I pursed my lips and blinked back tears.

"I'm going to head out. I'm not really in the mood to party

tonight." Hatchet spun around, heading for his bike. He peeled out, gravel flying behind him, as Merrick pulled into the parking lot.

I wrapped my arms around my body, willing the tears to go away.

Merrick closed the distance between us, and I met his concerned gaze.

He wiped a tear away on my cheek with his thumb. "Breathe, Wildfire," he commanded. "You should have let me tell him."

I shook my head. "I needed to."

"He was pissed?"

I shrugged. "He was blindsided. He accused me of leading him on."

Merrick leaned forward, pressing a kiss to the top of my head. "You didn't. Hatchet says things he doesn't mean when he's angry. He just needs a ride to clear his head. Let's go inside. You need a drink."

He snaked an arm around my waist and pulled me tight to his side as we stepped back into the clubhouse. The room hummed with energy, loud voices, and gruff laughs.

As we approached the bar, Eva caught my eye. She raised a brow. Shit. My best friend was going to be pissed that this was how she found out about us. To be fair, there hadn't been an "us" for more than a few hours, and I was still wrapping my mind around it.

Eva nudged Reaper, his glance following hers. Instinctively, he looked around the room—no doubt to see if Hatchet was present— before shifting back to Merrick with a question in his eyes.

"What do you want to drink?" Merrick asked, pointedly ignoring him.

"Whatever you're having is fine," I murmured.

Merrick placed our order with Leah as he gently stroked my back before moving his hands up to knead the muscles at the base of my neck. His thumbs worked in slow circles as I leaned into him.

He turned me to face him, wrapping his arms around my waist to pull my body against his. "Stop. Hatchet will be fine. Trust me. We'll give him the night, and by tomorrow, he'll be as happy as ever, with a blonde with big tits and no brain on his lap."

I grimaced and let out a forced laugh. "I'm not sure how that mental picture is supposed to make me feel better."

He squeezed my waist, then brushed his lips across my forehead.

Before I could respond, Eva strolled over and grabbed my arm. "Sorry, Merrick. I need to steal my best friend away from you for a few. She's apparently forgotten to tell me a few things."

I shot Merrick an apologetic look as Thane and Fuse surrounded him, and Eva pulled me to the quiet hallway.

"I mean this with so much love, but what the fuck is going on?" Eva asked, her tone insistent and confused.

"Um, so, Merrick and I are a thing."

"Yeah, I gathered that. When did this happen?"

"Today. It's a long story," I explained, launching into the strange events of my morning and afternoon.

Eva mimed her mind exploding. "I thought for sure you'd hook up with Hatchet. I thought you might even be the woman to settle him down. It always seemed like you both had fun together."

"We did. We do. But kissing him made me realize we couldn't be more than friends. It felt like how I imagine kissing you would feel."

Behind me, I heard a throat clear. We turned to see Reaper's imposing form before us.

"You planning to kiss my woman?" he asked me with a smirk.

"I think I've kissed enough of my friends today."

Chapter Twenty-Three

"You finally went for it," Fuse said, a statement rather than a question. He swirled the scotch in his glass. "Took you long enough."

Thane glanced between us. "You knew about him and Kenna?"

"There wasn't a 'me and Kenna' until this afternoon," I explained evenly, meeting Thane's stare without flinching. "We're figuring it out."

"I don't really give a fuck what's going on, as long as it doesn't affect the club," Thane growled, his stare sharp enough to cut. "Where's Hatchet?"

I shrugged. "He left after Kenna spoke to him. He needed air. Nothing a night with a sweetbutt or two won't fix for him."

Thane grumbled under his breath, shaking his head as he walked away.

Fuse caught Leah's attention with an almost imperceptible nod and pointed at his scotch of choice before returning his eyes to me. "I know losing Rose was hard. Hatchet'll come around. Once he realizes the Merrick he knew ten years ago is back, once he realizes you and Kenna just work, he'll be happy for you, too. Let him work through his shit on his own, and don't lose sleep over claiming that woman."

His tone left no room for argument, his advice echoing through me like an order.

I followed his gaze toward Kenna, my heart both filling with the sight of her and wrenching at the memory of Rose.

"It feels different this time," I murmured. With Rose, I'd mistaken her chaos and intensity for passion. I'd thought the fighting and make-up sex meant we cared. But the truth settled in my chest—we'd been burning down, not burning bright.

"You finally see it, don't you?" Fuse asked as if he'd read my mind. "You and Rose were fire and gasoline. You couldn't see through the smoke."

My jaw tightened. He wasn't wrong.

Fuse nodded toward Kenna. "You're different with her. You don't brace yourself for a fight when she looks at you. You've both buried love. Lived through the kind of loss that strips you to bone. Not everyone comes back from that. But you two? You get it. You both crawled out of the wreckage and somehow found each other through the smoke."

"I don't know what this is yet between us, but it feels like the first good thing I've had in a long time. And after everything we've been through, I don't want to waste time or fuck this up."

Without looking away, Fuse slid a glass toward me. "To not fucking this up," he said, raising his glass in a toast.

I savored the way the bourbon cut all the way down. He was right. Kenna had rekindled something within me that had been snuffed out when I buried Rose. My gaze returned to Kenna.

"You don't get many chances like this in life. Go get your woman before she changes her mind," Fuse said, pushing my shoulder.

I shot him a glare that only made him smirk, then turned toward the hallway to stalk away. Reaper's eyes narrowed at me as I approached.

"We'll be talking about this little surprise tomorrow," he said.

"You're one to talk," I reminded him. He gave a half shrug—a silent acknowledgment that he'd hesitated to admit his obsession with Eva at first, too.

I caught Kenna's hand and threaded my fingers through hers, tugging her toward the shadowed hallway at the back of the clubhouse.

Eva caught my eye over her shoulder, grinning like she already knew exactly where this was going. She waggled her brows at me before disappearing into the main room with Reaper.

"Where are you taking me?" Kenna asked breathlessly.

I spun her gently until her back pressed to the wall, one hand braced beside her head. "I needed to do this," I growled, tipping her chin up before crushing my mouth to hers.

She let out a small chirp of surprise that I swallowed with a kiss. I trailed my lips down the slope of her neck, breathing her in. Sweet. Floral. Mine.

"I've wanted to touch you all day," I murmured against her skin. My teeth grazed her collarbone. "Kiss you. Bite you. Taste you."

I pulled back to gaze into her eyes, her pupils blown wide and cheeks flushed.

"Then do it," she whispered.

A low rumble escaped my chest as I claimed her mouth again, taking our kiss deeper. My hands traced the lines of her body through the thin dress, memorizing every curve until my palm cupped the perfect round of her ass. She pressed against me instinctively, hips meeting mine. Lust and desire ignited between us, and regret for not making a move sooner coursed through me. I should have claimed this woman the day I met her.

I pulled back just enough to meet her eyes. "You can tell me to slow down. If it's too much—"

"Don't stop. I want more. I want all of you."

"Good," I said softly, my tone deceptively smooth as my hand skimmed beneath the hem of her dress. My fingers toyed just shy of her inner thigh.

"Merrick," she breathed, darting a glance toward the open end of the hallway. "What are you doing? Someone could see us."

I adjusted my stance, half shielding her with my body. "They'll only see my back." My fingertip teased the edge of her thong before brushing it aside. "And even if they did see you ..." I drew slow circles over her clit with my thumb, watching her grip the wall for balance "... no one here would care. We're outlaws, Wildfire."

A reluctant moan slipped from her throat. "We should stop."

I kissed just below her jaw. "You don't want me to stop. Eyes on me, Wildfire."

She whimpered, hips tipping forward when I slid my fingers through her slick heat.

"You're soaked for me," I murmured, my thumb finding her clit again before I slid a finger inside her, curling it in precisely the way I knew would undo her. "And so fucking tight."

Her breath came faster, more shallow. "Merrick ..."

"I can't wait to be inside you. Feel you strangle my cock the way you're squeezing my fingers right now."

She let out a clipped laugh. "You are not fucking me in the hallway. We're going to get caught."

I smirked. "No one's looking."

I continued to stroke her, and when I pressed my palm hard against her clit, her knees nearly buckled.

"Come for me, Wildfire."

Her answer was a strangled gasp as she shattered against my hand, her body tensing as she pulsed around my fingers. I kissed her through the waves of pleasure, holding her upright until her breathing steadied.

When I finally drew my fingers from her, I held her gaze as I pressed them to my mouth, sucking them clean. "Better than I imagined."

Shock flashed over her face.

I adjusted my painfully hard dick, smirking. "Another drink?"

Her eyes flicked to the bulge between us. "What about ...?

"This was just the appetizer," I murmured. "I want you in my bed for the main course."

She bit her lip. "We should go to my place then. I need to feed Brisket before we spend the night together."

I dipped my head and nipped at her neck. "Fine. But we leave now. I've held back long enough." Wrapping a possessive arm around her waist, I led her out, glaring at any man who dared to look at her as we weaved through the crowd. She was mine—

A familiar ringtone sang from my phone, cutting the thought in half.

Merci.

A ripple of unease slid down my spine. My sister never called. She mostly communicated in short text messages and GIFs, and never when she was on shift at the hospital.

"Merci, what's up?" I answered.

Her tone was urgent and clipped. "It's Hatchet. He's been in an accident."

My stomach dropped as she continued. "An ambulance just brought him in. He's in triage with the trauma team right now."

The words were a punch to the gut. My grip on Kenna tightened, and she looked up at me, confusion etched across her face.

"We're on our way."

The music and chatter blurred together as I shoved my phone into my pocket, my focus tunneling as I scanned the room.

I crossed the room in quick strides to where Thane and Reaper sat at the bar. "Merci called. Hatchet's in the trauma center," I explained.

Kenna's hand shot up to cover her mouth, and her eyes widened in shock.

"Goddamn it," Thane growled. His stool screeched as he stood. "Did the dumbass lay down his fucking bike again?"

"I don't know. I'm headed there now." My fingers locked around Kenna's as I pulled her to follow me. My mind replayed Merci's frantic tone, every worst-case scenario spiraling through my thoughts.

"If he dies because of me ..." Kenna started, her voice cracking.

I jerked to a stop and cradled her face with my hands. "Stop. This isn't your fault. Hatchet rides his Harley like it's a dirt bike. It's not the first time he's crashed."

Still, the guilt poisoned her expression. "But he was upset when he left. Because of me. If I hadn't—"

I interrupted her again. "No matter what happens, this isn't your fault. Let's get to the hospital so we can see how the dumbass is doing."

The night air whipped through the windows of my truck as I sped down the backroads to the hospital. I reached for Kenna's hand across the console and squeezed it tight. Her eyes glistened with tears under the moonlight.

As we burst through the doors of the ER, I searched the busy space for my sister before shooting her a text. She responded within seconds, promising to bring us an update in a few minutes.

I turned to face Kenna and frowned at the fear and tension etched into her face. I pulled her into my body and wrapped my arms around her.

"He has to be OK," she whispered, voice muffled against my jacket. "I can't lose someone else. Not like this."

"Me neither," I admitted.

She looked up, desperate. "What if he—"

I shook my head and pulled her closer. "We don't break that easy. Hatchet's made of steel and luck. Merci should be out soon to give us an update."

I glanced up to see Reaper, Eva, Thane, and Fuse streaming through the automatic doors.

"Any updates?" Thane asked.

"Not yet."

Seconds crawled by. The buzz of the waiting room faded under the weight of what wasn't being said. Finally, a set of double doors swung open. Merci strode out in her blue scrubs, spattered with blood. A mask hung around her neck. Her tired eyes flicked from me to Kenna in my arms, and I could see the questions forming.

"How is he?" I asked.

"He's in surgery to stop some internal bleeding. But, all things considered, he's in decent shape. Could've been a lot worse."

"What happened?" Fuse asked.

"He hit a deer on his bike. Laid it down. Fortunately, he wasn't going fast, and he was wearing his jacket and helmet, for once. He was conscious when he came in and recognized me, which is a good sign. I need to get back there. We're busy as hell tonight because some gangbanger kids robbed a drugstore. I'll let you know if anything changes."

"Thanks, kid," Thane said, smiling at Merci and pulling her into a hug.

Merci glanced back at me with raised brows. "Are you going to introduce us?"

I rolled my eyes. "Kenna, this is my pain-in-the-ass baby sister, Merci. Also happens to be smart enough to be a doctor."

"It's nice to meet you, Kenna." Merci shifted her eyes to me. "I didn't realize you were seeing someone."

"I'm as surprised as you are," I said with a short laugh.

Chapter Twenty-Four

The group of us sat in the waiting room, each of us lost to our own thoughts while time crawled. The faint scuffing of nurses' shoes sounded through the hallway, and monitors beeped in the distance.

My mind looped the same image over and over—Hatchet tearing out of the parking lot after what I'd said to him. My stomach churned. I kept thinking about what could have happened. The worst case. And how much of it might be my fault.

Choosing Merrick had almost cost my friend his life

Eva appeared in front of me and held out a paper cup. "Stop beating yourself up," she said gently.

I kept my gaze trained on the floor and wrapped my hands around the thin cup, savoring the burn and the bitter steam curling into my face. "It's my fault," I murmured.

Merrick's heavy, sure footsteps approached. His presence hovered above me before he lifted me from my seat and tugged me into his lap. "Breathe, Wildfire. This isn't on you. Look at me."

I tore my face from his chest and gazed into his eyes.

Merrick wiped away tears from my cheek. "It was in no way your fault."

"He's right," Reaper added from across the room. "This is the third bike Hatchet's wrecked in as many years. He's impulsive and reckless as hell."

Eva crouched so we were eye level. "Stop catastrophizing. Merci said he's OK."

My shoulders shook with a silent sob, and Merrick's arms locked around me like iron, holding me in place until I could breathe again.

"We're heading home," Eva said after a beat. "I'll pick up Brisket and take him to our place for the night."

"Thanks," I whispered, forcing my voice not to crack. "Be sure to grab his dinner. He's probably starving by now."

Hours crawled by. Around midnight, Merrick's phone buzzed with a message from Merci: Hatchet was out of surgery. Relief punched through my chest.

I drifted off after that, waking to the murmur of low voices and the faint rustle of magazine pages. Merrick's heavy leather jacket was draped over me. Across the room, he stood with Merci, whispering.

"Is he OK?" I rasped.

Merrick helped me to my feet and settled the jacket over my shoulders, the weight of it grounding me.

"He's awake," Merrick confirmed. "We'll come back in the morning during visiting hours."

I glanced at Merci for confirmation.

"He's in good spirits. He's already trying to flirt with the nurses," she said with a laugh.

"See?" Merrick murmured, brushing a thumb along my cheek. "Hatchet's fine. Let's go home. Get a few hours' sleep."

"Home?" Merci asked. "You live together?"

I smirked at Merrick. "I haven't even been to his house yet. For all I know, it's a gross bachelor pad."

Merci laughed. "It's more sterile than the OR. My brother is a clean freak."

"Oh, I'm certainly a freak," Merrick murmured. He nuzzled my ear. "In the sheets."

Merci wrinkled her nose. "Gross. I'm leaving."

Merrick threw his head back and laughed, the deep rumble echoing through the waiting room.

Merci stilled for just a second. "Now that's a sound I haven't heard in a long time. It was nice to meet you, Kenna."

Merrick didn't say much on the drive back, but he never let go of my hand. His thumb traced slow circles over my knuckles as the headlights cut through the dark Texas night. Instead of pulling into the main lot of the clubhouse, he took a turn down a long drive, the truck rocking over the ruts until a lodge-like house appeared out of the shadows.

"I expected something more rustic," I said. "This looks like a vacation home."

Merrick shrugged. "It's a benefit of working for the club. Thane likes to have me on site, so they built this a few years ago."

Inside, log walls and high ceilings greeted me. The scent of cedar lingered in the air. The space was open and organized—everything in its place, nothing left lying around.

"Let's get some sleep," he said quietly, hanging his keys on a hook by the door. "Visiting hours start at ten."

"Can I take a shower first?"

"It's connected to the bedroom through that door. Towels are in the cupboard on the left."

I closed the door behind me and released a ragged sigh. I needed a moment to let myself fall apart. I twisted the knob until hot water sprayed across the tiles, and steam billowed out from the enclosed glass shower. I pulled my dress over my head and dropped my panties to the ground before stepping inside.

The heat of the water hit my shoulders, and the first sob ripped out before I could stop it. After hours of holding it in, my chest finally caved under the weight of it. I pressed my hands to the tile and let the steam blur my vision.

I'd been terrified to lose Hatchet. Even though whatever romantic feelings I thought I might have for him had dissipated, he'd become one of my closest friends since moving. I had no words for the terror that shot through me when I heard he'd been in an accident and the lingering fear that choked me as I continued to worry. The thought of losing him—of another funeral, another goodbye, another hole in my heart—clawed inside my chest.

By the time the water began to cool, my body felt wrung out. I wrapped myself in a towel and cursed under my breath when I realized I had nothing to change into. A quick rummage through the dark oak dresser turned up a soft, worn T-shirt. I slipped it over my head, the hem falling mid-thigh. It smelled faintly like Merrick.

I padded out to the kitchen. Merrick stood, staring out the window into the night sky.

"Hey," I said softly, brushing my hand on his back.

He turned, and for the first time all night, the mask was gone. The guarded control he'd worn at the hospital had slipped, letting me see the worry lining his face.

"Hatchet's going to be OK," I assured him.

He scrubbed his face with his palm. "The man has cheated death more times than I can count. One of these days Merci's going to call me from the ER to tell me I have to bury my best friend."

I couldn't bring myself to tell him it wouldn't happen. Because we both knew it could. We'd both watched accidents rip away people we loved in a heartbeat.

I yawned as the heaviness of the night settled over me.

"Let's go to bed," I suggested.

He led me toward the back, into the bedroom. "Not exactly how I pictured our first night," he grumbled as he pulled back the covers.

I slid in, the sheets crisp against my flushed skin. He stood at the edge of the bed, pulling his shirt over his head. In the soft light, his tattoos looked darker. The strong black lines coiled over muscle and scars. His jeans hit the floor, and my breath hitched. Despite my exhaustion, every nerve in my body lit up as he slipped under the sheets beside me.

His arm circled my waist as he pulled me flush against his

chest. His nose tucked into the curve of my neck, warm breath feathering my skin. The scent of leather and his cologne clung to his skin.

And despite everything—Hatchet's accident, the fear, the adrenaline—I fell asleep fast, surrounded by the solid weight of him.

* * *

I woke to cool sheets and an empty pillow where Merrick had been, his faint scent filling the air around me.

The kitchen was still. A lukewarm, half-drunk cup of coffee sat abandoned beside the carafe. I dumped it in the sink, filling the cup with hot coffee, and carried it to sit at the table beside the large picture window.

Outside, a squirrel darted across the wooded yard, scattering a few startled birds from the rustic feeder. Their chirps and flutters were the only music in the quiet lodge. I sipped the bitter coffee and let my mind drift.

The low rumble of Merrick's truck cut through the stillness. I stayed seated, watching the door as the sound of a code punching in echoed, followed by the creak of hinges.

He filled the frame of the doorway before stepping inside, holding a hot-pink polka dot duffel bag.

My brows rose, but I kept sipping. "Is that mine?"

"I thought you might want a change of clothes," he said casually. "Found it in your closet."

He set it on the table like it was no big deal. I stood and unzipped it, sorting through the clothes. Jeans. T-shirt. A dress. Then—

I held up a lacy black thong by one finger and grinned. "You went through my panties?"

"They were the first ones I grabbed," he claimed.

"Liar." I laughed. "Those were at the back. I never wear them. That lace is so uncomfortable."

He didn't flinch at being caught. Instead, he reached in and pulled out a set of silky red boy shorts and—fuck—a pair of cotton panties patterned with tiny T-rexes.

"I grabbed a few that I want you to wear for me," he said with a half grin. "I've never seen a woman in dinosaur underwear."

Heat flushed my cheeks. I snatched them from his hands. "I'm still deciding how I feel about you going through my clothes before you've even seen me out of them."

I went to walk away, bag in hand, but he caught my wrist and spun me before I could take a step. In one move, I was seated on the table before him, the wood cool against my thighs.

"We can change that," he murmured, lips brushing my ear. His hands skimmed up the bare skin beneath the oversized T-shirt I'd borrowed. He traced my curves as he pressed his lips to mine. The air shifted with the promise of pleasure as he ran a hand up my thigh. He paused when he realized I was bare.

"Wildfire," he growled as his mouth claimed mine. I melted into him, my anxious thoughts drowned out by the delicious ache of desire.

Then his phone shattered the moment.

Merrick glanced at the caller ID and sighed as he stepped away to answer.

"Prez," he said in a flat, professional tone, greeting Thane without a hello. He shot me an apologetic glance as he stepped outside the front door. He didn't have to explain. Club business.

I rolled my eyes and slid off the table, taking the duffel to the bedroom. Dumping it out across the bed, I started to sort through the pile and froze.

Nestled between a few tank tops and my favorite pair of jeans was my vibrator.

My hand flew to my mouth. Shit. I'd left it out on the bathroom counter yesterday morning to dry, so Merrick hadn't just tossed it in. He'd found the case in my nightstand, handled it, and packed it in my bag.

Heat flashed through my core, pooling low and deep as I imagined those big, tattooed hands examining the suction at the tip before curling the flexible base into the clamshell case. I pressed my thighs together and swore under my breath.

I shook my head to clear it as I heard the front door close. I'd figure out what to do about that thought later. I shoved the rest of the clothes back into the bag and picked a T-shirt and jeans for the day, stuffing the rest on top of the toy to deal with later.

I slipped into the bathroom to change, brushing my teeth and pulling my hair up into a messy bun. When I stepped out, I collided straight into Merrick's chest. His hands caught my shoulders automatically, steadying me.

"Merci texted. Hatchet's awake."

Relief loosened something inside me, but the tension in his jaw still hadn't fully eased, stress still tightening the corners of his eyes.

"How's he doing?"

Merrick shrugged. "She said he's OK. In a bit of pain, but the doctors are optimistic."

"That's good," I said, searching his face. "Can he eat yet? We should grab him something to eat. Maybe those breakfast tacos he loves."

"A peace offering?" he asked in a sharp tone. "Sorry Kenna chose me, but here's a taco?"

I flinched. I could see how Hatchet might take it that way, though it wasn't my intent.

Regret flashed over Merrick's face as he took in my pained expression. "Shit. That was out of line," he admitted. "I just ... don't know how he's going to take it when I walk through that door."

I bit my lip, sucking in a breath through the heaviness in my chest. "It's fine. Let's just get over there."

I grabbed my purse off the counter and turned to head to the door. His hand hooked my arm, turning me back to face him.

"Don't do that. Don't say it's fine when it isn't. And don't brush it off when I fuck up. That wasn't fair to you."

I blinked at him, feeling the crack in my chest widen. "I don't want to come between you and him. Maybe it's better if we all just ... stay friends. I can't be the reason—"

Merrick interrupted me with a kiss, gripping my shoulders tight. "You're not the reason he's in the hospital. Like you told me last night, he was blindsided. Hatchet's never been a relationship guy. And you didn't feel that way about him. Right?"

"But—"

"Let's table it," he cut in gently. "Let me talk to him first. I'll text Merci and see what he can eat. Donuts from Maisie's, tacos from his favorite place. If there's a way to soften the blow, it's with food. Man thinks with his stomach and his dick in equal measure."

A corner of my mouth twitched upward.

He kissed me again. "I really am sorry."

I let out a shaky sigh. "I know. Let's go."

Silence filled the cab of Merrick's truck. The pink donut box sat warm in my lap while I downed a latte with a triple shot of espresso from Maisie's. Merrick drove with one hand on the wheel, the other tapping restlessly against his thigh until we made the stop for tacos without a word.

When we walked into the hospital, Merci waited outside Hatchet's room.

"I just finished my shift," she said, looking between us. "Kenna, why don't you join me in the café for some coffee? Give the guys a minute alone."

I glanced at Merrick. He gave a terse nod as he reached for the tacos and donuts.

I followed Merci down the hall, glancing back once to see him pacing outside Hatchet's room. He rolled his shoulders like he was loosening up for a cage fight, before finally squaring himself and walking through the door.

Chapter Twenty-Five

HATCHET

The smell hit me first. Sausage, egg, grease, and heaven. Was I dead, or was it my imagination after I'd thrown a hardened bran muffin across the room just an hour before?

My eyes cracked open to see Merrick in the doorway, holding a pink Maisie's Bakery box in one hand and a grease-stained paper sack in the other.

"Hey, pumpkin tits. Is that for me?" I asked, waggling my brows.

Merrick didn't even crack a smile. He just tossed the bag in front of me. "So, you crashed your bike. Again."

The way he said "again" carried the weight of years of lectures and silent looks over mangled chrome. Sometimes Merrick acted more like a father than a friend.

"The deer is more at fault than I am," I offered, tearing into the bag for a taco.

Merrick sank into the stiff plastic chair beside my bed. "Coast hauled your bike back to the clubhouse this morning. It's completely totaled. You got lucky."

The words left unsaid echoed louder. *One day, your luck'll run out.* We'd had the conversation too many times.

I took a giant bite of my taco and nodded approvingly. "So ... you and Kenna, huh?" My words came out muffled through a mouthful of tortilla.

Merrick hesitated. "I wanted to tell you," he said, bracing his elbows on his knees. "She just beat me to it."

I balled up the foil from my first taco and lobbed it at his head. "Yeah, fucker, you should've told me. I didn't even know you liked her." I ripped open the next taco and doused it in hot sauce. "This is so much better than the shit they fed me this morning. Fucking oatmeal. They made me eat oatmeal. Fucking hospitals, man."

He let me rant, giving me space to get the noise out until I figured out what I was trying to say. And somewhere between bitching about oatmeal, bran muffins, and endless episodes of *Judge Judy*, I found it.

"You guys make sense."

Merrick stared at me with shock. "You're not pissed?"

I shrugged, licking a trail of hot sauce running down my hand. "I guess not. Don't get me wrong, I liked Kenna. Hoped we'd hook up when she was ready. Never thought I'd see the day that your old ass gets the girl instead of me. You think you can keep up with her?"

He chucked the foil ball back at me, nailing my temple.

"Seriously, though. A part of you will always belong to Rose. A part of her will always belong to her fiancé. Maybe two shards can make a whole."

Pain flickered across his expression. That old grief, buried and raw underneath all the walls and steel. It was why most of us never mentioned Rose. Seeing the man who could carve apart a traitor under a skilled blade with a broken heart was jarring.

"I've never felt this way about anyone. Even Rose," he admitted.

That made me pause. *Even Rose.*

"Does she know that?"

Merrick scoffed. "No. We haven't exactly had time to talk."

I raised a brow. "Ah, too busy fucking?"

His eyes narrowed. "We haven't even had time for that."

I chuckled. "Brother, have you learned nothing from me? You've got to close the deal."

Merrick just shook his head with that long-suffering expression he always reserved for me. "I didn't want to go behind your back. I wanted you to know about us before anything happened. Then you had to pull the ultimate cock block and get in an accident."

I threw my head back and laughed, holding my side where the stitches pulled. "Yeah, sorry about that. I needed a ride to clear my head. I didn't realize the local wildlife would ignore the road crossing signs."

His humor softened, voice dipping. "Kenna was worried. She blames herself."

That wiped the grin off my face. "Shit." My chest tightened. "I didn't even think of that." I rubbed a palm over my face, my fingers lingering in the rough stubble of my short beard. "Where is she? I should talk to her."

"Merci took her to get coffee." Merrick pulled out his phone and typed a quick message. "They'll be back in a few."

"Since we've got a minute ..." I paused, taking a bite of another taco. "Are you ready for the sitdown in Fort Worth?"

Merrick nodded. "I think so. I've spent a lot of time wrangling Serpent and Jag. The last thing we need is for them to piss off the consigliere."

I couldn't help but chuckle, but it came out rough with the stitches in my side. "If it goes well, it'll be a windfall for the club. I'm going to need the money after all of this. Mafia's got the hardware we asked for?"

"Fresh shipment," Merrick said with a nod. "Not the usual stash, either. Automatics, some custom jobs, and even a few grenade launchers. Serious heat. That's why Thane's having us facilitate the deal. High risk, high reward."

"Damn." I whistled. "Wish I could be there to get my hands on a fucking grenade launcher. Think I can still get my cut even though I'm laid up?"

"We got you. With this deal, everybody's getting a cut, assuming Jag doesn't pull some stupid shit and piss off the mafia boss. And Merci is moving some things around in your record, so your bill won't be nearly as high as you might think."

Thank fuck for that. Without insurance, I'd be up a creek—and I already had shit credit to begin with.

Merrick grinned, but his eyes stayed tight with worry. "You just focus on not dying."

I raised my taco in a sarcastic toast, wincing but grinning anyway. "To not dying."

Chapter Twenty-Six

Merci led me through the labyrinthine corridors of the hospital. Clipped footsteps and the steady beeping of distant monitors trailed us until she ducked us into a tucked-away café. The air shifted instantly—from bright lights and an antiseptic sting to the cozy hum of espresso machines and low chatter.

The barista, a bored-looking guy with a mohawk and a silver lip ring, took our order and set about making two lattes.

Merci led me to a corner table, the surface scratched but clean.

I leaned back in my chair. "How long have you been a doctor?"

She smiled sheepishly. "I'm barely a doctor. I'm an intern. I just graduated from med school. I got lucky landing this residency so close to home."

"You're a lot younger than your brother," I observed.

She laughed. The bright sound eased the awkwardness between us. "Fifteen years. I was a surprise."

The barista called our names. We retrieved the steaming cups and returned to our seats.

"Enough about me." Merci tried to school her face into a serious expression. "What are your intentions with my brother?"

We burst into a fit of laughter. A woman reading a thick tome at the table beside us threw us an annoyed glare.

Merci tapped the table impatiently with her fingers. "Seriously, though. I can already tell he's different around you. Lighter. Is it serious?"

I chewed the inside of my cheek. "It's new. We've been friends for a while now, and I only realized there was something more right before Hatchet crashed." Guilt twisted in my gut. "He crashed because of me. God, I feel so bad."

"What do you mean? He hit a deer on his bike." Merci raised a brow. "Are you Snow White? Do you give orders to the creatures of the forest?"

I huffed a laugh. "Hatchet tore off on his bike after I told him that I'd felt nothing when he kissed me."

"Wait. Hatchet kissed you? Where does Merrick come into play then?"

I covered my face with my hands and shook my head. "Hatchet kissed me, and I felt nothing. So I ordered Merrick to kiss me."

"You ordered him?" she asked skeptically. "Merrick doesn't do anything he doesn't want to do, so I don't exactly think you bullied him into it."

I laughed. "We'd been skating around how we felt for a while, I think. After everything we've lost ..." I trailed off.

Merci tilted her head in question.

"I know about Rose. My fiancé died, too. Car accident."

Her smile faltered, and her eyes softened with sympathy. "I'm sorry." Her fingers tapped on the table. "I know it's an unimaginable loss. It changed Merrick."

I nodded. "He's the first person who truly understood me. I think that's what drew us together. He seemed to really love her."

Merci bit her lip, seeming to weigh her words. "I lived with Merrick and Rose for a few years. Our dad died when I was fourteen, and our mom planned to move away. I wanted to stay to finish high school. Merrick remembers their relationship with, well, rose-colored glasses. I think his guilt got tangled up in that. He remembers the relationship he wishes it'd been."

A tall man in a crisp white coat appeared beside our table. His badge read Dr. Luca Marchetti, Thoracic Surgery. He bent to kiss the top of Merci's head. His cologne, sharp and expensive, wafted around us.

She looked up at him and smiled. "Luca, this is Kenna, my brother's ... girlfriend."

She glanced at me with a slight question in her eyes, like she wasn't sure whether we'd put a label on our new relationship. I offered a small smile, not even sure what Merrick would call me.

"And Kenna, this is my fiancé, Luca. He's a surgeon."

Luca extended his hand, his expensive Rolex catching the light as he spoke with a thick Italian accent. "A pleasure," he said, his accented voice smooth. "Merci, amore mio, I have a few more patients to see before we start our holiday. You should shower and change so we can get on the road as soon as I'm done." There was an edge to his voice, a quiet command beneath the charm.

Merci's smile was tight as she nodded. Luca's gaze lingered on her for a beat before he strode away.

"A surgeon fiancé," I teased, trying to shake the tension. "Should we start calling you Meredith Grey?"

Merci snorted. "Fortunately, I was never his intern. We met at a charity gala in Chicago. We're getting away this weekend. Though apparently, one day of it will be spent with his family." She rolled her eyes. "Which means endless passive-aggressive questions from his mom about when I plan to ditch this pesky little career and start pumping out babies."

I cringed. "Ah, one of *those* future mothers-in-law."

Her fingers clenched tighter around the cup. "Yep. His mom thinks a woman's place is in the kitchen, preferably barefoot and pregnant."

I cringed.

"But Luca knows who I am. And Merrick would murder me if I gave up my career to play house."

I raised a brow in question.

"Merrick paid for my college," she explained.

I blinked, caught off guard. "He what?"

Merci nodded. "Books, rent, everything. Told me I was the smart one. He wasn't going to let me waste it by staying in the club and becoming someone's old lady."

For a moment, I didn't know what to feel. Warmth flooded my chest at the thought of Merrick quietly funding his sister's future. But underneath that was a ripple of unease. I couldn't help wondering just what kind of blood or deals had padded those tuition checks.

Merci's phone pinged, interrupting my thoughts.

"We're being summoned. Merrick says Hatchet wants to see you."

My stomach fluttered as we made our way back. I wrung my hands as I followed Merci into Hatchet's room. She pulled the chart at the foot of his bed while I stood in the doorway. I bit my lip as I searched Hatchet's face.

"Hey, beautiful. Come on in."

Merrick stood and stepped toward me. When his hand wrapped around my shoulder, my tension eased slightly. "I'm going to give you two a few to talk," he said as he pressed a kiss to my cheek. I flushed as Hatchet shot me a look that promised endless teasing.

"Everything is looking good," Merci said briskly, closing his chart.

"Thanks, doll. Can I get a sponge bath later?" he asked with a wink.

The comment earned a snarl from Merrick.

"It's Dr. Doll to you, asshole. And I'm sure one of the nurses will be happy to give you a sponge bath. Nurse Jason is working today. He's got nice, big hands. I'll ask him to fit that in his schedule," Merci said with a devious grin.

Hatchet held his palms up. "On second thought, I think I'm all set."

"Good. I'm off for the next few days. My fiancé is taking me away for the weekend, so Dr. Soos will be taking over your case. Take it easy."

Merci and Merrick slipped out, leaving me standing stiffly in the corner. I chewed my bottom lip and wrung my hands.

Hatchet patted the spot next to him. "C'mere."

I moved closer and perched on the side of the bed facing him, still uncertain of what to say.

"It'll take more than Bambi to take me out."

The little laugh I tried to let out broke into a sob, and before I knew it, the whole dam burst. "I am so sorry," I whispered as tears streamed down my face.

"Hey, hey," he said, pulling me against his chest. "You have nothing to be sorry for."

I sobbed something unintelligible, and he held me tighter.

"Kenna, I'm fine. It was an accident. Could've happened to anyone."

"But if I hadn't blindsided you—"

He hushed me with a firm squeeze. "Stop that. Like I already told Merrick, you two make sense. If I'm gonna be pissed at anyone, it's me—for not seeing it sooner."

I pulled away. "You really think that?"

"Yeah, I do," he said, wiping the tears from her cheek with my fingers. "Can you do something for me, though?"

"What?"

"Share a donut with me?"

I stood, grabbing two donuts from the box. "I want my own," I said as I bit into a jelly-filled donut and handed him a bearclaw.

"Unbelievable. I almost died, and you won't even share the best one."

A knock on the door interrupted our laugh.

"Maybe we should start calling you Crash," Reaper called as he walked in, Eva tucked under his arm.

Hatchet grinned. "Too late. No take-backs on the road name once it's given. Those are the rules."

As the men drifted into a debate about the salvageable parts on Hatchet's bike, I turned to Eva. "How's Brisket?"

Her grin spread. "Having the time of his life with Hawk. I'm asking Rhetta to make them little matching cuts with Maverick patches."

Reaper's head jerked around. "Dog cuts are not a thing."

Eva stuck out her tongue at him. "Don't think I won't parade them into Church once they're officially patched in."

Reaper rolled his eyes, and Hatchet wheezed out a laugh, wincing as he grabbed his side. "Fuck, you can't say shit like that."

Reaper shook his head, returning the conversation to something about exhaust pipes.

Eva leaned back in her chair. "Seriously, though, it's been nice having Brisket around to keep Hawk occupied. I might need to get a dog for my dog."

"Wow," I teased. "Already expanding the family? Jesus, you two move fast."

Eva chuckled. "We move fast? Pot, meet kettle."

"You and Hawk moved in with Reaper after, what, twenty minutes?"

"Under duress," she shot back. "Big difference."

Before I could retort, Merrick walked in. His gaze flicked across Eva and Reaper, then landed on me, softening as his lips curved. "How's my second-favorite PR consultant?" he asked Eva.

Eva gasped, hand over her chest. "Second?"

Merrick hooked me by the waist and lowered his mouth to mine, the kiss slow and deliberate. When he pulled back, there was a satisfied smirk tugging at his lips. "Sorry. Kenna's my number one now."

Eva rolled her eyes and grinned. "She's mine, too. Why don't I just keep Brisket another night?" She raised her brows as she threw a suggestive glance my way. I flushed.

"That would be great," Merrick said. "Kenna will be staying at my place tonight."

A sharp knock interrupted the room. A tall man in a white coat leaned against the doorframe. "Quite the party. I'm Dr. Soos. Unfortunately, we can only have two people visiting at a time. Perhaps a few of you can come back later?"

"We'll head out," Merrick offered. "Glad you're OK, brother, but you're running out of lives. Maybe we should start calling you Kitty Cat."

Hatchet grimaced. "I love pussy as much as the next man, but if you start calling me Kitty Cat at the club, I'll remind you why they call me Hatchet."

I hugged him carefully, mindful of the wires and his bruises. "Text me what you want tomorrow. Breakfast, lunch—whatever you need, I'll bring it."

Hatchet cursed. "Phone's toast. Shattered in the crash."

"I'll have a prospect bring you a new one," Reaper offered.

Merrick wrapped an arm around my waist, feathering light kisses across the side of my neck.

Hatchet groaned. "The fuck, brother? Get a room."

Reaper snorted. "Don't be jealous, Crash Cat."

Eva clapped her hands together. "Oh, I love Crash Cat. Such a good road name for Mr. Nine Lives."

Hatchet pointed a finger at them both. "Try it once at the clubhouse, and I'll carve it into your foreheads. And if you start sending me cat memes when I get my new phone, I'll make you regret it," he said, looking pointedly at me.

"There'll be no cat memes tonight. Don't text us at all," Merrick warned. "We're busy."

I glanced at Merrick, raising my brows.

He met my eyes, his smile tugging wider. "I'm taking you out on an official date."

Hatchet groaned dramatically. "I see how it is. I survived a horrific accident and lost a beautiful girl, but sure. Go on a date."

I glanced at him, my brows furrowed, and breathed a sigh of relief when I saw the mischief in his eyes. Relief loosened my chest.

When Merrick guided me out of the building, I finally breathed. The hospital's sterile air gave way to the sunny warmth of midday in May.

"I have to take care of some club business before I take you out tonight. Do you want me to drop you at your place so you can pack anything I missed?" he asked, pressing his hand to the small of my back.

I arched a brow. "Like my vibrator?"

That rare, wide smile I loved spread across his face. "Couldn't miss that, sitting out in the open."

A laugh bubbled out of me. "Drop me at my house and I'll meet you at your place tonight. How should I dress for this date?"

"Jeans and a leather jacket, if you have one."

"Are you taking me to the clubhouse? Because I hate to break it to you, that's not a date."

I jumped as a palm came down on my ass just hard enough to surprise me—and turn me on. Heat coiled low in my stomach.

"Smart-ass woman. I'm taking you somewhere on my bike. Get in the truck."

I gazed up at him as he opened the door for me. I'd never get used to the juxtaposition of hardened biker and sweet, yet commanding gentleman.

A few hours later, the wind whipped through my hair as I pressed my body tight against Merrick's back, enjoying the rumble of his Harley coursing through my body. The vibrations traveled up through my thighs and into my core.

I leaned with him around each curve as he drove deeper into the woods. He slowed as he turned down a narrow dirt road and stopped in what appeared to be an abandoned park lot.

"Did you bring me here to murder me? I listen to a lot of true crime podcasts, and this seems like a good place to kill someone. Remote. No one close enough to hear me scream."

Merrick shook his head with a smile. "Murder isn't a first-date topic. I won't discuss the ways to kill someone until at least the third."

I raised a brow. "I'm not going to ask if you're serious."

His only answer was to lace his fingers through mine and tug me down a short path. The trees broke into a clearing overlooking a lake, glittering under the fading light. A small table was set up with two chairs and wildflowers in a glass jar. A picnic basket and cooler waited nearby.

My heart pounded in my chest. "You did this for me? Is this the club business you supposedly had to take care of?"

Merrick pulled a chair out with one hand and tapped the back of it. "Sit," he said —more command than request. "One of the Mavericks owns the Onyx Taproom. I needed time to get him to put together a picnic for us."

I watched him pull small bowls from the cooler. He set one in front of me before taking a seat and settling with his own. "He told me these are called caprese bites."

I snickered as I popped a balsamic-drizzled tomato into my mouth. "So, where are we?"

"My property. I bought it years ago. This is my favorite spot. Someday I want to build a house here. Our house, if you'd like."

I raised a brow. "We've been together for like, five minutes."

He shrugged. "I want you, Kenna," he said, his gaze steady on me. "I want to watch the sun set over this lake with you every night and wake up beside you every morning. I want you wearing a cut of your own at the clubhouse beside Eva and Rhetta. Hell, I already know I want to marry you. I want to get down on one knee with a big-ass diamond and let the guys give me shit about how whipped I am. Tell me you don't want this yet, and I'll back off. I'll slow down if you ask me to. But I know exactly what I want."

I swallowed a bite of the salad as I tried to process his words. "It's not that I don't want that. But shouldn't we date for a while? Then move in together? And then do all the other big stuff, like get engaged and build a house together? Like normal people."

"I'm not normal, and I don't want to waste time following society's rules." He finished his last bite of the salad and watched me carefully, as if he expected me to run away.

But I was done running. "OK."

His eyes lit up. "OK?"

I smiled nervously. "I'm in. Conditionally. We move in together while the house gets built. I'm not in a hurry to get engaged."

Merrick cleared the table and handed me a plate with a pita filled with chicken salad. He sat before he spoke again. "I'll have the prospects pack up your place this week."

I bit into the pita and narrowed my eyes at him as I chewed. "Stop abusing your power. I'm packing my own shit. I don't need them going through my things like you did." I blushed. "I don't need more men pawing through my panties or my toys."

His eyes gleamed. "Got more stashed away?"

My face heated. "That's none of your business."

Merrick continued, undeterred. "I have a storage unit behind the clubhouse for whatever you don't need to move into my place right now. Reaper might be able to have his crew get the house up in time for Christmas."

I shook my head with a smile. "You're insane. This is our first date. You should be asking me about my hobbies and favorite color, not moving in together."

"Fine," he said, his tone amused. "What's your favorite color?"

Merrick peppered me with first-date questions as we finished our plates. From childhood memories to first concerts, we fell into comfortable conversation as the sun set across the shimmering lake.

When the plates were cleared, Merrick pulled out a blanket and spread it across the grass. He handed me a plastic cup and filled it with red wine before cracking a beer for himself. Vibrant oranges and pinks streaked across the sky as we settled in to finish watching the sun sink below the lake.

His mouth captured mine, and my breath caught as the rough pad of his thumb stroked my cheek. He broke away just enough to murmur against my lips, voice low. "I have one last question for tonight." His hand curled in my hair. "Wear my patch. Be my old lady."

I looked to the sky and responded in an exasperated tone. "First of all, that wasn't a question. Second, what is it with you bikers? I don't want to be called an old lady. I'm only thirty-one, for fuck's sake."

Merrick smirked as he listened to my tirade. "How about I just call you my lady? We'll let you hit forty before we add the word 'old'?"

"Forty isn't old," I shot back. "You're forty."

"Exactly."

"Maybe fifty." I huffed. "I'll become an 'old lady' when I turn fifty."

Merrick smirked. "Eva accepted her cut without a fight."

I scoffed. "That's because Reaper fucked her into submission."

Merrick's eyes darkened. "Is that what it'll take?"

A wide grin spread across my face. "It's worth a shot. You won't know until you try."

His growl vibrated through me before his mouth crashed to mine. He gripped my hip hard enough to bruise. His hungry, demanding kiss lit every nerve ending in my body.

A low moan slipped from me as his hand slid beneath my shirt, calloused fingers skimming my ribs until he tugged the fabric up and over my head. The cool night air licked at my skin, and my nipples tightened under the thin lace of my bralette. A shiver rippled across me in a way that had nothing to do with cold.

Merrick shoved the flimsy lace aside and sucked one puckered nipple between his teeth, biting sharp enough to sting before smoothing the sensation with his tongue. Heat coiled tight and low. I writhed under him, jeans already unbuttoned with one flick of his fingers.

As I wiggled them down, he leaned back on his heels, eyes blazing. The jingle of his belt filled the air before he yanked it free, looping it around my wrists in a smooth, practiced motion.

"Hands stay up here," he ordered, pressing them above my head and tightening the leather. "You move, I stop. Understand?"

My pulse jumped. "Yes."

"That's it, Wildfire. Good girl."

Excitement coursed through my body at his praise. I'd never understood the appeal of being bound, tied up at someone else's mercy. Not until this moment. Surrendering to Merrick, trusting him completely, intoxicated me.

Reaching back, Merrick pulled his shirt over his head. I bit my lip as I took in his inked pecs and abs, sculpted by the hardened life he lived. My eyes traced the tattoos that covered nearly every inch of him. He leaned over me and began to gently kiss a slow-burning path down my chest and stomach. I instinctively moved my hands toward his hair, and he growled.

"Arms up."

I sucked in a breath and obeyed. Yep, I was gone for this man. I finally understood the appeal of the dominant alpha male featured in the romance books stacked in my bedroom.

His mouth traveled down my chest, slow, deliberate, licking and biting a trail toward my stomach. My body arched toward him, craving more.

Then he settled between my thighs and glanced up with a wicked glint.

"As you noted earlier, no one will hear you scream. So scream for me, Wildfire."

Before I could retort, his mouth was on me, tongue dragging over my clit.

A gasp ripped from me as my hips jerked off the blanket. "Oh, fuck—" He pressed my thighs down firmly with his hands, mouth devouring me with obscene precision. He alternated between tormenting licks and sucking pulses that scattered my thoughts. I couldn't tell if I was seeing stars because of the night sky or because of the way he ignited pleasure within me.

"Merrick," I moaned. I clawed the picnic blanket with bound hands as I arched into him.

"Say it louder," he rasped against me. His tongue flicked mercilessly.

"Fuck—Merrick!"

Sensation charged through me, and I panted as he edged me closer and closer. He was relentless, drawing out every sensation.

When I was teetering, he pulled back just enough to blow cool air across me, smirking at my desperate whine. "So fucking wet for me. You taste like both heaven and sin."

Overwhelming pleasure consumed me as he slipped two fingers within me and flicked his tongue over me one last time. I cried out as the climax slammed into me, stars exploding behind my eyelids, my body bucking helplessly. The sound tore from my throat and echoed across the quiet lake.

Merrick moved up my body slowly, kissing my stomach and chest before pressing his lips to mine. "Don't move," he ordered in a rough voice as he leaned back on his heels and stood before me.

He unbuckled and dropped his pants, boots thudding against the ground. My gaze darted over every inch of him—the tattoos, the scars, his thick cock.

"See something you want, Wildfire?"

"Yes please," I whispered.

He kneeled, straddling my hips.

"Then be mine."

"I am yours." I raised my arms to wrap them around his neck, but he grabbed my wrists with one hand to stop me. Pinning my hands above my head once again, Merrick crushed his lips to mine.

"You know what I mean." His dark gaze peered into mine.

"Fuck me first and then we'll talk," I promised.

His eyes lit up. "You think that's how it's going to be? You make demands, and I follow your orders?"

I giggled. "It's called compromise."

"Compromise? I'm not sure that's a concept I understand."

He slid into me slowly, stretching me almost painfully. "Fuck, Kenna. This is the tightest pussy I've ever had. Like you were made for me."

A sharp gasp ripped out of me. "Give me a second. It's been a long time, and you're a fucking beast."

He chuckled, kissing me softly. "I'll give you a second. But then you're going to take every inch of me like the good girl you are."

He drove deep, swallowing my cry.

I met him, thrust for thrust, as the friction between us caused tension to coil once again in my core.

"Oh-my-fucking-fuck-fuck," I rambled. My body shook as another orgasm washed over me.

"Wildfire," he groaned in my ear as I felt his cock swell inside me before he found his release.

He tugged the blanket up around us, pulling me tight against his chest.

He kissed my forehead, his voice soft. "You're mine now, Wild-fire. Even if you're not ready to wear my patch on your back."

I hummed in response, not having any words. I traced a finger along his inked, scarred chest before pressing my palm over his heart. The steady rhythm beating below centered me.

"You know, I'm not sure I'll ever be ready for the whole 'property of' thing."

Merrick combed his fingers through my hair. "It's not about possession. Anyone who fucks with you answers to me. To all of the Mavericks."

I rolled onto my side, propping my head on my hand so I could meet his gaze. His eyes glinted fierceness and tenderness all at once. "Hasn't that already been the case? You protected me when we were just friends. What makes this any different?"

He tensed before exhaling. "Because being with me puts a target on your back. The life I live is dangerous. If you're mine in every way, then you're safer. There's an unspoken rule among clubs that old ladies and kids are off limits. I'll be more comfortable bringing you into my world if I know you're safe."

I bit my lip and sighed before nestling into the warmth of his body. "I just don't want to lose myself in all of this. I want to be with you. But I want to be me, too."

He kissed the top of my head and tightened around me. "You will be, Wildfire. Always. That patch doesn't change who you are. It just tells the world you're mine—and that I'm yours."

I smiled against his skin, the tension in my chest easing. "Well, when you put it like that ..." I trailed off. Was I ready for this? Was I OK with the entire concept?

Merrick pulled away, looking into my eyes. "Is that agreement?"

I shrugged. "You seem to have at least fucked me into agreeableness."

He chuckled and pulled me closer. "Property of Merrick. Has a nice ring to it."

I rolled my eyes. "You would think that."

He brushed a hand on my bare shoulder, noticing the chill on my skin. "Let's get dressed and go back to my place. As much as I'd love to sleep under the stars with you, my back will hurt for a week if we stay out here."

I giggled, and he kissed the tip of my nose. "Old man."

He stood, zipped his jeans, then offered me his hand. "Just wait until you're my age."

Chapter Twenty-Seven

I woke up tangled in Merrick's arms, the weight of his body heavy and grounding. Carefully, I slid out from under him, grabbed my phone from the nightstand, and slipped quietly out of the bedroom.

In the kitchen, the smell of brewing coffee filled the air as I sat on the couch, scrolling on my phone. The device pinged, and my chest tightened in anguish as I read the text message. Over the past few weeks, I'd avoided calls from Alec's mother and sister. Now I knew why they'd been so insistent. Grief cracked open in me raw and fresh, like no time had passed at all. They wanted me to return to our alma mater for the ribbon cutting of a new child development lab—one they were naming in his honor.

I didn't even hear Merrick until the deep timbre of his voice cut gently into the silence. "What's wrong, Wildfire?"

Startled, I handed him my phone, not trusting myself to speak without my voice cracking. His brow furrowed as he read it, then lifted his steady gaze back to me.

"You should go," he said, his voice low and steady.

Tears pricked hot, and I shook my head. "I don't think I can."

He sat beside me, pulling me into his chest in a tight embrace that told me I didn't have to hold myself together. His lips brushed my temple. "I'll go with you."

I blinked up at him. "Really?"

"Really," he said firmly.

I swallowed hard. "It's just ... going back there, seeing everyone, remembering ..."

Merrick squeezed my hand. "I know. But sometimes, the only way through is to face it. Alec deserves to be remembered. And you deserve to heal."

I wiped at my eyes, trying to steady my breathing. "Maybe."

He smiled, just a little. "So, a child development lab?"

Grateful for the distraction, I exhaled. "Alec was a child psychologist. He wanted to work in public schools and help kids who were struggling. He always said if he could change just one kid's life, it was enough."

Merrick nodded, his expression thoughtful. "He sounds like a good man."

"He was," I whispered.

There was a silence, heavier but not uncomfortable. Then Merrick cleared his throat, almost uncertainly. "You want kids?"

I let out a short, humorless laugh. "No. Alec did, though. It was always a pain point between us."

Relief flickered in his gaze. "Good. I've never wanted them either. Why bring kids into this fucked-up world?"

I managed a shaky smile. "Exactly. Plus, they're sticky and loud and smelly. I do want a few dogs, though," I added. "And a goat. Maybe two. Oh, and some chickens. And a peacock."

Merrick tilted his head at me, exasperated. "So no kids, but you want a goddamn petting zoo?"

I grinned, shrugging. "Pretty much."

He shook his head, muttering under his breath. "The things I am willing to put up with for you, Wildfire."

A loud honk sounded from outside the window, startling us both. I looked up, confused.

Merrick stood and walked to it, pulling back the curtain. "Looks like the prospects are here with the furniture."

"What furniture?" I followed him, peering over his shoulder. A moving truck idled in the driveway, a club prospect leaning against the hood, arms crossed.

Merrick turned to me, a hint of a smirk on his lips. "You're moving in. First load's the big stuff—couches and tables. Whatever you want to keep here, we'll bring in. The rest can go into storage."

I blinked, still processing. "But I haven't even packed anything."

He shrugged, his tone casual but his eyes warm. "You can pack today. "

I stared at him, torn between surprise and something softer, something that made my chest ache in the best way. "You're serious about this, aren't you?"

He stepped closer, brushing a loose strand of hair from my face. His knuckles grazed my jaw, making me meet his gaze. "Dead fucking serious, Wildfire."

I laughed, shaking my head. "You asked me to move in less than twelve hours ago."

"And?" He brushed a loose strand of hair back from my face. "Life's short. I don't waste time when I know what I want."

I laughed. "Old man logic."

"Smart man logic," he countered with a grin. "Get dressed. I'll unload with the prospects before heading to Fort Worth for club business."

I wrinkled my nose. "Just say you're doing shady biker shit you can't tell me about."

His grin widened. "I'm doing shady biker shit today. Put some clothes on before the prospects see you. I'd hate to have to rip their eyeballs out."

I shook my head and pressed my lips to his.

"If you need anything while I'm doing said shady shit, ask one of the prospects or call Fuse. He'll be hanging out with Hatchet today," Merrick said.

An hour later, I faced a stack of moving boxes and a small army of new prospects assigned the unfortunate duty of helping me.

"What can I pack?" asked Arson, a lanky man with jet-black hair and flame tattoos licking up his arms.

"The entire kitchen? Merrick owns like two cups and paper plates," I said with a laugh.

Arson chuckled. "Perfect. I can take this room if you want to take another. You'll have to tell the guys what you want them to pack, though, because Merrick said, and I quote, 'Don't go through her shit without asking first.' And none of us wants to piss off the boss."

I shook my head. Overprotective alpha males.

"Bayou, can you pack up my office? I have a lot of books."

"Yes, ma'am," he said in his deep Southern accent, nodding at me as he grabbed a set of boxes and headed down the hall.

"And Zen, I think you could handle anything that's in the main room and the closets. I'd like to take the blankets and throw pillows to Merrick's, but everything else can go into storage for now. I'll handle packing my bedroom and bathroom."

Zen nodded, his mop of dark-blue hair falling over his face.

I lugged a box into my room, shut the door, and yanked open the nightstand drawer. My hand closed around the small collection of toys I wasn't about to let a prospect stumble across. I tossed them into the bottom of the box, then buried them under T-shirts and leggings.

"Sorry, boys, no bonus finds for you today," I muttered to myself.

By the time I emerged after packing my room, nearly the entire house was boxed and taped. The men were loading the truck like an efficient machine.

Arson wiped sweat from his brow. "We'll get the rest of your boxes in the truck and over to Merrick's. Just send us a text if you need anything else," he offered.

I thanked the men, sending them off with bottles of ice-cold water from my nearly empty refrigerator.

Alone in the house, I started cleaning the kitchen. The counters were bare except for a stack of library books I'd set aside while packing. I picked them up, frowning at the overdue notices tucked inside. They needed to go back downtown.

I considered waiting for Merrick to go with me, but he was busy with whatever secretive club business kept him unavailable today. Asking a prospect to escort me to the library felt absurd. Besides, the sooner I got the books returned and cleaned up the house, the sooner I could pass the keys back to Eva so she could rent it out.

I grabbed my keys and jumped into my Range Rover, heading downtown. The streets buzzed with the lunchtime crowd, and parking in front of the library was full. I circled the block twice before finding a spot farther down the street.

Inside the cool library, I dropped off the books and breathed a sigh of relief—one less thing to worry about. As I walked back to my car, I pulled out my phone to check for messages. I sent a funny GIF to Hatchet and responded to my brother, who was asking when I'd be returning for a visit.

The street was quiet, the sun high and hot overhead, but something prickled at the back of my neck. I slowed and glanced backward casually.

A man in a dark bandanna stood twenty yards back.

My heart skipped a beat as his eyes met mine.

I quickened my pace, turning the next corner. I glanced back again, my gut clenching as I realized he'd closed the gap between us.

I forced myself to walk faster. *Coincidence*, I lied to myself. He wasn't following me. We just happened to be heading in the same direction.

My paranoia felt ridiculous, but the feeling in my gut wouldn't go away. I chanced another glance. He was closer. My walk turned into a clipped power stride. I turned another corner and glanced around. In my haste, I realized I'd passed the street where I'd parked and headed toward an abandoned construction site on a more industrial block. The hospital where Hatchet lay loomed in the distance, its sign a beacon, but it might as well have been miles away.

I ducked behind a stack of wooden pallets, crouching low. My hands shook as I tried to call Merrick. Voicemail. Damn it. I dialed Fuse next, my breath coming in short gasps.

He picked up immediately. "Kenna. What's wrong?" I could hear Hatchet in the background, demanding to know what was happening.

"I think I'm being followed," I whispered, my voice barely audible. "I'm hiding in a construction site near the hospital. But maybe I'm being paranoid."

"Trust your gut," Fuse urged. "If you felt it, you're not imagining it. Stay hidden, but run if you can get away."

My stomach dropped as the man crossed my line of vision. His boots crunched slowly across gravel. Hunting me.

"Kenna Walsh," the man sang, his accented voice echoing across the abandoned space. "Come out, come out, wherever you are ..."

I whispered a curse. "He's here. And he knows my name."

"Listen to me," Fuse said, his voice steady. "Stay silent, and stay on the line so I can listen in. I'm coming. Do you know the cross streets? Or see any signs that can help me find you?"

"It's the abandoned Zaide building not far from the library."

"I know where that is. I'm on my way. Stay calm. And Kenna, if he gets to you, you fight with everything you've got."

I pressed myself deeper into the shadows, my pulse pounding in my ears. Even from a distance, I could hear the man's footsteps crunching on gravel as he moved closer.

Chapter Twenty-Eight

Fuse's phone rang just as I was changing out of my hospital gown, ready to ditch this sterile hellhole. I'd been cleared for discharge an hour ago. The stitches tugged when I bent, my ribs ached like a motherfucker, but I was mobile enough.

The doctors were probably booting me because every nurse on the floor had a hard time keeping out of my room. I didn't blame them —I looked fantastic in a gown that showed way too much ass.

Fuse's voice turned razor sharp. "Stay calm. And Kenna, if he gets to you, you fight with everything you've got."

My blood iced over.

Fuse met my eyes, jaw tight. "Kenna's in trouble. Merrick was right. The Jackals have been watching her."

Every ache vanished. "Where?"

"Construction site, two blocks north."

"Let's go," I snapped. "You got a spare piece?"

Fuse pulled a tiny Ruger LCP from his ankle holster and thrust it into my hand.

"Cute," I muttered at the small handgun, jamming it into my waistband.

I laced up my boots. Adrenaline drowned the fire that every movement sent through my ribs.

"Why her?" Fuse asked as we strode out of the hospital in a rush.

"Kenna's family is loaded," I explained. "My guess is ransom. What I want to know is what the fuck she's doing downtown on her own. There's no way Merrick left her unprotected."

We hit the street at a jog, Fuse scanning alleys, me clutching my side.

Two blocks. Two fucking blocks that felt like two miles. The construction site loomed ahead—chain-link fence torn open, scaffolding abandoned.

I heard her before I saw her. The thug in the bandanna wrenched her from behind a stack of rebar, her cry slicing through the air.

"Thought you could hide from me, puta? Jefe's been looking for you. If we can't get your rich mami to pay up, we'll sell you to the cartel. Bet they'd like a redhead."

Kenna struggled against him. "Get your hands off me, asshole."

"Let her go." My voice was ice.

The man spun, shoving Kenna against a concrete mixer. He eyed the Ruger in my hand and laughed, a harsh, grating sound. "With that toy gun? Fuck off."

Fuse melted into the shadows, stalking behind him.

I kept the guy's eyes on me as I moved closer. "Last chance. Walk away."

He sneered, one hand gripping Kenna's arm, the other reaching for his waistband. "Or what? You'll—"

I lunged. Not at him—at Kenna. I shoved her clear just as he drew his weapon. The gunshot exploded, searing through my side. White-hot pain blinded me. Fuck.

Fuse didn't hesitate. Two shots from the shadows. The man dropped, a dark stain blooming over his chest.

Kenna scrambled to me, eyes wild. "Hatchet!"

"I'm fine," I gritted out, but she was already ripping off her shirt, pressing the fabric hard against my side to stop the bleeding.

"But I don't mind the strip show, doll. Nice bra. Black lace. I like it."

Kenna glared at me, but I could see the fear in her eyes.

Fuse crouched beside us. "You're going to need to go back to the hospital. I'll call an ambulance."

"No," I rasped, grabbing his arm. "If they find you here with that gun, you're going back to prison. Go. Now. I'm good. Kenna can call."

Fuse hesitated, then nodded grimly. He wiped his Glock clean of prints, pressed it into my hand, and vanished into the maze of scaffolding.

Kenna's hands trembled against my wound. "Why'd he leave? You're bleeding—"

"Protecting him," I groaned. Sirens wailed in the distance. "Call 911 and tell 'em I fired the shots when they get here."

She didn't hesitate. One hand pressed hard against my wound, and the other fumbled for her phone. Her voice was surprisingly steady as she spoke to dispatch. The ambulance screeched to a halt minutes later. Paramedics swarmed us, and Kenna clung to my uninjured hand as they loaded me onto a gurney.

"I'm riding with him," she insisted to the paramedics.

I squeezed her fingers. "I'll be fine, doll. This isn't even the worst gunshot I've had. Not even in the top three."

The look on her face told me that it wasn't as comforting as I thought it'd be.

The ER doors flew open as the paramedics wheeled me in, fluorescent lights as blinding as the midday sun had been outside.

Merci stood, arms crossed. "Back so soon, Hatchet?"

I groaned, but a laugh escaped through the pain. "Thought you might enjoy more practice on GSW patients. Wanted to make sure you didn't get bored."

She snorted, falling into step beside the gurney. "Get this asshole to Trauma 1," she ordered a fellow intern. Her tone softened as she glanced at Kenna. "You OK?"

Kenna nodded, though her knuckles were white where she gripped the rail.

Merci's eyes flicked to the wound on my side, professional and sharp. "Clean entry and exit. You're lucky, idiot."

Kenna hovered in the doorway, her face pale. Merci waved her in. "You can sit with him while we get this cleaned up. I'll get a nurse to bring you a scrub top. It was smart to use your shirt to staunch the bleeding."

As the docs worked, Kenna never left my side. Her hand stayed in mine, her thumb tracing circles on my skin. Merci kept up a steady stream of dry commentary, helping Kenna laugh through the tension.

As Merci left the room, she gave me a long look. "Rest. And try not to get shot again between now and your next discharge. The cops will probably be in shortly to take your statement."

Kenna's phone dinged. "It's Fuse," she said. "I'm going to step out and update him. Do you need anything?"

I gave her a lopsided grin. "I'm good. Just try not to get in trouble between here and the waiting room. Merci will be pissed if I rip these stitches."

Her lips twitched as she slipped out. I let my head fall back against the pillow. The adrenaline had burned off, leaving nothing behind but fire in my side and the hollow ache you only notice when the fight's over.

Kenna had been seconds away from—fuck, I couldn't even let myself finish the thought. Another loss like that? I'm not sure Merrick would survive it. He was my brother, my oldest friend, my family. Losing her would've gutted him worse than any bullet ever could. Hell, it would've gutted me, too.

Bruised ribs, busted stitches, hole in my side—small price. Better me than leaving Merrick hollowed out again. He couldn't live with another ghost.

I exhaled slowly, trying to let the pain drown out the thought clawing at the back of my skull: what if we hadn't made it in time?

Chapter Twenty-Nine

I dug my phone out of my saddlebag. The screen lit up with a barrage of missed calls—Fuse, Kenna, Hatchet—and a single, brief text from Fuse that sent a cold spike of dread straight through my gut.

FUSE:

Kenna's safe. Hatchet is back in hospital. GSW. Call me.

A roar of fury tore from my throat. The consigliere of the Fort Worth Mafia had insisted on a closed-door meeting with us and the Red Rock Riot. No distractions, no phones—protocol for these kinds of deals.

Reaper and Thane looked up, their expressions hardening as they caught the storm in my eyes.

"What happened?" Reaper asked, already moving toward his bike.

"I don't fucking know," I growled, my voice barely controlled. My hands shook as I dialed Fuse, thumb jabbing the call button. He answered on the first ring.

"Merrick," Fuse said, his voice steady but edged with tension.

"Talk," I demanded, thumbing the speaker on so Thane and Reaper could hear.

"Kenna was followed downtown. You were right. The Jackals were watching her. Waiting for her to be alone," Fuse said, his words clipped. "She hid in a construction site, called me when she realized she was being tracked. Hatchet and I got there just as the guy found her. Hatchet took a bullet to the side. I put the guy down. Wiped my prints from the weapon and left it with Hatchet. He ordered me to get out of there, so I didn't land back in the pen."

My chest tightened, every muscle in my body coiled. "Kenna OK?"

"Shaken. But she's fine. Merci's letting her sit with Hatchet."

"We're leaving Fort Worth now."

Thane cursed under his breath. "Go. We'll be right behind you. I'll get the lawyer there before the cops question Hatchet."

I didn't wait for another word. I was on my bike, engine snarling, the road blurring beneath me. Despite Fuse's assurances, my mind raced with every worst-case scenario. I'd buried too many friends to believe tomorrow was promised to any of us.

The hospital parking lot was a blur as I skidded to a stop. I stormed through the doors, scanning the waiting area until I saw Fuse sitting beside Kenna. Relief slammed into me, but it was short-lived. Kenna was pale, her jeans splattered with blood, a pink hospital scrub top replacing whatever she'd been wearing. She looked small and exhausted, but she was alive.

I crossed the room in three strides and pulled her against me, crushing her to my chest. She clung to me, her fingers digging into my back. "Wildfire," I murmured into her hair.

"I'm fine. Hatchet's the one who got shot. It was the same gang."

"You sure?" I asked, looking to Fuse.

Fuse nodded.

White-hot rage burned through me. "We end them tonight."

Fuse met my gaze, his eyes hard with resolve. "Consider it done." He turned and left, his steps quick and purposeful.

Kenna's hand found mine, her fingers cold. "Merrick—"

I squeezed her hand, my anger tempered by the need to keep her safe. "I'm taking you home."

She nodded, her eyes searching mine for reassurance. I brushed my thumb over her cheek, my heart aching with the weight of what could have happened.

* * *

I nodded at Coast as I slipped from my home in the dead of the night, Kenna fast asleep in my bed. Despite the prospect monitoring the gate, I wanted assurance that someone was watching my place as well. The former Navy Seal was a well-trained weapon. Besides Fuse, Reaper, and Hatchet, he was the only bastard I'd bet my life— and hers—on. It'd be a shame if he had to prove it, but after tonight, the Mavericks patch was his. I'd ask Thane to put it to a vote early.

Blood roared in my ears as I ripped down the highway on my bike. The silenced Sig Sauer offered a comforting weight in the holster beneath my cut. It usually took forty-five minutes to get to this part of the city, but I made it to the rundown Jackals' clubhouse in just over thirty.

I parked my bike and appraised my surroundings. This part of the city was like a mausoleum. The clubhouse sat between abandoned homes with peeling paint, sagging plywood, and boarded-up windows. Crabgrass clawed through cracks in the sidewalk, and trash rolled by like tumbleweeds in the soft breeze. A dog barked in the distance.

Reaper stood, a deadly sentinel at the doorway, his Glock comfortably in his hand, finger resting above the trigger.

"Any problems securing the place?" I asked.

He snorted. "Cleared the shithole in less than five minutes."

"Who's inside?"

"Thane, Fuse, and Archer."

I let out a gravely laugh. "Been a while since the prez got his hands dirty."

Reaper grinned. "Disappointed he's missed out on all the fun lately. He's still salty that you didn't let him get a piece of Tyler or Danny."

I lifted a shoulder. "Let's get this party started then."

Reaper trailed behind me as I stepped into the ramshackle house. It stank of weed, mildew, and fear. Ripped, stained curtains shifted as the wind blew through the cracked windows.

"'Bout damn time you showed up," Thane growled.

"I had to get the old lady settled," I explained as my eyes swept the room.

Thane gave me a wolfish grin. "Good for you. Glad you have her."

Fourteen men kneeled facing the wall, their hands zip-tied behind their backs. I closed my eyes for a moment, imagining Kenna hiding in that goddamn construction site. If my brothers hadn't been nearby, she'd be gone. And that was enough to justify what I was about to do.

"Turn around," I ordered.

Archer, Reaper, and Thane began to jerk the men around to face me. I stalked from one end of the small living room to the other. Each step was a sticky fight with the linoleum, beer, piss, and filth gluing my boots down.

"Who's in charge?" I demanded. "Which one of you is Jefe?"

Silence. I glanced down the line expectantly. "I said who the fuck here is in charge?" My thundering voice echoed through the room, the simmering anger in my chest boiling to the surface.

I watched their eyes dart toward the end of the line at the oldest man, who couldn't be more than twenty-five. I grasped my hand around his throat and lifted him off the ground. His eyes bugged out as he gasped for air.

"I want every single one of you to remember my face. Because the last thing you'll see before you die tonight is how pissed off I am that you came after my woman. Again."

I hurled the man to the ground and drew my blade from my hip.

"Hold him," I ordered. Archer and Reaper pinned his arms as the man struggled, fear shining bright in his eyes.

I dragged my blade down his sternum, blood pouring from his chest.

One of the zip-tied men pissed himself. Another prayed quietly. The rest glared at me with hatred. I straightened and wiped the blade on the ripped sofa.

"No one hunts my woman and survives. As of tonight, the Jackals are extinct."

One of the men—probably only seventeen or eighteen—began to beg and plead. I pulled my silenced Sig Sauer from my hip and shot him in the head in one clean, muffled shot. Blood and brains painted the peeling floral wallpaper behind him.

"Is the place wired?"

Fuse nodded. "Ready to blow when you make the call. Added some Tannerite for a bit of flare."

I huffed a laugh. "Dramatic. Hatchet would appreciate that."

I methodically stalked down the row of men, slitting every throat. "See you all in hell," I growled.

We mounted our bikes and drove around the block, taking cover behind a sturdy brick church. Fuse hit the detonator, and the explosion rattled the stained-glass windows before us.

Smoke billowed into the sky as we closed a chapter for the city.

Chapter Thirty

Morning sunlight slanted through the hospital blinds. I lounged back, remote in hand, flipping through channels until the local news caught my eye.

The anchor's voice was smooth, almost bored, as she reported an explosion that had flattened part of a block. The camera panned over charred wreckage, flashing to a shot of police tape and shell-shocked bystanders. No survivors. Gang-on-gang violence, the reporter explained. The house was a known hangout for the dangerous street gang called the Jackals that had plagued Houston over the past few months.

I smirked, muted the TV, and settled deeper into my pillow. Fuse worked fast.

The door swung open, and Merrick strode in, his expression unreadable as always. He glanced at the TV, then at me. I grinned. "Morning, boss. You catch the news?"

He nodded, pulling up a chair. "Looks like the problem took care of itself."

"Miraculous," I deadpanned.

Merrick leaned forward, elbows on his knees. "Thank you. For saving Kenna."

I waved him off. "She's family. What else was I going to do? But you'd better make things official with her soon, before I try to win her over again."

Merrick growled. "Like hell you will. She agreed to be my old lady. It's official. I already moved her in with me. Her cut should be here soon."

I chuckled. "You move fast."

Merrick cracked a rare smile. "Life's short. I'll wife her up as soon as she'll let me."

Before I could rib him more, Merci breezed in wearing her white coat, clipboard in hand. "Morning, troublemakers." She checked my vitals, her touch brisk but gentle. "You're looking better. I might let you out of here soon—if you promise to take it easy. No throwing yourself in front of stray bullets or bike accidents for at least a month."

I shot her a grin. "No promises, doc."

She rolled her eyes and turned to Merrick. "I like Kenna. I expect a double date soon. I want to get to know the woman who's melted the ice around your heart."

"We'll see," Merrick gruffed.

I piped up. "Can I be the fifth wheel on this date?"

Merci shot me a look. "Maybe you should stop whoring around and settle down."

I clutched my chest in mock offense. "I tried! But Merrick stole her instead."

Merrick snorted. "You never stood a chance."

Merci laughed, shaking her head. "Let me see what I can do about getting you discharged."

I winked at her. "Admit it. You'll miss me."

She sighed, but her smile was real. "Yeah. I'm sure I will."

As she left, Merrick and I lapsed into comfortable silence, the morning news still flickering on mute. For the first time in a long time, everything felt right. Kenna was safe and happy. And if I had to take a bullet for that? Well, I'd do it again in a heartbeat.

Chapter Thirty-One

I stretched beside Merrick in bed, awoken by the sound of barking. The backyard squirrel was probably taunting Brisket again. The morning ritual woke us nearly every morning.

Merrick stirred as I shifted, his arm tightening around my waist as he pulled my back closer to his chest. He buried his face against the curve of my neck, scruff rasping against my sensitive skin. A shiver ran down my spine when his mouth turned from soft kisses into possessive nips.

"Good morning, Wildfire," he whispered in my ear, his voice still gravely from sleep. His breath sent goose bumps cascading down my body.

His large, rough hand slid down my naked side, tracing the dip of my waist and the swell of my hip. A needy sound escaped my throat before I could stop it.

Merrick nibbled on my ear, stroking my hip. My breath hitched as he inched closer to the apex of my thighs. I moaned at the agonizing slowness of his movements, unhurried like we had all the time in the world. Finally, he slipped a finger between my legs, and a primal growl emanated from his chest.

"You're already soaked for me, aren't you?" he asked, stroking. The friction of his hand made me arch into him.

He lazily circled my clit, his touch teasing and unhurried, while his hard cock pressed insistently against my backside.

But then—just as my hips rocked for more friction—his hand disappeared.

"Merrick," I gasped, heat spiking into frustration.

He only chuckled, reaching across me for the clamshell case on my nightstand.

"I'm curious about this," he said, pulling the curved silicone toy from the case. "I searched it online and read a few interesting examples of how it can be used."

He pressed the button, and the toy whirred to life, its low hum filling the room. Hovering over me, he slid the vibrating end inside me easily, the buzzing curve pressing perfectly against my G-spot. The other end curved up, the suction sealing over my clit. A jolt of overwhelming pleasure ripped a cry from my throat.

"Fuck!" My hands knotted in the sheets. My hips bucked helplessly.

"That's it," Merrick groaned.

"I–I'm not gonna last long," I gasped, the sensations overwhelming, teetering on the edge before I'd even caught my breath.

"I don't give a fuck," he growled.

He grabbed my hips, flipped me onto my stomach, and spread my legs with his knees. The slim silicone toy buzzed mercilessly inside me and sucked at my clit, making my entire body tremble.

"Goddamn, look at you," Merrick said, spitting into his hand before stroking himself. The slick sound sent a pulse of anticipation straight through me.

"You're going to take me with that toy in your pussy."

He lifted my hips slightly before sliding into me in one smooth, brutal thrust, filling me to the hilt and pressing the vibrations harder against my G-spot.

"Fuck," I sobbed, overwhelmed with the fullness. The toy

pressed harder into me with every stroke of his cock, and the pressure of his body over mine pressed the suction end harder onto my swollen clit. Every movement sent me spiraling higher, the pressure nearly unbearable.

Merrick leaned down, voice rough against my ear. "You like that, Wildfire? My cock stretching you while that toy ruins you?"

"Yes," I moaned.

"You're mine. This pussy is mine."

His pace was maddening—slow, steady, deliberate. He forced me to feel every inch until my legs shook.

"Say it," he commanded. "Say whose pussy this is."

My breath hitched. "Y–yours," I stuttered.

"Louder." His thrusts deepened, hitting that same devastating spot with each roll of his hips.

"Yours, Merrick!" I cried, clutching the sheets so tightly my knuckles ached.

"Damn fucking straight," he growled in a savage tone. "Mine to fuck. Mine to fill. Mine to make scream. You're fucking mine."

He rolled his hips harder, and the toy sent vibrations ricocheting through me until I shattered.

A violent, all-consuming orgasm tore through me, my body pulsing around him and the toy as wave after wave wrecked me.

"Good girl," Merrick whispered, his release chasing mine. He tightened his grip on my hips as his strokes became frantic. He roared my name as his climax hit, pulsing deep inside me.

He collapsed beside me, dragging me back into his arms. I slipped the toy free and turned it off, hypersensitive following my orgasm. Still trembling, I curled against him.

Merrick kissed the top of my head, his voice soft. "You ready for tonight?"

I sighed, my fingers tracing idle patterns on the tattoos covering his chest. "Not really."

He squeezed me gently. "You don't need to be OK. You don't need to be ready. I've got you."

I nodded, but my stomach twisted at the thought of seeing Alec's family in Boston for the ribbon-cutting. The idea of facing them for the first time since his funeral made my chest ache.

* * *

Hours later, the Boston air hit me. The crisp sixty-five-degree weather felt unfamiliar following my time in the humid Texas heat. I clutched my bag as we stepped off the plane, memories of my former life rushing back.

As if sensing my anxiety, Merrick's hand found the small of my back, the gentle pressure steadying me as we walked through the busy terminal.

Outside, he tugged my arm. A sleek town car idled by the curb with a man in a suit and hat holding a sign with my name. I stared, irritation flickering through me. "They sent a car?"

Merrick chuckled, squeezing my hand. "Guess they wanted to make sure you got there. You're a bit of a flight risk."

I rolled my eyes but let him guide me into the car. As we pulled away from the airport, the city skyline rising in the distance, I leaned into Merrick to draw strength from his presence. His warmth, his quiet confidence, made the tightness in my chest ease just a little.

The dedication ceremony was held in a sunlit atrium at the university, surrounded by glass and greenery. The sound of laughter and soft conversation filled the space, but all I could hear was the pounding of my own heart.

The ribbon cutting was brief but poignant. Alec's mother spoke about his passion for helping children, his kindness, and his dreams for the future. I stood in the front row, Merrick's hand in mine, as tears burned hot paths down my cheeks.

At the reception afterward, I finally faced Alec's mother. Her eyes widened as she took in Merrick beside me—his broad shoulders, the tattoos peeking from beneath his rolled-up sleeves, the quiet intensity in his gaze. But without his cut, he looked less intimidating.

He stood tall, his posture respectful, his smile polite—the most approachable I'd ever seen him.

"This is Merrick," I said, my voice steady despite the lump in my throat.

Alec's mother blinked twice, then extended her hand. "It's nice to meet you, Merrick."

Merrick shook her hand gently. "It's an honor to be here, ma'am. Alec sounds like an incredible man."

Her eyes softened. "He was. And Kenna, I'm so glad you came. I wasn't sure you would."

I tried to smile. "I wasn't sure either. But I'm glad I did."

"Kenna!" My mother's sharp voice cut through the crowd. I braced myself against Merrick as she appeared in a tailored navy pantsuit and pearls.

Her mouth pinched as her eyes flicked to Merrick. "I've been trying to reach out all day. You should have called me when you landed."

I sighed. "Just coming was a lot," I said, my tone flat. "I didn't feel like talking."

She huffed. "Sweetheart, people will talk. Couldn't you come to an event like this alone? For Alec's family? Who is this man?"

My fingernails carved crescents into my palm. "If you'd give me five seconds without criticizing me, I'd introduce you."

Merrick's jaw ticked. "Merrick Morris." He stretched his palm toward her.

She shifted at the snarl in his tone. She glanced down at his hand, taking in the dark tattoos. She took it gingerly. "Sutton Walsh," she squeaked. "And what exactly do you do, Mr. Morris?"

Merrick's tone stayed polite, but his steely gaze didn't waver. "I work in private security," he said evenly.

Her eyebrows shot up. "And you met Kenna ... how?"

I couldn't hold back a laugh, the interrogation lighting up my rebellious streak. "Merrick is in a motorcycle club. The club is a client. He's one of the officers."

Her eyes widened, lips parting in silent horror. Before she could collect herself enough to respond, my oldest brother's smooth baritone interrupted.

"Mom, Senator Greenfield's looking for you. Says he needs to talk to you about next week's fundraiser." Everest gestured to the corner, where the suited man was engaged in a heated conversation with a constituent, clearly not looking for my mother.

My mother nodded sharply. "Of course," she said, smoothing her hands down the front of her pants. She threw me an icy glare. "We're not done with this conversation," she said before stepping away.

Everest let out a low whistle. "I overheard most of that, sis. For a second there, I thought Mom was going to have a full cardiac event. Thanks for the entertainment."

He turned to Merrick, giving him an appraising scan, then offered his hand. "Everest Walsh. Eldest brother and the one always saving Kenna's ass from Mom's wrath. But it looks like you might be able to handle it."

Merrick shook his hand. "Happy to handle anything for Kenna."

I hugged my brother tight. "Thank you. Are Logan and Kendall here, too?"

Everest shook his head. "Logan has some big case she's working on right now and practically sleeps at the law firm. And Kendall is ... well, doing what Kendall wants." He shrugged. "She's trying to steal your crown as 'Most Difficult Daughter.' She changed her major to social work, of all things."

"The horror. How will she ever find a husband?" I scoffed sarcastically. "I'll see her major change and raise her one tattooed biker."

Everest chuckled. "You always did like to win. Why don't you go say hi to Alec's sisters, and I'll introduce Merrick to the best bourbon in Boston?" He clapped Merrick on the shoulder.

As the guys peeled off toward the bar, I found myself exhaling. The tension drained from my shoulders as I wove through the crowd to Alec's sisters, letting the conversations and laughter settle the nerves my mother had frayed.

Throughout the rest of the reception, Merrick mingled like a gentleman. He listened, smiled, shook hands, and made small talk beside Everest before returning to my side. He stood close enough to remind me he was there but never crowded me. He let me have moments with Alec's family and friends, and the memories that still lingered.

After, we slipped away, ducking dinner invitations and well-meaning questions. With nerves worn raw, all I wanted was a bed and a glass of wine. The city lights glittered as the town car took us back to the hotel. When we checked in, I frowned at the key card in my hand. "They upgraded our room," I muttered. "Of course they did. Always meddling."

Merrick smirked, wrapping an arm around my shoulders. "They just want you to be comfortable, Wildfire."

I sighed, but I couldn't help but smile. "I know. It's just … a lot."

He kissed the top of my head. I leaned into him, grateful for his strength and patience. I let the exhaustion slide between us, feeling for once as if I could let someone else help carry my grief.

Chapter Thirty-Two

I nudged open the front door, juggling an iced latte in one hand, black coffee in the other, a sack of burritos, and a small, wrapped gift pinched awkwardly in my elbow. Brisket woofed before barreling toward me, his nails scratching against the hardwood floors.

Even though I'd lived in this house for years, Kenna made it feel like a home with pillows and throw blankets scattered everywhere like she was building a fort, and candles flickering on every surface. The scent of vanilla lingered in the air, mixing with the familiar smell of woodsmoke and leather.

I deftly avoided tripping over the overzealous dog and dumped the burritos and gift on the counter before I made my way across the room to Kenna. Her red hair caught the sunlight slanting through the window, shining like dancing flames as she stood in front of a bookcase. She reached high on her tiptoes to place books on the top shelf.

I smirked as I read the titles. "You really do like true crime," I observed. "Should I be worried?"

"About what?" she asked innocently.

I raised a brow and handed over her latte. I wiped the dampness on my jeans before catching her chin between my fingers, tipping her head up so she looked into my eyes.

"Sometimes I think you're the most dangerous one in the room," I said.

She leaned into my touch and smiled. "I might know how to kill a man twelve different ways, but I know I'll never need to. Not with you by my side."

I pressed her gently into the bookshelf and kissed her, grounding myself in her warmth. It would never be enough. I'd regret every lost minute until I met her, but I planned to spend forever making up for it.

"What did you bring me?" she asked as she attempted to peer around me.

I glanced over my shoulder at the box, and nerves fluttered in my chest. "I'll give it to you later."

Kenna pouted, pursing her lips in a way that made me want to bite them. "You're seriously going to make me wait?"

"Fine," I relented.

I stalked across the room and held the box out to her. She shook it, the thunk echoing through the room.

"Well, it's not a puppy," she joked.

"It's not a chicken or a goat either."

She grinned. "There's always next time." She ripped the hot-pink wrapping paper off the box. "This has Eva written all over it," she observed.

I nodded and watched her as she slowly separated the leather vest from the sparkly tissue paper. She bit her lip as she held it in front of her, taking in the Mavericks insignia and the bottom rocker that proclaimed "Property of Merrick."

For a heartbeat, air stalled in my lungs. The silence was killing me. Did she hate it? Did she understand how important this was to me?

Kenna slipped one arm through and then the other. There was a custom patch on the front licked in flames surrounding an embroidered "Wildfire." She brushed her fingers across it before gazing into my eyes.

"We both know how fast things change. I love you. I want you to be mine in every way possible."

"So, this means I belong to you?" she asked, challenge in her tone.

I shook my head. "This means every part of me belongs to you. For the rest of our lives."

"Do I still have the right to vote?" she asked in her sassiest tone.

She yelped as my palm hit the curve of her ass, and I pressed my lips to hers to silence her protest.

"This patch gives you full veto power on me," I whispered, sliding my hand from the curve of her ass to her hip. "This gives you the right to tell me what you want. Tonight and every night. I'll give you any damn thing you want, Wildfire."

"Really?" she drawled as she ran her fingers down my chest slowly. "You sure you're ready for what I want?"

Before I could answer, my phone rang. Thane's name blared across the screen—a summon I'd never ignored. I silenced the call and tossed the phone onto the counter.

Kenna blinked, surprised.

"I'm yours, Wildfire. Your home is with me."

"Speaking of home ..." she trailed off.

I pulled back, my brows raised.

"I may have invited some people over tonight for a housewarming party."

I groaned, feigning exasperation. "I've lived here for years. How much time do we have before people start showing up?"

"A couple hours."

"Good. Now go to our room, take off your clothes, and wait for me. I want to see you ride me wearing nothing but that cut."

She burst out laughing. "That's one order I won't veto." She turned to head toward our bedroom.

"One more thing," I said. "Marry me."

She paused. "I love you. I'm wearing your patch. That's enough for me for now."

I rubbed the back of my neck. "Life's short, and I'm not getting younger."

She scoffed. "You're not old. I watched a TikTok last night that said forty is the new thirty. Let's settle in. Build our house. And then we can get married."

* * *

Merci arrived first, letting herself in without knocking like always. Brisket lost his goddamn mind, barking and wagging his whole body as she scratched his ears.

She hugged Kenna, pressing a bottle of wine into her hands. "Luca couldn't make it," she said. "Another long shift at the hospital."

Soon enough, our backyard filled with our friends—Eva, Reaper, Thane, Rhetta, and Fuse. Music played as we chatted and ate hot dogs.

Hatchet was late, as usual. When he finally showed up, I caught the scent of something sweet—expensive perfume, from what I could tell. He had that smug, just-got-laid look, and I rolled my eyes. "Took you long enough," I muttered.

He grinned, slapping me on the back. "Had an early date. Knew there weren't going to be any single chicks here tonight."

"Hatchet, you ever show up on time for anything?" Fuse called out.

"Only for funerals and court dates, brother," he said as he beelined for the cooler. Hatchet grabbed a beer and then sauntered over to Merci, who sat perched on a lawn chair.

He flashed her his charming grin. "So, you planning to patch me up tonight? Or are you off duty?"

Merci smirked, swirling her wine. "I'm definitely off duty. So try not to get yourself shot, stabbed, or otherwise maimed."

Hatchet chuckled, leaning in a little closer. "But I like it when you play doctor with me."

Merci rolled her eyes. "I might just let you bleed out next time so you'll shut up."

I narrowed my eyes, watching him. Hatchet knew damn well Merci was engaged, but that never stopped him from turning on the charm. He was harmless, mostly, but I still didn't like it. Not when it came to my sister.

"Relax. I don't think Hatchet knows how to have a conversation with a woman without flirting."

I grunted, not taking my eyes off him. "He's doing it to push my buttons."

She squeezed my hand. "Yeah, that's half the fun for him. At least he's toned it down around me."

I huffed. Only because I'd threatened to smash his face in. I glanced down at Kenna, the firelight catching the mischief in her eyes. She was right, of course. Hatchet lived to get a rise out of me.

Hatchet caught my glare and grinned wider, raising his beer in a mock toast.

We sat in a loose circle around the bonfire. The flames flickered and popped, casting long shadows across the faces of my family. Kenna sat beside me, her bare feet propped on my lap. I pressed my thumb into her arch, finding the spot that made her melt.

Kenna tossed an empty beer can at Hatchet. "So, what's the story behind the nickname? Did you chop down a tree or something?"

Hatchet smirked. "It's a road name, not a nickname. And no, I didn't chop down a tree." He took a slow sip, clearly enjoying keeping her in the dark.

Kenna rolled her eyes. "Oh, come on. You're not going to tell me?"

"Maybe someday," Hatchet teased. "When you've earned it."

She laughed, then turned to me, curiosity bright in her eyes. "Why don't you use a road name like some of the other guys?"

The question caught me off guard, but not in a bad way. I'd laid that part of my past to rest long ago, but with Kenna, it didn't feel like an open wound anymore. "I had one, but I buried it with Rose."

She pulled back to look into my eyes, her expression softening. "Oh, I'm sorry. I didn't realize—"

"Don't apologize," I said, my voice steady. "When we crashed, my cut was shredded. I buried Rose in hers. I went nomad for a while without one, and when I came back, I was just Merrick."

"What was your road name back then?" she asked, her voice quiet.

"Bowie."

"Like David Bowie?" she said, eyebrows raised.

Reaper and Thane chuckled.

I shook my head. "Like a Bowie knife."

Kenna bit her lip, her eyes searching mine. She was smart enough to figure out why a biker like me, the sergeant-at-arms, would've been called Bowie. She didn't push, but I could see the questions in her eyes. I didn't mind. She deserved to know who I was, even the parts I didn't talk about. I'd tell her if she asked.

Then she surprised me again. "What about Damascus?" she asked.

"Damascus?"

Kenna nodded. "Yeah. Damascus steel is strong. Resilient. Forged in fire. It's the perfect road name for you. You've been through hell, but you're still standing. You're sharp when you need to be, but you're also ... layered. Complex. Like a Damascus blade."

Fuse leaned forward, nodding. "Damn, Kenna. That's good. Fits better than Bowie ever did."

I stared into the fire, letting the name settle over me. Damascus. It felt right. More than that, it felt like a new beginning—like maybe I wasn't just the man who'd buried his past, but someone who could be forged anew.

I glanced at Kenna, a small smile tugging at my lips. "Damascus, huh? Do I need to order you a new patch? Property of Damascus?"

She smiled back, her eyes bright in the firelight. "No, you'll always be just Merrick to me."

The group fell quiet, the fire crackling between us. I felt the weight of my past lift, replaced by something new—something forged in fire but tempered by love.

Epilogue

One Year Later

I leaned against the porch railing, watching the sun rise over the lake. The water shimmered with rippling reds and pinks, the colors so vivid they brought back the memory of my first date with Kenna—right here, on a blanket spread over this very spot.

Kenna had torn into my life like a wildfire, burning away the loneliness and loss, leaving something new and stronger in its place.

I drained the last of my coffee, the warmth lingering in my chest as I turned to head inside. The house still smelled of drywall and fresh paint, but with the boxes unpacked and Kenna's touches everywhere, it finally felt like home.

It'd taken us longer to get it built than we'd expected—construction was delayed by a few months when Eva was hospitalized with life-threatening complications early in her pregnancy. The entire club had rallied around her and Reaper, stepping up wherever we could so they could focus on getting their twins to term.

We hadn't minded, though. Living together at the club's property had given Kenna the chance to truly come into her own as an old lady.

Inside, Kenna was already dressed for the day in a short, off-shoulder floral sundress, her auburn hair falling to her shoulders in loose waves. She clutched a clipboard in one hand, a purple pen in the other. She moved through the kitchen with purpose, probably set on checking the flowers, the cake, or some other damn thing for the wedding. I snagged her as she scurried by, pulling her close.

"Merrick!" she screeched at the disruption. Brisket woofed at me in a shared protest.

I plucked the clipboard from her hand and lifted her onto the countertop, pressing my body between her legs. I fluttered kisses along her collarbone, up her neck, my hands roaming her smooth thighs. I sucked in a breath when I realized she wasn't wearing panties.

"I have so many wedding things to get done. I don't have time for this," she protested, but her breath hitched as I trailed my hands higher.

"The ceremony isn't until seven. You have plenty of time for me to remind you who you belong to before this fucking goat rodeo gets started."

She glanced down as I slowly pushed her dress higher, her eyes catching on the new tattoos on my knuckles—bold script that read "WILD" and "FIRE."

"Besides, who knows if he'll even show up," I grumbled. "There's still time for him to run."

She laughed, shoving my shoulder. "He's not going to run. Besides, it's your job as the best man to make sure he doesn't."

I chuckled. "Or maybe it's my job as the best man to be his getaway driver."

Kenna smacked my chest. "You'd better behave today. No getaway stunts."

"I promise," I grumbled. "I just never expected Hatchet, of all people, to get married. Especially before us."

She shrugged. "You haven't asked me yet."

I glared at her. "I asked you on our first date."

"More like demanded." She scoffed.

I pushed her dress up higher, kissing the inside of her knee, then trailing my lips slowly upward. "Will. You. Marry. Me?" I punctuated each word with a kiss. At the end of my proposal, I ran my tongue up her bare center, and she gasped, arching against me.

"You did *not* just propose with your tongue," she panted. "Propose like a normal person. With a ring."

I chuckled, my laughter vibrating against her, making her moan.

"Knock, knock," a cheery voice called out as our front door opened. Brisket barked, his paws slipping on the wood floors.

Kenna scrambled to pull her dress down, but the flush across her neck and chest gave us away.

"Gross," Merci complained, balancing two handfuls of bags in her hands. "Really? The kitchen counter? People eat there."

"I know," I said with a wry grin. "You're interrupting my breakfast. Maybe you should try knocking."

Kenna hopped off the counter. "Let me help you with those."

"I'm just dropping these off, and then Jessa and I are heading to the airport to pick up Mom," she said, setting the bags at the bottom of the stairs.

"I can pick her up," I offered. "As long as my getaway driver services aren't needed, I don't need to do anything else today."

"You need to pick up your tux," Kenna reminded me.

"Right," I said, scrubbing my hand over my face. "I can grab that after. When does she land?"

"In two hours," Merci said.

"Consider it handled. Now get out of here. I was just proposing to Kenna when you walked in."

Merci raised a brow, glancing at Kenna. "Proposing?"

Kenna laughed, shaking her head. "He wasn't serious."

"I'm completely serious," I growled.

Kenna sucked in a sharp breath as I turned to stalk toward her.

"Goodbye, Merci," I said, not bothering to look at my sister and not caring whether she was out the door by the time I got to Kenna. "I know you have wedding planner shit to do. And I have an hour and a half before I need to go. So, I'm going to take you upstairs, and by the time I leave, you'll have agreed to marry me."

"Merrick," she said in exasperation.

I needed her to know I meant every damn word. I threw her over my shoulder, and she shrieked as I carried her up the stairs.

"Put me down. You can't just manhandle me into marrying you."

Despite her protests, I could hear the smile in her voice. She laughed breathlessly as I tossed her into the middle of the bed.

I slid the straps of the sundress down her shoulders. I kissed her throat, but I couldn't stop thinking about what I really wanted from her. An answer.

"Stay here," I commanded, pressing a kiss to her forehead before rolling off the bed. I crossed to the dresser and rustled through a drawer to find the velvet box.

She sat up, swinging her legs over the side.

I knelt beside the bed and took her hand. Her eyes widened at the sight of the ring box. She stared at the shimmering oval-cut sunstone inset on a gold band. The fiery orange and yellow gem reminded me of her radiant strength and fierce spirit.

"Marry me, Wildfire."

She leapt forward, wrapping her arms around my neck and knocking me back to the ground. With her legs straddling my hips, she pulled the ring from the box and held it up in the morning light.

"This is beautiful. How long have you been holding onto this?"

"I ordered it a week after you moved in."

"What?"

"I've always known you were the one. You insisted on waiting until we were settled, though, so I've held onto it. I don't want to wait anymore. I love you."

"I don't want to wait either. But, after planning someone else's wedding, I want to elope. Just us."

"Whatever you want, as long as you're mine."

* * *

The bride and groom said their vows beneath a magnolia tree in full bloom, and a makeshift dance floor had been built over the spot where Kenna planned to plant a garden next spring.

Lights strung from trees hung above us, casting a warm, honey haze on Kenna's floor-length champagne lace bridesmaid dress. Our family—the Lone Star Mavericks Motorcycle Club—milled about the yard, while Hawk and Brisket trailed behind guests, angling for treats.

"Show it to me," Hatchet said, sliding between me and Kenna as he slung an arm over each of our shoulders.

"What?" Kenna asked innocently.

"The ring. I can't believe Merci had to be the one to tell me this asshole finally proposed. I'm wounded."

Kenna rolled her eyes. "It's upstairs. Besides, it wasn't a real proposal."

"What do you mean it wasn't a real proposal?" I growled, shrugging off Hatchet's arm to face Kenna. "I asked you to marry me, I gave you a ring, and you agreed. And hands off my fiancée, Hatchet."

Hatchet chuckled as I tugged Kenna closer.

"You asked as you were trying to paw off my clothes. It's not exactly a story I can tell. We don't need to announce it tonight. This isn't our day. Let them have the spotlight."

Hatchet shoved Kenna's shoulder gently. "Tonight is about family and love. You're family, and you're in love. Go upstairs and put that ring on so we can toast," he demanded. "If you don't, I'll tell everyone about your proposal, in detail, during my speech."

"You wouldn't."

Hatchet's wicked grin grew. "From what Merci told me, it was pretty scandalous. And I can be creative and fill in the other details." He stroked his short beard, eyes glinting with mischief.

Kenna sighed dramatically. "You're not going to let up on this, are you?"

Hatchet shook his head.

"Fine. You know, I would have never become involved with the Mavericks had I known you would all be so bossy."

We chuckled as she stomped away, muttering to herself.

"Thought you'd never ask her," Hatchet harped. "When's the big day?"

I shrugged my shoulders. "After planning your circus of a wedding, she wants to elope."

"You're already in a tux and everyone's here. Get married tonight."

My brows jumped. I didn't hate the idea.

Kenna approached, hand outstretched as if to prove to Hatchet she'd slid the ring onto her finger. The sunstone glittered as it caught the light of the nearby fire.

"Merrick says you don't want to plan another wedding," Hatchet said.

Kenna shook her head. "Between work and opening the center next week, I don't have time."

"Then get married now," Hatchet schemed. "Everyone's already here."

Her jaw dropped. "What? No," she protested. "I can't steal your day."

"It'll be perfect," he promised. "Then Merrick and I can remind each other of our anniversaries. My bride'll loan you her 'something blue.' Merrick's age covers 'something old,' and this bouquet works for 'something new.'" He shoved the flowers into her hands with a smirk as he strode away.

Kenna's wide eyes flicked to me. "You want to get married tonight?"

I smirked. "It's a good idea. Almost everyone we care about is here."

Before she could argue, Hatchet climbed onto a chair and clanged his fork against his beer bottle. "Listen up, assholes!" he bellowed. The bride glared at him. "I mean, wonderful guests. Shut up for two seconds."

The crowd quieted.

"First of all, I want it on record that I never thought I'd choose marriage as a life sentence."

"Neither did we," Fuse hollered.

Laughter rippled through the small crowd. "I found my match. But tonight ain't just about us. It's about love, family, second chances, and the people you'd lay down your life for. Like Kenna and Merrick. Who, by the way, are going to get hitched right now."

The backyard erupted in cheers.

Less than five minutes later, Everest walked Kenna down the aisle. Hatchet stood beside me, and Eva stood in as Kenna's maid of honor. Merci and Reaper each cradled a sleeping newborn in their arms, smiles wide on their faces.

Thane officiated our wedding before our family and friends, and they cheered as we sealed our improvised vows with a kiss.

Hatchet lifted his beer. "So, here's to the Mavericks. The family we've found and the friends we've lost. Here's to all of you who are there for us even when the roads get rough."

"Or when one of you crashes," Merci added with a laugh.

"Yes, to those who lift us up when we crash. Literally. I'm going to try not to do that again. I promise. So, here's to love and family."

The toasts echoed as I leaned down to kiss my wife, claiming her in front of our family and sealing my promise to love and protect her.

Kenna

The scent of rich coffee and spice filled the bedroom, stirring my senses from a deep, dreamless sleep. Warm sunlight fanned across my bare shoulders wrapped in the tangled sheets. Heavy boot steps echoed down the hallway, followed by the clicking of Brisket's nails on the wood floors.

"Wake up, Mrs. Morris," Merrick said, his deep voice making my pulse rise before I even opened my eyes. "I have a surprise for you."

In the week since our impromptu wedding, Merrick had woken me with a latte and a new surprise every morning. So far, he'd given me breakfast in bed, a new leather jacket, an enormous bouquet of flowers, and a ruby necklace. I insisted it was unnecessary. I didn't need gifts to feel cherished. Merrick made me feel that way every second just being himself.

I groaned and buried my face deeper into the pillow, refusing to give in just yet. Something thudded softly on the mattress beside me. Moments later, a soft muzzle sniffed my hair and a warm, rough tongue licked my ear.

"What the fuck?" I shrieked, rolling over just in time to see a small, wriggling furball launching for my face again.

Merrick scooped up the puppy into his arms. "Sorry." He chuckled. "I didn't expect her to attack you like that."

I sat up and stared, barely processing. "Hold up—did you ... get us a puppy?"

He cradled the fluffy bundle against his chest, one big palm easily holding her squirming body still. "Remember the puppy you kept showing me on Instagram last week? The one Maisie found behind the bakery? No one claimed her. She's yours now. Ours."

Merrick set the puppy back onto the bed ,and she bounded into my lap. I ran my hands through her light tan and black fur. Her tail whipped against the mattress as she snapped her tiny jaws at my chin.

"The vet thinks she's a purebred Malinois," Merrick added.

"What should we name her?"

"That's up to you, Wildfire," he said as he petted Brisket, who leaned affectionately against his thighs.

I held the puppy up, gazing into her warm, brown eyes that shone with the promise of mischief. "How about Waffles?"

"Waffles?"

"Yeah, Belgian Waffles." I snickered at the joke. The puppy yawned in agreement, and I set her back onto the bed.

Merrick shook his head. "Christ, woman. What am I going to do with you?"

"Feed me breakfast?" I asked hopefully as he handed me the latte.

Merrick grinned. "I can do that. Are you nervous? Today's the big day."

Waffles bounded to the end of the bed and attempted to dive off the side like a canine Evel Knievel. Merrick caught her mid-air as she let out a bark of protest. He set her on the floor and leaned in to cage me with his arms. He kissed me, his tender yet possessive touch grounding me. Brisket approached, tail wagging as Waffles began to nip at his paws.

I took a long sip of the latte, letting the cardamom and cinnamon sweetness coat my tongue. "I'm excited. I can't believe it's finally opening."

We'd worked our asses off to open the Ignite Strength Center. Today, we would begin to welcome women and girls who deserved safety and hope. For those who didn't have a family like the Mavericks to protect them. And through our partnership with the local women's shelter, we already had a waiting list of women and girls who were ready to reclaim their power.

"I'm proud of you, Wildfire," Merrick said warmly. "We all are."

The entire Mavericks family had rallied around me to make my dream of empowering women in the community a reality. Built within an old firehouse, the Ignite Strength Center offered a full gym, an art studio, and a computer lab.

My phone pinged with a text message.

EVA:

I have every local news channel lined up to cover the ribbon cutting today!

ME:

You're on maternity leave. Stop working.

EVA:

The twins are asleep. By the way, one of my clients wants to make a donation so you can add more art classes. He wants to know how much for naming rights to the art studio.

Merrick's mother, Maren, had moved back to the area six months ago and volunteered to teach classes in painting and pottery. But with the cost of supplies, we'd only been able to offer ten spots.

ME:

Wow! I don't even know what to ask for.

EVA:

How about $500,000 for naming rights to the art studio? And I think I can get him to give another $250,000 to support the other classes you have planned.

Fuse and Coast led the monthly self-defense classes, Hatchet was putting together a workshop on basic auto maintenance, and Linc's basic computer programming class already had a wait-list.

ME:

That would be great. Thank you for making it happen.

EVA:

Of course! Love you!

I stood, still staring at my phone. "I think Eva just landed us three-quarters of a million," I told Merrick, my voice a little wobbly with disbelief.

He beamed. "Told you you're unstoppable. Thane called too—said the Mavericks want to go all in on building the clinic you and Merci dreamed up."

My brows jumped. "Really?"

It was Merci's idea to recruit a team of doctors, nurses, and social workers to open an attached medical clinic and counseling center. But we'd nixed the idea when we realized how expensive it would be to stock the required supplies.

Merrick shrugged. "It's a good investment. The Mavericks would probably use it the most."

I scoffed. "Yeah, because you guys get hurt when you're doing nefarious biker shit." I ran my fingers over the newest scar on his forearm. "You still haven't told me what you were doing when your arm was fileted open."

Merrick smirked, covering my hand with his over the scar. "Club business."

I rolled my eyes.

"Ow." A litany of colorful swearing followed as Merrick bent over to pick up Waffles. "She bit my ankle."

I patted the pup on the head. "Good girl. He deserved that, didn't he?" I cooed.

"Get in the shower. I'll be back with breakfast in a few."

I laughed. "I thought you were making me breakfast."

Merrick shook his head. "Wildfire, you know I can barely scramble an egg. I'll go grab a few breakfast tacos so you can start out your day on the right foot."

I kissed Merrick, a spark zinging between us as his hand stroked down my side. I popped a smooch on Waffle's snout before leaning down to peck the top of Brisket's brindle head. I watched as my husband strode out of the room, a wiggling Waffles in his arms. Brisket trotted behind him with a squeaky toy in his mouth.

The morning sunlight spilled across the room, catching on the framed photos scattered on the dresser. Some new, some old, but all of them proof that love, loyalty, and friendship could burn away the pain of loss.

If anyone had told me that the hole Alec left in my heart could ever be filled—not replaced, but filled and expanded, and by a biker, no less—I'd have laughed. But love found its way in, burning hot like a wildfire. And in the ruins left behind, new life bloomed. The Mavericks weren't just Merrick's brothers-in-arms—they were my family, too.

I ran a hand through my tangled hair as my heart filled with happiness. I had a husband who saw every part of me—even the scars and shadows—and loved me all the more for them. I had friends who'd step between me and a racing bullet. And I had a purpose, a place to pour all the aching and hope and hard lessons into helping women stand up and reclaim their own power.

Life wasn't what I'd planned.

It was better.

Even after all the heartbreak, I woke up surrounded by love.

And I'd never take it for granted.

Hatchet & The Hellcat

Lone Star Mavericks MC Series, Book 3

In a world ruled by loyalty, love is the most dangerous betrayal.

When Merci Morris walks away from her high-society fiancé after discovering his betrayal, she's left questioning everything she thought she wanted. While her father helped build the Lone Star Mavericks Motorcycle Club, she's spent years playing by the rules, carving out a future beyond the chaos, loyalty, and expectations that come with it.

Reckless, impulsive, and impossible to pin down, Hatchet has always been the club's charming playboy—until an unexpected obligation forces him to look at his life differently. But no amount of growing up prepares him for Merci walking back into his orbit.

Hatchet knows the Maverick's code better than anyone: protect the innocent, respect the rules, and keep his hands to himself when it comes to the sisters and daughters of club members. But Merci isn't the quiet, good girl he remembers. In her place is a fierce, unpredictable woman determined to prove she doesn't need the club—or him—to keep her safe. And she's done asking for permission—not from the club, not the code written by her father before she was born.

As new threats surface, the line between protecting Merci and wanting more starts to blur. And the closer they get, the more dangerous their connection becomes.

Because in a world built on loyalty and consequences, crossing the line could cost them everything.

Read **Hatchet & The Hellcat** on Amazon Kindle or purchase signed copies directly from the author at rachelesterlineauthor.com.

* * *

Dear Reader:

Buying direct from rachelesterlineauthor.com is the best way to support my work as an independent author. It ensures the most support goes toward my next release, and allows me to give back to you! Every order placed here is hand-packed by me and includes bookmarks and stickers as a thank you for your support.

Sincerely,
Rachel Esterline

Subscribe for Updates and Bonus Content

Visit rachelesterlineauthor.com/subscribe to receive updates about release dates, event announcements, and bonus content, and more.

* * *

ABOUT THE AUTHOR

Rachel Esterline is an independent author based in the Lansing area in Michigan with her partner-in-crime of more than twenty years, Jeremy, and their two rescue dogs—Kimber and Ranger—whose wild spirits and stubborn loyalty wind their way into every canine character she writes. She has two degrees from Central Michigan University—a bachelor's in integrative public relations and a master's in higher education administration—and her Accreditation in Public Relations from the Public Relations Society of America.

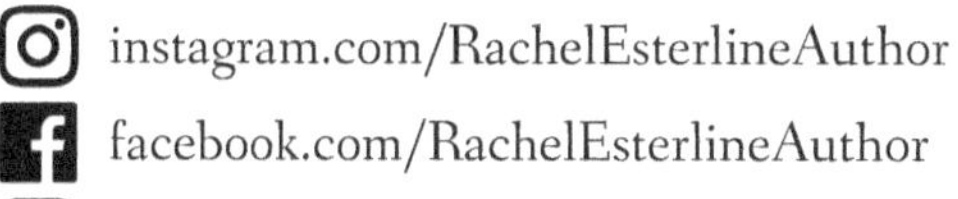

Book Club Experiences

Kick your book club into high gear with an author-led experience.

I love connecting with readers and bringing the gritty world of my motorcycle club romances right to your group. Depending on the group, I can offer:

Interactive Activities: Fire up your creative side with MC-inspired extras—like a road name generator, story-based mad libs, coloring pages, games, and more.

Custom Stickers and Goodies: Every club deserves its colors. Deck out your meeting with themed stickers and bonus swag that make your gathering unforgettable.

Live Q&A Sessions: Let's ride together for a live conversation about the book. I'm available to join your meeting in person (within driving distance of Lansing, Michigan) or virtually for an interactive, behind-the-scenes chat.

Visit **rachelesterlineauthor.com/book-clubs** for info.

About the Malinois & Dutch Shepherd Rescue

Malinois and Dutch Shepherd Rescue, Inc. (MAD Rescue) is a 501(c)(3) nonprofit organization dedicated to saving Belgian Malinois and Dutch Shepherds who have been surrendered, abandoned, abused, neglected, or impounded. Operated entirely by compassionate, like-minded volunteers across the United States, MAD Rescue relies on a network of dedicated fosters and donors to provide care and second chances. Visit **madrescueinc.org** to learn about volunteering, fostering, or adopting.

From left to right: Kimber, Jeremy, Rachel, and Ranger in October 2023, following Ranger's official adoption from the Malinois & Dutch Shepherd Rescue.

Acknowledgments

Writing a book is a lot like I imagine building a motorcycle from scratch would be—equal parts reckless optimism, busted knuckles, and desperate googling.

First, thank you to my family and friends for cheering me on and to every reader who found me on TikTok. Your support is what keeps these stories roaring down the highway.

Huge thanks to my cousin, **Stephanie**, who not only read my messy early manuscript on a family vacation, but also provided a live commentary as she tried (with admirable dedication and wild theories) to predict who Kenna would end up with.

To **Brooklyn Powers**—my writing buddy, beta reader, and all-around advocate for the Lone Star Mavericks MC universe. Thanks for answering my random messages and sharing ideas on how to make the Mavericks even hotter in our weekly writer chats.

Mel Purdy, your skill and creativity as a designer elevate my books. I appreciate your patience with my "what if we tried ..." design experiments more than you know.

And, of course, **Evelyn**, my sharp-eyed editor. Thank you for tightening my prose and never shying away from a little blood, darkness, and chaos.

Here's to the village behind the Lone Star Mavericks and the women who match them mile for mile, bruise for bruise, and never back down.